UNWRITTEN RULES

A DICKIE FLOYD DETECTIVE NOVEL

DANNY R. SMITH

COPYRIGHT

Cover by Jon Schuler

www.schulercreativelab.com

"The L.A. cop novel is different from the New York cop novel, from the Miami cop novel, and, thank God, from the Minneapolis cop novel. It has become nothing less than a peculiarly American art form, a chronicle of the deterioration of what Scott Fitzgerald called the last and greatest of all human dreams. L.A.'s cops and killers and the streets they troll have attracted the very best American crime writers. People like Raymond Chandler, Ross Macdonald, James Ellroy, Joseph Wambaugh, Walter Mosley, and Michael Connelly. To that list, you now need to add one more name: Danny Smith. Nobody has ever written the L.A. cop novel better than Danny Smith does. Nobody. Ever."

— Jake Needham, author of the Mean Streets Crime Novels

"Unwritten Rules is a fast-paced thrill ride filled with colorful characters, true to life dialogue, and police procedural details that have defined the best detective series since Connelly's Harry Bosch novels."

— Phil Jonas

"Danny Smith brings every character, event and neighborhood to life. Exhilarating, thrilling and suspenseful. This is an OUTSTANDING book!"

— Daryl Wayne Knight

"Dickie, the old time cop, Josie the independent woman cop. She has his back even when she fears they will both lose their jobs. They are a high performance duo. You won't want to miss one word of it. Really. Truly. Honestly."

— Michele Kapugi

"Spellbinding. Smith's novels make the absolutely the best police procedural series that is currently being published."

— Henry "Bud" Johnson

"I have read all of the books in the "Dickie Floyd" series and each one left me yearning for more."

— Moon Mullen

"Unwritten Rules is Danny's finest work to date. All I can say is 'Wow.' I thought I had everything figured our early in the storyline and just when I did the plot twisted in a completely different direction."
— Scott Anderson

"Unwritten Rules is a thrilling journey into an underworld inhabited by thugs and cops—and by those who blur that line. You won't want to put it down."
— Patricia Barrick Brennan

ACKNOWLEDGMENTS

I would like to offer a special thanks to my beta readers, whose eyes for detail have helped me polish this novel: Scott Anderson, Ernie Banuelos, Jacqueline Beard, Michele Carey, Teresa Collins, Andrea Hill-Self, Henry "Bud" Johnson, Phil Jonas, Michele Kapugi, Ann Litts, William "Moon" Mullen, Ralph Kay Reeves, Dennis Slocumb, and Heather Wamboldt. Also my wonderful wife, Lesli, and daughters Jami and Randi Jo. I am beyond grateful for this wonderful team of all-stars!

As always, a big thanks to my terrific editor and great friend, Patricia Barrick Brennan. I honestly couldn't do this without her.

For the partners and loved ones of the four Compton police officers killed in the line of duty

Officer Dess K. Phipps, EOW 10/12/1962
Officer Ralph Kay Reeves, EOW 03/26/1968
Officer James Wayne MacDonald, EOW 02/22/1993
Officer Kevin Michael Burrell, EOW 02/23/1993

And in memory of California Highway Patrolman Dana Everett Paladini (EOW 07/04/1972), who, with only nine months on the job, was killed when struck by a ricocheted bullet fired by a deputy sheriff who was putting down a badly injured horse.

A CROWD HAD GATHERED ACROSS THE STREET, IMPEDING THE FLOW OF commuters arriving at the civic center for another day of American justice, Compton style. Cops, lawyers, witnesses. Dutiful civilians responding to their juror summonses. Defendants out on bail, free to live their lives of crime while the wheels of justice crept along. Each of them likely speculating as to what had happened here, correctly assuming that someone had died. Suddenly. Violently. The telltale signs their clues: yellow tape strung from an apartment building to the center of the street, a highway patrol car sitting ominously in the center of the cordoned area, its front end pointed at the apartment. Pointed at me, in fact—the detective in the window.

Focused on the crowd but speaking to my partner, I said, "Did you know that the first highway patrolman killed in Compton was shot by a deputy sheriff?"

From somewhere in the apartment behind me, she said, "How have I never heard that?"

I turned and looked at her. If anyone could rock disposable blue gloves and paper booties, it was Josie, a veteran detective whose dark blue pinstripe suit and cream-colored blouse blended nicely with the usual accessories one wears at a murder scene. Her dark hair hung loosely at her shoulders, offsetting the otherwise professional look of a lady cop. She appraised me as if I were a suspect in an interrogation, clearly skeptical about what I had said.

"You never heard that story?"

Her eyelashes fluttered, but not in a come-hither way. "No, Dickie, I never heard it."

I continued, "What happened, the deputy was trying to shoot this horse—"

"A *horse!* Why would he shoot a horse? And why was there a horse in Compton?"

The uniformed deputy at the door, stationed there to protect the integrity of our crime scene, turned and looked at me, his eyebrows raised. I smiled at him and turned back to my partner. "Back then—this was in the early seventies—there were several riding stables around here. Black cowboys were a thing, and let me tell you, nobody messed with them. Anyway, there had been an accident and a horse inside a trailer was badly injured. Chippies had the handle because the accident happened in the county, just outside city limits."

Looking back at the crowd outside, I visualized a dead horse in *our* scene, seeing it as it might have appeared on the news that day. There would be a crowd of course—there was always a crowd. Shaggy haired men wearing bellbottoms, Elvis sideburns and shades. The women, well, they might have taken more care with their hair and clothing than the ones who were here today. I grinned at the thought of women with their Farrah Faucet feather-cut hair and brightly-colored dresses that fell well above the knee. The newscaster, a man—almost always a man then—solemn while speculating about the horse. *Why would deputies shoot a horse?*

I said to Josie, "The deputy pulled his thirty-eight and shot the poor bastard in the head—*BAM!*"

"The horse," she clarified.

I turned to face her again. "Yes, the horse. He was trying to put it out of its misery, but the bullet ricocheted off the trailer and hit the chippie in the chest. There were no vests back then, so the bullet ripped through his ribcage and lodged in his heart. He was D-R-T."

"D-R-T?"

"Dead right there."

Josie rolled her eyes and moved away, scanning the scene.

I lifted my fedora and wiped sweat from my forehead with the palm of my hand, while eyeing the fan that stood next to me at the open window. It was off when we arrived, and it would remain so while we conducted our investigation. That was the first rule of homicide work: never alter a crime scene.

I left the window and returned to the body that lay facedown near the doorway. Staring at the dead highway patrolman, I did the math. It had been fifty years since the chippie was killed by the deputy's errant bullet. That was 1972. Two years earlier, in 1970, four chippies were killed during a shootout in Newhall, a place that was then, and remains, a world away from Compton. My gaze fixed on the dead man at my feet, I uttered, "Almost fifty years."

Josie appeared at my side, her fresh, floral scent washing over me. She said, "And that's the only other time a chippie's been killed in Compton?"

"There've been other cops killed here over the years: MacDonald and Burrell, the two Compton coppers killed over near Rosecrans and Dwight, back in the early nineties—"

"I remember."

"And others. But the chippie, the one who was killed by the deputy, he was the first and only CHP killed in Compton, to my knowledge."

"Until now," she said.

"Until now."

Josie continued making some notes for an affidavit. At this point, we didn't know anything about the dead highway patrol officer who lay prone on the floor of the modestly furnished apartment, which was otherwise unoccupied. We didn't even know how he had died. There were no obvious signs of trauma and no indication that he had encountered violence here—at least nothing we could yet see. It appeared as if he had walked—or more likely, run—into the apartment and keeled over. Nonetheless, we would investigate it as a homicide until the manner of death was established. We would need judicial blessing to seize the private residence as a crime scene. If this turned out to be a murder, we had to consider that his killer might have lived here and could have legal standing inside the apartment, meaning he would be protected against unwarranted searches of his residence. There were no *dead cop* exceptions, which was the essence of Mincey vs. Arizona, and

3

the genesis of the crime scene search warrant. Simply, a Mincey warrant.

Josie, meandering through the kitchen, said, "The tenants are Hispanic."

I glanced around at the various pictures on the walls: Jesus on the cross, Jesus at The Last Supper, Our Lady of Guadalupe with her head bowed. There were figurines and candles adorning shelves, and a small shrine on a table in the corner. "Ya think?"

She slapped her notebook closed and slid it into her pocket. "Are you ready?"

I retrieved my phone from my pocket and tapped the button that would call the main line to Homicide. It was first on my Favorites list, programmed as '187,' the California penal code for murder. While waiting for the call to connect, I tucked the phone beneath my chin and said to Josie, "I'm going to have the office put a hold on the coroner while we get a warrant signed."

Josie scanned the small apartment once more, likely making sure she had everything noted for the affidavit.

After finishing the call, I followed Josie through the doorway, pausing to address the deputy whose name tag identified him as Parker. "Nobody in or out while we're gone."

"Got it, sir."

"If the crime lab shows up, tell them we've gone to get a warrant. Also, make sure you leave the door open just as you found it, but keep the looky-loos at bay. If the landlord happens by, see if you can get some information on the tenants."

"Yes sir."

Josie and I walked down the driveway, past the CHP car where a second deputy stood. We ducked under the yellow tape and got into Josie's Charger. She started the engine and I got the air conditioner going and adjusted my vents. The plan was to go one block over to the Compton sheriff's station where we could type a search warrant and affidavit and print it out before walking next door to the courthouse.

An hour later, we returned with a signed warrant and saw that Phil Gentry had arrived from the crime lab. He was snapping photos of the outside while awaiting our return.

We signed back in on the crime scene log, gloved up, and went to work. Phil took scene photos and then dusted for latent prints. Josie and I searched through drawers and cabinets, in the closet, and under the bed in an attempt to identify the tenants or their landlord.

After a short while, I met Josie near the small kitchen and held up a black book. "This is all I came up with, some names and numbers, everything in Spanish."

She traded me the black book for a handful of mail. "Utility bills in the name of Maria Guadalupe Gomez Hernandez. By the looks of it, I'd say Maria is an elderly woman."

I looked around again and couldn't disagree with her. *Old* was the first word that came to mind. *Orderly* yet another. But who was she, and why was there a dead chippie on her floor?

Josie said, "Should we call for the coroner?"

"Sure," I said.

As Josie made the call, I stepped over to the window again. The number of onlookers had doubled, and I wondered how many of them were supposed to be inside the courthouse by now, handling their business. Two news crews had arrived and were aiming their cameras toward us.

Josie ended her call and said the coroner would be here in thirty minutes.

I said, "I'm going to canvas the neighbors. Why don't you try calling a few of those numbers, see if you can find out who Maria Guadalupe is and why she isn't home."

Josie took a seat at the dining area, which consisted of a card table under a plastic cover and two folding chairs. I walked out.

Twenty minutes later I was back with an announcement. "Coroner's ninety-seven," I said, using the radio code that indicates a unit or person's arrival at a particular location.

Josie set her phone down. "No luck with the phone numbers. Did you get anything from the neighbors?"

I shook my head. "Nobody's home next door. One of the two upstairs apartments is vacant, the other is occupied by an elderly man who said he hasn't seen or heard anything all day. Then again, he just got out of bed."

"Great. What about a landlord? Did he at least give you that?"

I held up my notebook. "He gave me the name of a property manager and the address where he sends his check, but no phone number. That can be one of our next stops. We also need to talk to court security before we leave today."

"The parking lot guards?"

"And the guys inside, see if there's any cameras that pick up the apartment."

Coroner's Investigator Nick Stewart appeared in the doorway and signed in on the deputy's log. Stewart, all business beneath his blond flattop and furrowed brow, stared at the body of the deceased traffic officer while stretching a pair of disposable gloves over his hands. "What's the story on this?"

Josie said, "Compton got a nine-one-one call, a female reporting that a CHP officer had jumped out of his car and run toward the apartment building across from the courthouse parking structure. Deputies responded and found the patrol car as it sits with its driver's door open."

Stewart didn't look up. He was busy tucking his tie into his shirt, a habit of men who wear business attire and hover over dead people.

Josie continued: "The deputies searched the area and found the door to this apartment open, just as it is now. They saw the chippie down, so they cleared the apartment for suspects, checked his vitals, and called for paramedics. He was pronounced at zero-eight-forty-six."

Stewart scanned the small room, as if something seemed amiss.

I said, "Window was open, as it is now."

He nodded and returned his gaze to the fallen officer. "Let's have a look."

Josie said, "There were half a dozen deputies here within minutes, and none of them found anything that would give us a clue about what happened."

Stewart ran his gloved hand over the officer's head, probing for evidence of trauma beneath the thick black hair. He then turned the dead man's head both directions, gently, while inspecting all areas of the head and neck. Stewart lowered the head to the floor and retreated to the briefcase he had set behind him. He made a few notes on a coroner's investigation report, then went back to the body. Keeping his eyes on it, he said, "I'm going to roll him, guys."

Josie and I both stepped up for a closer look. I would have expected to see blood oozing from beneath the body had he been shot or stabbed. The absence of any obvious trauma had me puzzled. Maybe he had been struck in the head or knocked out by a punch to the jaw. Neither of those things would necessarily cause bleeding. But would that have killed him? It was possible. The more I saw of death, the less I was surprised by the peculiarity of it. Death could be strange business.

As Stewart tried to roll the officer's body, it hung up on the pistol holstered on his hip. I wondered what might have caused an officer to run into a building that hadn't also raised concerns for his safety. But chippies were wired differently than deputies. The bulk of their contacts with the public were traffic related, and the majority of those contacts resulted in citations. Deputies, on the other hand, had at the forefront of their minds the notion that every contact had the potential to turn deadly. It would be rare to see a deputy chase a man into a building without having drawn his weapon. Especially in this neighborhood.

But had this officer actually chased someone into the building? This was only an assumption on my part, which was a violation of Rule Two in homicide work: never assume anything. I reflected on the briefing as it had been told to us by the handling unit when we arrived. The officer had jumped out of his car and run into the building. No mention of him chasing anyone. I wondered who might have made the call, and what they had seen that caused them to call 9-1-1.

I tapped Josie's elbow and said, "Let's make sure we get a copy of the nine-one-one."

The deputy at the door said, "I'll have the watch deputy take care of that for you, sir."

I looked over at him. "Thank you, sir."

Stewart had lowered the officer's torso to the floor and released his grip on the dead man's shoulder. "No sign of any significant trauma, just a small contusion on his forehead." He stood up and took one step backward while peeling off his gloves, staring at the chippie.

I knew Stewart would forgo probing the officer's liver to document the body temperature relative to the ambient temperature. It was unnecessary to do so when the circumstances of the case removed any question of the approximate time of death. Some coroner's investigators might have been inclined to do so anyway, in order to check off each box on the crime scene procedures list. Stewart was a seasoned professional who had the confidence to allow common sense to guide him, and he was also one who would handle a dead officer with great reverence.

"Did you see his name tag, by chance?" Josie asked, her pen posed over her notebook.

"Officer Gomez," Stewart answered, his voice low and melancholy. "Let's see if he's got his ID with him."

I waited while Stewart went through the dead officer's pockets one by one. This was a task that, by law, police officers and detectives were not allowed to perform. The body belongs to the coroner. Until a representative of the coroner's office was there to do it himself or available to give a detective permission to do so, we were not allowed to move the body or search through any clothing or belongings that were worn by or attached to the decedent.

The license was in a breast pocket. Stewart held it at arm's length to read it. "Antonio Carrera Gomez."

I turned to meet Josie's gaze. "Gomez. That was the name on the utility bill, right?"

She nodded. "Could be a coincidence though. It's a common name."

"How's that work again, with the two last names?"

"So, traditionally, the two last names are the first last names of one's parents. In this case, you would have Carrera as the first last name of his father, and Gomez as the first last name of his mother. Does that make sense?"

"You're saying that Maria Guadalupe could be his mother, right?"

"Technically, yes. But again, it's a very common name."

"But here he is, dead on her floor."

Stewart reconfigured his tie while saying, "You think he's related to someone here?"

"We don't know," I said. "We'll find out though."

Stewart looked at me. "If you identify the next of kin and make notification, let me know."

"You bet," I said.

Josie asked, "What do you think, Nick? I mean, with such little trauma, what might have killed him?"

He shrugged. "We'll see what they find during the post. Could be a natural."

The thought that it might have been a natural death had crossed my mind. Though the officer appeared fit, it didn't mean he couldn't have dropped dead from a heart attack after running from his car into the building. When it's your time to go, it's your time to go.

From the hallway, the patrol deputy said, "Sir, CHP brass is ninety-seven."

I nodded and looked at Stewart. "Are you ready to take him downtown?"

"Transport's outside waiting, and I've done all I can here. Are you guys finished?"

"I think so," I said, moving back to take a glance through the window. There were half a dozen CHP cars out front now, men and women in their tan uniforms with blue leg stripes standing together. Several deputies stood scattered not far from them, set apart in their tan uniform shirts with dark green pants. One of them waved his hand from the CHP car toward the building, perhaps hypothesizing what may have happened. I turned from the window. "Would you mind if we gave the CHP brass a walk-through before we move him, Nick?"

Stewart shrugged. "I've got no problem with it."

Gentry had packed up his equipment. "I'm out of here, Dickie. Are you going to want aerials? I could probably go up in a bird this afternoon if I don't get another callout."

I thought about it briefly. "Yeah, why not. It's a dead cop."

He gave me a thumbs up and walked out, his gear slung over his shoulder.

I went outside and addressed the CHP brass that had arrived, telling them we didn't yet know what caused their officer's death. I said, "There are no obvious signs of significant trauma, so at this point, it's anyone's guess. He may have had a heart attack."

A heavyset man, gray hair matching his neatly trimmed mustache, said, "But we have no idea *why* he was here in Compton."

The two bars on his collar told me this man was a captain, and I assumed he would be the commander of their South Los Angeles office, located not far from where we stood.

9

"Could he have had court?" I asked, turning to glance at the court-house behind me.

The captain shook his head. "Not down here. Officer Gomez was assigned to the Newhall office, and he was on duty since zero-six-hundred. We had no knowledge of his departure from his assigned beat this morning."

2

Two uniformed deputies took down the yellow tape and stuffed it into the trunk of their radio car to be thrown away back at their station. Most of the gawkers moved away, slowly, talking among themselves. As I walked to my car, I heard someone say, "He prolly got what he had comin'," her way of expressing a general grievance against law enforcement. She was glad an officer was dead. I didn't bother turning to see who said it. We all had something coming, and I had learned to count on karma for the appropriate dispersal; she usually got it right.

Josie followed me as we drove across the street and into the civic center parking structure. At the gate, I brandished my badge, a six-point star with the state bear whose hair had been polished off and now looked more like a pig. The security man said, "You have a subpoena?"

"No, sir," I said, hiking my thumb toward the sedan behind me. "My partner and I are investigating the death of a highway patrolman across the street. We were pulling in here to park so we could talk to you and the other security officers to see if anyone saw anything, and then head inside to look at video footage."

"But you no have a subpoena, yes?" he said, in a thick Spanish accent.

"I no have a subpoena, yes," I agreed.

"Okay, you pay, I give you ticket."

11

I pictured the contents of my briefcase wondering if I had a subpoena handy. Anything would do, no matter if it was for Pomona court and from 1989. The mere display of a subpoena could get you into most county lots, and it was easier than trying to reason with someone who was unreasonable. Fairly certain there were no subpoenas in my briefcase, I dug a five out of my pocket and flicked it toward him. He took it and raised the gate. I said, "Hasta la tacos, amigo," and drove through.

In the relative darkness of the parking structure, I paused to remove my sunglasses and glanced in my mirror. Josie drove through the gate with a smile and a wave, no five bucks, no ticket, no bullshit. It reminded me of when I was partnered with a deputy named Hernandez, working patrol. He and I would stop to a taco stand together, order the same meals, and I would be charged full price while he would get half off or pay nothing at all. If white privilege was a thing, it must've been happening somewhere other than Los Angeles.

I drove to the top level where there was plenty of parking, and Josie and I both wheeled into our spots. When we met and began walking back to the guard station, I said, "He didn't make you pay?"

She shook her head. "Nah, he never does."

I shook my head and we continued on, the sounds of clicking heels and squealing tires echoing through the concrete maze.

The security officer sat in his booth at the gate looking down at his lap and didn't notice us walking up to him. Our timing was good as there were no cars coming through at that moment, so we'd be able to chat with him free of disruption. Having spent a lifetime going to the various court-houses around the county and beyond, I knew that the mornings were the busiest, and, to a lesser degree, early afternoons following the lunch hour. Over the years, security had been significantly tightened at all of the court-houses in L.A. County. At Compton, everyone, other than those with court-house identification or a badge, went through metal detectors. The lines could resemble airport security stations or Dodger games, since they, too, had gone to metal detectors at the gates.

"Excuse me," Josie said, taking the lead as we approached the booth.

The security officer jerked his head up as he sprang from his stool and stuffed something into his front pocket. "Yes, how may I help?"

Josie tucked a lock of hair behind her ear and smiled warmly, stepping closer to the thin man in the oversized uniform. "Have you been here all day?" she asked, flashing her badge again to reaffirm our authority.

"Yes," he said, glancing at me but then settling his gaze back on Josie. "I come at seven, and I no leave until three, not even for lunch."

I looked around the structure but didn't see any restrooms from where we stood. He might bring his lunch, but everyone has to have a potty break.

"Did you see that highway patrol car there in the street?" she asked, pointing to where the vehicle had been until just moments ago when it was loaded onto a flatbed tow truck and hauled away, on its way to police impound where it would be held for evidence.

He set his gaze in that direction as if the car still sat in the street, covering his chin with one hand as he concentrated on his memory of it. "I see it, yes. It is there long time, no? All morning."

"Did you see the officer who parked it there?"

He shook his head. "He came at the busy time, many cars in a line, I don't see him."

"How do you know it was a man?" she asked.

"Huh?"

"You said, 'he' and 'him'. How do you know it was a man?"

The security man shrugged. "I don't know. I don't see him."

"You didn't see anyone get out of that car?"

He shook his head, and then sat back on his stool, retreating from the line of questioning.

"You didn't see someone run from the car into that apartment building?"

He shook his head again. "No, *señora*. I tell you already."

Josie watched him for a long moment, and then looked at me. "Do you have anything?"

I turned my attention to the guard. "What is your name, sir?"

"Eduardo Gustavo, *señor*."

I opened my notebook and jotted the date and time, *CPT courthouse security*, and his name. I looked up. "I'm Richard Jones, and this is my partner Josie Sanchez."

"*Mucho gusto*," she said.

13

"*Mucho gusto*," he replied, holding her gaze until I shot another question at him.

"Were you the only one on duty this morning, *señor*?"

"No, there are two in the morning. Then, is jus' me." He shrugged, no big deal.

"Who was your partner this morning?"

"Is Sergeant Hill, *señor*."

I wrote the sergeant's name in my notebook. "Where is he now?"

Officer Gustavo turned to look over his shoulder, toward the courthouse which couldn't be seen from where we stood. "Prolly inside, all the day. He suppo' to come at lunch so I can go, but he don't, the *pendejo*."

The only other question I debated asking was what he had shoved into his pocket when we walked up. From what I could see of its shape and apparent weight through his uniform, I assumed it was a phone. Maybe there was a policy against using cell phones during his shift. He was probably playing a game, or maybe texting his woman—or someone else's. Instead I pulled my badge off my belt and held it up for him to have a close view. "*Señor*, from now on, you see the star with a piggy, you no charge. Yes?"

He smiled, showing gold and silver teeth. "*Si, señor*, is no pro'lem."

The glare of a hot summer midday sun against the walkways and white concrete courthouse raised the "feels like" temperature past the three-digit mark, at least in my mind. I had worn my lightest-colored suit for the occasion, with a pale green shirt beneath, and topped the ensemble with a natural-colored straw fedora. No feather. Regardless of my thoughtful choice of summer fashion, sweat beaded on my forehead, my nose, and my neck, and was now trickling down my back. It was the type of day I preferred to be indoors or working during the hours of darkness, but it wasn't to be.

Inside the courthouse, the temperature dropped twenty degrees. I paused, removed my hat, and wiped the sweat from my face and head while taking a moment to enjoy the change in climate. I also took this time to size up the various security personnel who manned the metal detectors and x-ray machines, and others who meandered about in the lobby. I spotted a heavyset black man with sergeant stripes and assumed he was

Sergeant Hill. I pulled my hat back into place and pointed my chin in his direction. "Let's go talk to the sergeant."

He met my gaze as Josie and I walked directly toward him. As we drew nearer, I reached to shake his hand. "Sir, Richard Jones, Sheriff's Homicide."

His grip swallowed my hand and I hoped he wouldn't squeeze it, the latent power evident from his light grasp. I was no small man, and my hands were at least medium-sized and strong from decades of weight lifting and exercise. But I felt weak and vulnerable in the grip of this sergeant who had the natural strength of a mason or steelworker.

"How ya doin', Detective? I'm Sergeant MacDonald Hill," he said, pronouncing it as three separate names: Mac Donald Hill. "Everyone call me Mac, or Sarge."

Josie said, "Sarge, did you go to Long Beach, by chance?"

He cocked his head. "Yes ma'am, I did. How did you know?"

"You played ball, right?"

He smiled. "It's been a long time, but yeah, I did."

She looked at me. "The sergeant should've gone pro, if you ask me and a whole lot of other Long Beach State fans."

Mac chuckled and waved his hand, dismissively. "Oh, I don't know about all that. These old knees of mine barely got me through college." He smiled, and for a moment, his gaze seemed to take him back twenty years.

"When did you play there?" I asked.

"Eighty-nine, ninety, and ninety-one—the last years of the program. But that was a long time ago, man, and now I'm just a regular ol' dude tryin' to get by with what's left of what the good Lord gave me."

His smile was contagious, a big dimple on one cheek and light brown eyes that sparkled when he spoke. After a moment, I said, "Sarge, is there an office we can talk in?"

"Yeah, man." He turned and started across the lobby, glancing over his shoulder at us. "We'll go upstairs." He lumbered toward the elevators, a man whose body had been broken down during his prime years, leaving him old before his time.

I said, "What position did you play at Long Beach?"

It was clear that football was still his passion. Rule Three of homicide: connect with people. The key to having success as an investigator was

15

learning how to relate to people from other walks of life, and getting them to relate to you. Eventually the conversations would ease into the uncomfortable topic that brought you together—that someone had been killed. The person you needed to open up had just lost a loved one or witnessed a terrible event. Or, they were involved in it. They pulled the trigger or they drove the car and now they were looking at serious time in the slammer, yet you expected them to speak with you. A seasoned investigator never sat down and said, "So what happened?" My strategy was to search for a topic the person seemed comfortable talking about. Preferably, a topic that brought them pleasure, and anything other than the topic at hand. If I could find a shared interest, I would spend substantial time on the subject before moving toward the dark business of death. At the home of a reluctant witness, I once spent twenty minutes talking about dogs before getting to the subject. You had to prime the pump.

"I was a linebacker through high school," Mac said, "running a four-nine forty at two-thirty-five. Then they moved me over to the O line, man, pullin' guard." A goofy grin spread across his face. " 'Fore you know it, I'm toppin' two-fitty and runnin' the forty up in the mid fives. Now, here I am, a quarter-pounder shy of three-hunnert and two Big Macs from heart failure. It takes me fi'teen minutes to walk to my car at the end of the day."

"I hear ya, brother."

The ride stopped on the fourth floor, and we stepped out, Mac holding the doors open with a tree trunk he called an arm. At the end of the hallway, Mac keyed open a door marked Security, pushed it open and nodded for us to step inside. It was a large room with desks in the center and tables against one wall with security monitors and recorders. A south-facing wall offered a view of the parking structure. I stepped over and looked toward the apartment building where the chippie had mysteriously died, but the view of it was hindered by the looming parking structure. I walked to the other side and looked to the north where I could see the fountain and concrete monument dedicated to the memory of Dr. Martin Luther King, Jr. There were prosecutors in the Hardcore Gang division who called it the Monument to the Five-Year Prior. In 1982, Proposition 8 was passed by California voters. It called for a five-year sentencing enhancement for anyone facing a serious felony who had been previously convicted of certain crimes. It seemed the bulk of Compton cases qualified for the enhancement. Governor Brown later signed a reform law allowing judges to strike the enhancement, a move that puzzled the voters, but didn't deter prosecutors from their pursuit of justice.

I heard Mac's voice behind me. "Was you a 'Niner, young lady?"

Josie's voice: "I was."

I continued watching the few people who were walking across the plaza, some in business attire and others in street clothes, nobody in much of a hurry in the heat.

Mac said, "But not when I was there, I know that."

"No sir," Josie said. "I was there a while after you. But I'm a big football fan, and I remember your name. You were in the hall of fame there."

He smiled and nodded. "Yes ma'am, they was desperate to put a lineman on the wall, so I got lucky. Plus, they thought I was pretty."

I turned from the window to see both of them grinning. As I walked toward them, Mac lowered himself into a chair, and grimaced as he sat.

"Did you have a shot at turning pro?" I asked.

The big man shook his head. "I wasn't big enough or fast enough for the pros. But to tell the truth, I'm not sure my body would have lasted much longer anyway."

I could only imagine, thinking of the aches and pains that I had, the result of years of police work. It wasn't football, but there had been many violent encounters, all without the benefit of first warming up and stretching. From zero to ninety-nine wasn't good for any of your muscles, especially the heart. I again wondered if the chippie's heart had failed him.

"So what can I do for you folks?" Mac said, leaning back in a chair of questionable remaining lifespan itself.

I pulled a chair next to his desk. "Were you out at the parking garage this morning, around eight-thirty?"

"Yes sir," he said. "Every morning I back my boy, Eddie G, at the booth 'til the morning rush dies down. I'd rather do that than work the lines coming in downstairs. Half these youngsters come in with they attitudes, actin' like fools, and I ain't got the patience to deal wit' 'em."

I nodded. "Eddie G. That's Gustavo?"

He smiled. "Yes sir, Mr. Gustavo. You met 'im?"

"We did. I asked him if he saw the chippie bail out of his hoop on the street, right there in front of the parking entrance. We figure he must've been chasing someone, the way his car was left standing, and then he ran into the apartment building across the street. Gustavo said he didn't see anything, but mentioned you were there too, so we were wondering—"

The big man's smile was gone. "Yeah, I seen 'im. Did something happen? Y'all said you work Homicide, right?"

"Yes sir, we do. What did you see?"

"Well, I seen the officer pull up and run into the apartments, just like you said." He looked across the office toward the south-facing windows. "What happened?"

"Did you see what he was running after, who he was chasing?"

"No sir, he wasn't chasing nobody. It was jus' him, and he acted like he was in a big ol' hurry."

"You didn't call it in?" Josie asked.

He shook his head, solemnly, a look of concern showing on his face. "I didn't think—I don't know, man, it just didn't seem…"

"It's okay, Mac," I said. "We just need to know about whatever you saw."

Mac glanced at Josie and then his eyes settled back on me, darker now. "I should a known somethin' wasn't right, but I just assumed, I mean, I seen the dude there other times, so I figured it was just something domestic, ya know?"

"You've seen the chippie there?"

"Yessir. Different times, but not in his poh-lees car."

Josie and I exchanged a glance. "What do you mean? You've seen him at the apartment off-duty, in civilian clothes?"

Sweat rings spread beneath the sergeant's shirt sleeves, moisture gathered on his forehead beneath closely cropped hair. He said, "Uh-huh, I seen 'im, several times. That's why I didn't think much of it. I thought, homie must've forgotten his lunch, or somethin'. I figured he stayin' there, or he got people there. He stayin' there?"

I shrugged. "We don't know much yet."

Josie said, "Right now, Sarge, we need to see some footage from your cameras and find out how far back you keep your videos."

"We don't keep no video," the big man said.

3

THE BIG MAN—MAC—EXPLAINED THAT THE VIDEO SURVEILLANCE SYSTEM was completely digital now, that Compton had upgraded a few years back and that there was no longer any such thing as "tapes." He said, "C'mon 'round here, I'll pull it up on this computer for y'all. I can pull up ever'thing you need in seconds."

He motioned for Josie to sit next to him, and I stood behind her. Within moments the monitor displayed two perspectives from the court-house parking structure, each showing the flow of vehicles coming in, and picking up pedestrian traffic in the background. Only a small portion of the street could be seen beyond the curbing.

"Is that all you have?" Josie asked, no emotion in her tone. She had one arm folded over her suit jacket, the other holding a pen near her mouth.

"That's the best chance at seeing across the street," Mac said, frowning at the computer screen. "I thought it would show more of the street than that."

"I don't have that kind of luck," I told him.

He wouldn't give up. He clicked through a series of other views and we watched as black and white pictures appeared, one after the other. We saw views of the lobby, the elevators, the parking structure, the holding cells. Finally, we saw the underground secured parking wherein inmates arrive on buses in the early morning and are loaded up and sent back to the county jail at the end of the day. It seemed there were views of everything other than the small apartment building across the street from the public parking entrance on South Acacia Avenue.

I said, "Hey boss, can those cameras be moved? In other words, could someone have changed their points of view remotely?"

Mac, shaking his head, began scrolling through the same series of views a second time. "No sir, they fixed."

Josie said, "Sarge, are you certain that when you were at the security booth that nobody was out in front of those apartments? No kids walking down the street or anything?"

He stopped scrolling, swiveled his chair to face Josie and regarded her for a moment, contemplating. Finally, he shook his head. "The high school's just down the road, and there are a lot of kids walking by in the mornings or riding their bikes. But no, I don't think there was anyone out there when the officer went into the building. I think I would've remembered that. Seems to me this happened after the school kids gone by."

Josie made a quick note and then looked at me while tapping her cheek with the end of her pen. "Well?"

I shook my head—I had nothing.

We thanked the big man for his time, and the three of us gravitated toward the door. He said, "I wish I coulda helped. I'll keep my eyes on that building from now on, let y'all know if there's any funny stuff going on."

Mac stayed behind as Josie and I stepped into an elevator and took it to the ground level, the two of us alone and silent throughout the descent. The lobby was quiet with a few others leaving the building, nobody coming in now. A lone security officer in a light blue shirt and darker pants, wearing a bored expression as natural as any I'd ever seen, sat perched on a stool near the main entrance, his shoulders slumped. He gave a slight nod as we passed through, an acknowledgement that we were all on the same team.

Outside, I stopped in the shade of the building and fumbled in my suit jacket for my sunglasses, taking in the Monument of the Five-Year-Prior. I loved Compton. *The Hub City*. Its history was both rich and ugly, charming and frightening, lively and deadly. Settled in 1867 by thirty pioneer families led by Griffith Dickenson Compton, the city remained white until 1948 when the pre-existing covenants that restricted people of color from purchasing property inside city limits were negated by a Supreme Court ruling. African-Americans began moving in, and after several years of disharmony and sometimes violence between the two races, white families fled the community in droves. By 1960, Compton was 40 percent black. The 1965 Watts Riots drove more whites from the region, and by 1970 Compton boasted a black population of 65 percent. During the eighties, Compton, at that time nearly three-quarters black, saw the rise of membership in black street gangs—Crips and Bloods—and the attendant violence of gang rivalry, deadly turf wars driven by profiteers of the crack cocaine epidemic. Young black men killed one another at record pace, and rappers gained fame and fortune by singing about life and death on its storied streets.

Being a Compton cop in those days had its own challenges under a black-controlled city government. White officers who had worked for the city when it had its own police department—before the sheriff's department began providing law enforcement services in the year 2000—were routinely passed over for promotions and special assignments. They were, at times, shunned by their black colleagues, some of whom had gang affiliations themselves, and who were part of widespread corruption such as theft of money and drugs, and aiding in the concealment of certain crimes committed by those gang members they favored.

Following the white flights of the preceding decades, the seventies found the city mostly black with about a third of its population Hispanic immigrants. Unable to flee, they learned to live in the midst of the violence. Hispanics were assaulted and murdered disproportionately, and, because they were known to carry their life savings with them, they were often robbed. Many were reluctant to report such crimes because they were here illegally.

Soon the Hispanic population began forming gangs that became battle-hardened as they stood up to the black gangs and became the protectors of their people. They, too, began building wealth for their gangs through the trafficking and sales of narcotics, and soon these gangs were yet another scourge that local law enforcement needed to handle.

But now, in the early decades of the twenty-first century, blacks have mostly taken flight themselves, driven out by an explosion of Hispanic migration, legal and illegal alike. The media is loath to report it, but there are more interracial crimes of violence between blacks and Hispanics than have ever existed between either of those two races and whites. When blacks and Hispanics are at war in the jails and prisons, when they are killing one another on the streets, the factor of race is ignored because neither is white. I had investigated murders where gang members had set out to kill someone from a rival gang, and, after failing to find an appropriate target, chose anyone of the other race to murder on the way back to their hoods. They called those "thrill kills." On one such occasion, I had presented the case to the District Attorney and suggested we pursue a hate crime enhancement. There wasn't a moment's consideration preceding the declination.

Though today the city is mostly Hispanic, black roots still run deep in its politics.

Reflecting as I stared at the monument, I said, "Floyd and I got into a pursuit down here one time when we were working Firestone DB."

"Detectives aren't supposed to get into pursuits."

"I realize that, Sergeant," I said, and grinned, "but it wasn't our fault."

Josie started for the parking garage. "I'm sure you were both victims of circumstance."

I trailed behind her, watching her black hair bounce on her shoulders. "We were just cruising along, headed back to Firestone—I don't even remember why we were in Compton—and this dude in front of us starts acting hinky, watching us close in his mirrors.

"Floyd was driving, and we were chatting about something, probably hot Latinas or where to get dinner, as we cruised along, minding our business. Pretty soon, we're picking up speed to pace this dude in front of us. The guy looks like a convict and he's cruising in a '79 Buick Regal, the gangster ride of choice. We could hear the bass of his radio thumping, because you had to have tunes in Tune Town, even when you were running from the cops.

"Finally, I'm like, 'Are we in pursuit?' Floyd says, 'Sort of.' And the dude hangs a hard left, jumps a curb, tears across a dirt lot, and Floyd stays right on his ass, over the curb, across the dirt lot. I grab the radio and start to put something out, but I'm not sure what to say, because—as you pointed out—we weren't supposed to be in pursuit. So I go, 'Eight-oh-one Paul, we're following a failure to yield,' and I put out our location and direction, gave Dispatch the vehicle description and the plate."

We stopped at the threshold of the parking garage and Josie studied me with her big brown eyes and thick lashes. "'Failure to yield.'"

I nodded. "I mean, we were flying now, in full pursuit, but I couldn't say it. Floyd was over there going, 'Yeah, I'm pretty sure we're in pursuit now, Dickie.' I keep putting out our location and I was thinking in my head that some watch commander somewhere would do the math and go, 'Failure to yield, my ass, those bastards are flying!'

"Dipshit goes through a solid red light at an intersection on Rosecrans, traffic everywhere, three in the afternoon—you can imagine the outcome. He takes out a poor old lady, t-bones into her and then bounces off that car and crashes into a light pole. Before the car comes to a stop, the dude's out and running, and so is my asshole partner. By the time I get my fat ass out of the car, I look around and both of them idiots are gone."

"Nice. You guys pretty much follow all the policies."

"Yeah, and this wasn't long after the new foot pursuit policy about partners staying together came out. Before, something would go down, and he'd be off and running and I'd circle the block, call for backup. Most of the time, I was driving, so it worked out okay. But when they said we have to stay together, I told him he needed to knock that shit off, because I can't keep up on foot. And now that it was policy that partners stay together, I knew we'd be hung out to dry if something went bad, like if we got into a shooting or something. But sure as hell, he did it again—and this time, he was driving!

"So I come around the back of the car, thinking I'll jump in and spin around the block. But they're both out of sight already! I make note of the direction people are looking, and figure that's where they went. Of course, it had to be into the projects. I took off and headed toward the north side of the projects thinking that was likely the direction they would continue. I can see people between buildings, coming out and looking that way, but I don't see Floyd. I put it out on the radio that my partner's in foot pursuit—"

"Once again making it clear to your watch commander how many policies you two are violating," she said.

"Yeah, but at that moment, I was really worried. I mean, come on, Floyd, you're going to chase someone through the projects by yourself?" I shook my head. "I come around to the north side of the projects and there's a six-foot block wall. I stop and get out, and my plan was to look over the wall to see if I could see him. As I'm going up to the wall, dipshit comes tumbling over it."

"Floyd?"

"No, the asshole he was chasing. Lands right at my feet. He's out of breath, covered in sweat. Done. Like, take me to jail so I can get some rest, and hurry up before that crazy asshole behind me catches up. So I holster my gun and hook him up, leave him laying there trying to catch his breath. Thirty seconds later, Floyd comes over the wall. He's also out of breath and drenched in sweat. And I'm a cool cat, just standing there with my prisoner, relaxed. Floyd's searching for air, and I go, 'Dude, where the hell've you been?'"

"It's a wonder you two haven't killed each other," she said.

"We've tried," I assured her.

She grinned.

I said, "So what's next?"

Fishing around in her purse and coming up with a set of keys, she said, "I say we talk to the landlord. We need to find out who lives in that apartment."

"I'll follow you."

4

As it turned out, the apartment complex was owned by an investment group registered in New York, and managed by Moe Property, a local LLC with an office on Rosecrans, not far from the Compton Carwash. As I pulled out of the parking structure of the Compton Civic Center, I paused before turning onto Acacia Avenue for another look at the scene. Of course, it was no longer a scene—there were no radio cars nor uniformed deputies, and the yellow tape had been removed. Life had resumed for all except the chippie who had mysteriously died just hours before, only a short distance from where I sat. But this was Compton, a place where life was heavily discounted among many of its residents, where death of anyone other than a loved one was easily forgotten.

Josie tailed me the short distance around the block to Compton Station where I parked my aging Crown Vic and joined my partner in her bureau-issued Dodge Charger. The bucket seat accommodated me as if it had been tailored to my size and shape. I chose not to consider that too carefully, as the aging process and sedentary nature of detective work had begun taking their tolls. I was immediately overwhelmed by the fragrance of lemony leather conditioner mixed with the floral scent of Josie's shampoo or body wash. I had come to enjoy the body wash smell, but it didn't seem to mix well with car maintenance products.

I clicked my seatbelt and Josie proceeded through the parking lot, past the rows of personally owned vehicles and adjacent to the area reserved for radio cars and plain-wrapped detective units. None of those was new and shiny like Josie's charcoal-grey Charger with its throaty engine rumble.

"You have the address, right?"

I leaned toward her to reach for the notebook in my right rear pocket, deciding at that moment it was definitely a body wash I had come to recognize. I wondered if she had likewise come to know the musky smell of my Old Spice "Pure Sport" body wash or my mildly scented Nivea shaving balm. Back in my seat, I wondered why all of these thoughts were in my head and if they meant anything at all. Did others question these things? Or was it my naturally inquisitive mind that took me down every rabbit hole I passed, some of which I had no business in? I flipped through my notebook until I arrived at the last page I'd written on. "Nineteen eleven Rosecrans. Should be just down the road from the carwash."

I looked up to see her nod an acknowledgment.

"Moe Betta Property Management."

She glanced from the road just long enough to give me a frown.

I continued. "This dude is probably a hit in Compton. Moe Betta Property. Moe Betta Bail Bonds. Moe Betta Wines and Spirits. Endless possibilities."

Josie glanced my way again, stoic behind oversized sunglasses.

"Come on, that's a little funny."

"It's not really Moe Betta, is it?"

"Should be."

We arrived, and Josie pulled the Charger to the curb in front of a small brick-front business with a large, street-facing window that featured the company name in bold, colorful window paint: MOE PROPERTY MANAGEMENT. In smaller print below, each on its own line: BAD CREDIT, NO CREDIT, SECTION 8, and *By Appointment Only*. Also a phone number with a local area code.

I glanced at my watch and saw it was nearly five. "This dude's probably gone for the day, with our luck."

"And didn't pull the security gates?"

My gaze drifted to the sides of the storefront window and the entryway door, and noticed the accordion-type gates folded to the sides of each.

Josie glanced in her sideview mirror and popped her door open. "Come on."

The front door was locked, but a buzzing sound prompted me to push the wood-framed and glass door open and step inside, Josie following. There was no room for chivalry in police work. It was one thing to open an office door for a female partner or colleague, but quite another to do so while investigating a death. It had been my experience that women in law enforcement didn't expect nor want to be treated any differently than their male counterparts—especially in the field.

We were greeted by the sound of a chime and the sight of an empty wooden desk that held a phone and a computer. A chair sat tucked in on the other side. Behind the desk was a mirrored window flanked by two interior doors. The one to the right popped open and an elderly black man with a close-cropped gray natural and a matching beard appeared in the doorway. He wore brown carpenter pants over tan work boots and a white button-up shirt with the sleeves turned up and its collar unbuttoned. His stature was consistent with a man from his generation—medium every-thing—back when a man weighing more than a buck-fifty was either a giant or a fat slob. This was a man who was either blessed by genetics or preserved by a lifetime of labor.

"How can I help you officers?"

In South Los Angeles and Compton everyone knew the cops on sight. You could drive a Crown Vic or a sporty Charger and five-year-olds would wave and say, "Hi poh-lees." Sometimes they would follow that up with, "You got any baseball cards?" thanks to our blue brethren who, in the early eighties, partnered with the Dodgers to produce baseball cards featuring officers paired with players. The cards were handed out by offi-cers on patrol to youths throughout the city, especially to the children of low-income neighborhoods where any gift meant a lot. Over the years, departments around the nation had followed suit, and eventually my department, LASD, did the same. Though by the time our department caught on, I was far beyond my patrol career, and therefore no Dickie Jones card was ever produced. If it had been, I would have hoped to be paired with Tommy Lasorda, if for no other reason than to help slim me down in the photograph. Who wanted to be paired next to a ripped and handsome Steve Garvey? So whenever the kids asked for a card, I was left saying, "Sorry, son, that's LAPD; the sheriff doesn't have baseball cards." When they showed disappointment, I resisted the urge to say, "Hey, at least we didn't beat Rodney King."

The man at the door said, "Come in and close that door behind you so them winos don't follow you in. First, they gots to use the bathroom. Then, they ask can you spare a cup of coffee or some change for a brotha. Shee-it, can I spare some change... Maybe if yo mama paid her goddamn rent I could spare some.

"Now what can I do for y'all?" He had worked his way to us and was offering his hand to Josie as he finished, his gaze roaming over her as a smile spread across his face. His appraising eyes were almond-shaped, outlaw eyes. But not an outlaw in the criminal sense, perhaps mischievous in his youth, a joker of sorts but hardened by life as an adult.

He introduced himself as Teddy Moe and said he was the proprietor of Moe Property Management and a few other assorted businesses. Josie handed him a card and likewise introduced us to him, stating that we needed to ask him some questions about one of the properties he managed.

After he and Josie exchanged pleasantries, the old man turned to me and asked if it was take-your-daughter-to-work day as he reached to shake my hand next. I grinned in response.

His grip was firm and meaningful, and he seemed to appraise me during the brief contact. Satisfied, he released my hand, and then turned toward the door from which he had come. "Step into my office where the crackheads can't see us talking." Nobody wanted to be seen talking to the cops. Not in Compton.

We followed him into a wood-paneled office sparsely furnished with a modest desk and chair. There were two metal folding chairs on the other side of it for guests. One wall was lined with four-drawer metal filing cabinets, varying in shapes and shades of gray, beige, and brown. Each was secured by heavy lengths of iron placed vertically across the fronts and through the handles of each drawer, fitted over steel U-bolts and secured with heavy locks.

I indicated the cabinets. "Keeping the crackheads out?"

He glanced behind him to follow my gaze as he lowered himself in his chair. "Crackheads would only want the metal to cluck off at the local scrap yards. There's records of hundreds of tenants—past and present—with enough personal information to keep an identity thief in business for decades. But these niggas around here wouldn't know what to do with it. Hell, they'd dump gold bars on the floor to steal the metal boxes that secured them. What're they gonna do with a gold bar?"

"You keep gold bars in here?" Josie asked, incredulously.

He chuckled. "No, no, no, honey, I ain't got no gold bars. If I did, I'd be in Vegas and I'd have two girls that looked like you, one on each arm."

She smiled.

"The point is, I have to keep these records under lock and key by law, since applications are accompanied by credit reports and fall under Gramm-Leach-Bliley."

I frowned.

He explained, "Federal Trade Commission laws designed to protect consumers from identity theft and other things. But y'all ain't feds—I know that—so that's not what you came to talk about. Either of you want a cup of coffee?"

I shook my head and Josie said, "No thank you."

He opened a desk drawer on his right. "A taste of bourbon?"

I smiled. "Not yet, sir, but thank you."

The man named Moe who seamlessly shifted from legal speak to ghetto jargon without seeming to notice, removed a bottle and a coffee cup from the drawer and poured himself a generous allocation of Early Times. Before plugging the bottle and returning it to the drawer, he took a quick pull from it and wiped the back of his hand across his hair-encircled mouth. He closed the drawer and said—in the Queen's English—"Now then, how may I be of service to our local law enforcement professionals?"

"TEDDY MOE MAY BE THE MOST INTERESTING CHARACTER I'VE MET IN Compton, if you exclude the former city manager who graduated from Harvard only to return to her hometown to begin a career in politics, and is now serving twenty-five for murder."

Josie checked her mirror and pulled away from the curb before shooting me a questioning glance. "Who was that?"

"Brenya Love, and no, there is no relation to the Love family from Watts, as least as far as I know."

"You mean the woman in Watts who was killed by LAPD, attacked them with a knife?"

"Eula May Love," I affirmed. "Her family still lives up there near the Jordan Downs, kind of famous around Firestone. Lots of Loves used to go to jail for a variety of crimes, mostly gang- or drug-related. Not surprisingly, many of them wanted to fight when you tried to arrest them. Environmental insanity."

"Them or the cops?"

"Yes."

"So the city manager did a murder?"

"She contracted it, had her husband killed. She was having an affair with the mayor and had aspirations of a national stage. Hubby was a deadbeat, a drunk who caused her more grief than good, so, like another evil woman of international fame, she tried to get him suicided."

Josie snickered. "You're awful."

"Hey, am I lying? Anyway, even though she was highly educated, she didn't have the intelligence to hire a pro. She got a couple of thugs to do the dirty work, gunned him down right in his driveway while she was at a city council meeting, assuring her alibi. Of course, they were told to make it look like a robbery. You know, take money out of his wallet and fling it to the side or something. But these two mopes couldn't resist taking his 1979 Monte Carlo that he was preparing to depart in when they came out of the shadows and pumped him full of lead. It didn't take long before the cops were looking for the missing car and these two idiots were cruising around in it, having a great time. Hubby's blood was spattered across the driver's side door, and also on one of the dude's shoe and his pants leg. Apparently, he nudged the dead man away from the car so he could close the door and back out of the driveway.

"The detectives were homed in on the mayor's girlfriend before her husband stiffened on the driveway, and it didn't take long for the two gangsters to lay her out in order to receive lighter sentences."

Josie had pulled back into Compton station and was looking for a place to park as I finished telling a small part of the tainted history of the city.

I said, "But anyway, getting back on track, Mr. Teddy Moe has an interesting history himself, I bet. I'd love to share a bottle with him and hear it."

"Well maybe when we're not busy with a dead cop and a missing woman and child, maybe you could take the time to do that. Right now, we need to get details on this Maria Guadalupe woman, and find out where she's disappeared to and what the story is on the kid she had living there with her."

Josie twisted in her seat to look behind her as she began backing into an open space.

I said, "Leticia Carrera. That's an interesting name, a Hispanic surname but isn't Leticia more of a black name? And Maria Guadalupe is too old to have a child that age. What's Moe say, ten?"

She shifted into park and looked at me. "Leticia is Hispanic. And yeah, ten, I think."

We both got out and started for the station, notebooks in our "weak" hands. By the time you graduated from the academy you had learned through pushups and extra miles running that one must never occupy his or her "gun hand," lest it be unavailable when needed.

I said, "I've met black girls named Leticia."

"Whatever, Dickie. I know one thing Floyd was right about—you'd argue with a wood post."

5

THE CALIFORNIA HIGHWAY PATROL OFFICE IN NEWHALL CLOSES AT FIVE. I've never been able to say that without rolling my eyes. Josie, fixated on the computer screen in front of her, didn't notice, though she had clearly picked up on my tone.

"Just because you can't walk into their office doesn't mean they aren't working."

"What, are you dating a chippie now? Or wait, you wanted to be a chippie, but you washed out because you wouldn't write your own mother a ticket."

Josie sat back in her desk chair and swiveled it to face me. "I'd totally write her."

I chuckled and glanced around the office. It was nearly eight now and most of the investigators were gone for the day. Yet there we were with no clear direction, two hunters alone on a mountain as a sudden fog stole away the last moments of daylight. We had no idea why our victim had gone to that apartment, much less who or what had killed him once inside. The tenants, whom we believed might have answers to our questions, were gone without a trace.

"Maybe we need to shut it down, be out there first thing tomorrow and see what we can learn."

Josie's fingers raced across her keyboard, her eyes fixed on the computer screen. I waited. After a moment, she hit the Enter key with resolve, and then turned her attention to me. "I can't find anything on Maria Guadalupe in the system. Not even an ID. She has to have relatives somewhere nearby, but how do we find them?"

"We need to have the girls down at Major Crimes run her through LexisNexis, see what pops. I don't know why we don't each have access to those databases here."

"I've already sent the request," Josie said, picking up her cell phone to check the time. "There's no way we'll get it back until tomorrow. I'm sure they're all gone for the day."

"We screwed up."

Josie raised her brows.

"Or I did," I said. "I let the lieutenant handle the CHP brass and I failed to give him a shopping list. We need Gomez's next of kin, his personnel file, and probably thirty days of activity reports, however the chippies catalog that type of information. Maybe sixty or ninety days. All traffic stops, reports—any activity that might have taken him out of his RD and down to Compton or anywhere near it. We need to find out who his immediate supervisors were and talk to them, and we need to talk to his partners or other officers on his watch. I mean, this might end up being nothing at all, but I don't think so. Something weird happened down there this morning, and now it's ours."

I PARKED MY CROWN VIC ON THE STREET IN FRONT OF MY APARTMENT complex after passing through the alley where tenant parking is accessed on a first-come basis. It was full, as it always was when I got home this late. Fortunately, there were always spots out front, and I had never heard of any vehicle thefts or break-ins. It was a quiet, peaceful place to live. That is, other than the shootout Floyd and I had gotten into not far from here when we were confronted by a contract killer who had been sent to take me out. Bullets had zinged around the bedroom community that afternoon, but nobody was injured. Ever since, I had been less confident that nothing could go wrong in sleepy Burbank.

I stepped out of my car and glanced around once more while retrieving my briefcase and suit jacket from the back seat. The soft glow of yellow streetlights allowed me to scan the interiors of parked cars for someone sitting in the dark, watching. Just as the killer who had come for me had sat, watching. But tonight, like almost every other night, the neighborhood was quiet outside of the muffled sounds of televisions and conversations spilling out through opened windows on the warm summer evening. I focused on Emily's apartment as I moved along the walkway toward the building, and a feeling of comfort and contentment washed over me. She greeted me at the door, her arms warm and soft, her red hair fragrant. Even dressed in a simple t-shirt and shorts, she was beautiful.

I set my briefcase down on a kitchen chair and folded my jacket over the back of it, removed my straw fedora and set it upside down on the table. Before I had moved three feet toward the fridge, Emily scooped all of it up and started for the hallway. Over her shoulder, she said, "I've got dinner in the oven, so your stuff needs to find a better place to hang out."

"We need a better place."

She stopped in her tracks and turned to face me, appraising me with her hazel eyes. I stepped toward her and took my hat from her hands and placed it on her head. I took my suit jacket and briefcase from her and leaned in for a kiss. She retreated slightly, placing her palm on my chest while looking up into my eyes.

"What are you saying, Richard?"

"I haven't stayed in my apartment for a month. Both of our places are small, and with the money we pay for the two of them, we could have a much nicer, larger apartment, or even a house."

"A house?"

I held her gaze for a moment and took a breath, having surprised myself with the suggestion. Yes, it had been something I had thought about lately, but I had also managed to suppress those thoughts, knowing my track record with committed relationships. Two divorces should have been enough to convince me, but then I had allowed a third relationship to evolve into cohabitation, something I viewed as convenient and also less confining or committed. But we might as well have been married, now that we had crossed that threshold. Emily now had a front row view of life as a homicide detective, the long hours, the never-ending communications —phone calls from partners, the desk, informants, and witnesses—at all hours of the day and night. The others hadn't really known what they were getting into until it was too late. That, or they believed I would change, become more domesticated. That soon I would long for nothing but evenings at home and weekend excursions, and that the job would be just that, a job. A paycheck and pension which could be as easily earned working Unsolveds or Missing Persons with steady hours and predictable schedules. That I would no longer desire working the floor—being assigned to one of the six homicide teams in the squad room—where the schedules were grueling and the caseloads unmanageable. What the exes had never understood was that I wasn't the type to change. Not yet. I still desired—*needed*—the steady diet of new cases, callouts in the middle of the night, fresh crime scenes, another victim, and another killer to pursue.

But maybe it would be different now with Emily. Not that I would change, but that she wouldn't demand it or long for it. Being a dedicated federal prosecutor with profound respect for investigators, she understood my lifestyle better than most. I had nearly convinced myself, yet on the other occasions when I considered having this conversation with her, I had managed to swallow the words and dodge the bullet.

Now here we were. Here it was. On the brink of the conversation all of those in budding relationships inevitably have at some point: *So where is this going?*

"A house or a bigger apartment, maybe a condo or something. A place with a garage big enough for us both to have a secure place to park, so you aren't walking in from the street at night and I don't have to worry about my county car being stolen." I looked around the small dining area adjacent to where we stood. "A place where I could set my things down without feeling like a guest."

Her gaze had followed mine toward the dining room, and then she turned to take in the small living room behind her. The move also separated us physically. I stood still behind her in the quietness, watching her, wondering what she was thinking. Was it too soon? Were we not on the same page? My feelings had grown rapidly over the last several months, and deep down inside, I knew that I loved her. But to what degree? And did she also love me? How much? Was she reluctant to give up her independence, or disappointed that I was leaving commitment out of the conversation?

In an effort to lighten the mood, I said, "Or we can just knock out the wall between us, turn our two apartments into a king suite."

Nothing.

After a long moment, she turned back toward the kitchen, pausing to take my hat off her head and hand it back to me. Moving away, she said, "We can think about it, Richard. Go put your stuff down; I'll get dinner served."

I stood for another moment as she walked into the kitchen. "Okay, babe. I'm gonna go next door and change, feed Cosmo, and maybe grab a bottle of something nice to have with dinner. What are we having, anyway?"

"Shepherd's pie," she said, now bent over as she glanced into the small window on the oven door.

Emily then stood and began collecting silverware from a drawer, busying herself. It seemed obvious she was bothered by something about the idea I had of getting a place together, but what it might have been, I didn't know. I turned to walk out, not certain I would come back, a part of me saying run out and never return, another part of me now wishing I had gone to a bar on my way home rather than walking into the honey trap.

As I opened the door, Emily called out from behind me, "Wait."

I slowly turned. She stopped across the living room from me, her head lowered as she nervously twisted a hand towel she held in front of her.

I waited.

She looked up, apprehension in her eyes. "There's something I need to talk to you about first."

"Before I change?"

"No, Richard, before we talk about moving in together, or whatever it is you're thinking about us doing."

"It was just a thought—"

"No matter," she said, taking one more step toward me but maintaining her distance. "We need to talk."

I stood frozen, uncertain of what to say, unsure of where this might go. Apprehensive about having this discussion, and now more than ever wishing I had stopped at the bar. This was exactly what I dreaded about relationships. There was always something. But better now than later, I thought; get this over and move on. It was coming to an end; I could feel it. I said, "Let me change and get that bottle. I'm not really all that hungry now."

6

THE NEXT MORNING JOSIE AND I HEADED NORTH TO NEWHALL, JOSIE behind the wheel of her county-issued Charger, sipping coffee from a Tiffany-blue Yeti mug. If I knew anything at all about my partner by now, it was that the mix was at about seventy-thirty, the thirty being coffee. I could never understand why people polluted coffee with some type of fancy creamer when the sole purpose of it was to get you moving in the morning. I considered this as I sat sulking in the passenger's seat, sipping bitter black coffee that I had grabbed at the 7-Eleven down the street from my apartment before the two of us met up.

So far, only a few pleasantries had been exchanged: Good morning. How are you? Fine. Good. Anything new? Nope. You? Nothing at all.

She said, "So what's up your ass?"

I looked over at her.

The traffic was light heading north at eight-thirty in the morning, not so much for the poor bastards coming south. Santa Clarita had grown over the years to a population of more than 200,000, and it seemed to me that half or more of those people commuted south every day for work. The percentage probably wasn't that high, but whatever those numbers looked like on paper, on asphalt it appeared that everyone in California had to go through the Newhall pass to get to wherever they were going.

I took a long sip of my coffee before answering, trying to decide what to say. What *was* up my ass, anyway? I knew what was on my mind. It had kept me awake all night and now it had my stomach tied in knots. I hadn't been able to eat, and now the coffee was mixing with acid and threatening to come back up if I didn't get something solid in my stomach before long.

But what was I going to tell Josie? That was the question. *What was up my ass?* If I'd been working with Floyd, or any other male partner, I'd have started the conversation about it the moment we joined up, before my door was even shut. I would have tossed my briefcase and suit jacket into the backseat and, while folding myself into the front, before either of us had bothered with "Good morning" or any other bullshit pleasantry, I would have been going off. *Jesus, women. You're not going to believe this shit.* But that's not a conversation you have with your lady partner.

I said, "Nothing, really. Just didn't sleep very well last night."

That was a true statement, so I hadn't lied. Though I also knew she would assume that I was lying and push me for more. The thing I hated about cops is how none of us believed the first thing anyone ever told us. Rule Four: everybody lies. It was a bitch being part of it and also trapped by it all at once. But I guess the chef had to eat his own cooking too, so we all had our crosses to bear.

Josie glanced over but her eyes were back on the road when she said, "Trouble with my buddy, Emily?"

"She's your buddy now?"

"I like her," Josie said. "She's cool. You could do a lot worse, I'll tell you that. Plus, she's hot."

"Women."

"What?"

"Men would never talk about other men being hot. We wouldn't even think about it. We might recognize that some men are more attractive than others, and we definitely judge each other's physiques—you know, that primitive instinct of sizing up foe or competition—but we don't see other men as 'hot'."

"You're avoiding the question," she said.

"What was the question?"

"Are you having trouble with Emily? I left you twelve hours ago, and you were fine. Now you have the weight of the world on your shoulders. I can see it. You're an easy read, partner. You wear your emotions on your sleeve."

I stared out the window, avoiding her glances that I detected in my peripheral vision. In between sips of the harsh coffee, I tried to formulate my thoughts so that I could share my personal troubles with Josie. That's what partners were for, right? Male or female, partners were partners. You trusted one another with your lives and most intimate thoughts, fears, and troubles. Having a woman's perspective right now would have been invaluable, but I wasn't ready to discuss it with her, any more than I had been open to conversation with Emily.

I turned and looked at my partner who stared straight ahead through big sunglasses, still sipping on her giant cup of caffeinated pudding. I said, "Let's talk about what we've got to accomplish on our chippie case today."

THE LOBBY OF THE NEWHALL CHP OFFICE GLISTENED WITH FRESHLY polished tile floors and spotless glass doors, windows, and partitions. The sheriff's department uses inmates to maintain the cleanliness of its facilities, people convicted of low-level crimes and classified as suitable to work as trustees. The smell of Lysol conjured images of a professional cleaning service sweeping through the lobby, a team of polyester-clad women unnoticed by the officer and civilian manning the phones on the other side of the bulletproof glass, a police radio squawking in the background.

"How can we help you?" the officer said as we came to a stop at the counter that separated them from the public.

"Howdy," I said, cringing when it came out. It had sounded corny, folksy, and contrived. I followed it up with, "Sheriff's Homicide," before the traffic cop had a chance to confuse us with a pair of civilians, there to report a crime.

Josie said, deadpan, "We're here to see Captain Walker."

The chippie, probably a twenty-year vet judging by the gray hair and tired eyes, picked up a phone and punched three or four buttons on its base. Soon he was telling someone that Sheriff's Homicide was here for the captain, and then he was saying, "Uh-huh… Yes… Okay, will do, thank you."

He looked up at Josie and then turned to address me. "Captain's on his way in now, ETA fifteen. You're welcome to wait here in the lobby, or you can come on back to our break room. We should have some coffee on."

I smiled and told him that would be great. He showed us to a small room with four sets of tables and chairs positioned in the center, a sofa along one wall, vending machines on another. A third wall featured a kitchenette with a microwave oven built into a set of cabinets, a sink in the center of a long countertop, and an office-style coffeemaker with three burners and an equal number of carafes. One was full, and I helped myself to it. Josie declined, and helped herself to a small bottle of water from a refrigerator.

We sat in silence, Josie staring at her phone while I suffered with my angst over Emily. The only distractions were the muted sounds of radio traffic that permeated the walls, and the sounds of vehicles pulling through the parking lot outside a small window on the far side of the room. I walked over and looked out at the CHP cruisers backed into their spots, a few officers milling about.

I went back to the pot for a second cup, glanced at my watch and made a mental note of the elapsed time—twenty minutes and counting. We had a lot to do, and I was beginning to get antsy. I needed to direct my energy and thoughts toward the task at hand in order to keep my mind off of the domestic issues. It had always worked like a charm before, though I wasn't so sure about this time.

Coffee in hand, I circled the room looking at the various posters, photographs of executives, and framed newspaper articles of historical Newhall events. There was the 1982 Bell UH-1 helicopter crash at the nearby Indian Dunes—a 600-acre ranch where many movies had been filmed—in which actor Vic Morrow and two child actors were killed during the filming of the movie *Twilight Zone*. I remembered it well from my childhood, having grown up not far from there.

The door came open and Captain Walker, whom we had met briefly at the crime scene yesterday, stepped inside. He came straight toward me with his hand extended, and we met in the center of the room. We shook hands, and Josie stood up from the table and did the same.

He motioned for us to follow him. "Sorry to keep you guys waiting."

"No problem, sir," I lied.

He turned toward the door. "Let's go down to my office."

As we followed him down a hallway adorned with officer portraits, he looked over his shoulder and said, "I just returned from Division a few minutes ago."

"Where is that, Captain?"

"Glendale. I try to avoid the place if I can." He opened the door to his office and directed us to a pair of leather chairs near his desk. "I had to meet with our division chief and bring him up to speed, even though there wasn't much I could tell him. Do you guys have any news for me?"

The captain's desk was flanked by a pair of standing flags: Old Glory and the state flag with its red star and grizzly bear. He lowered himself into the tall leather chair behind it, picked up a file that had sat on his desk, and held it toward us. Josie received it.

I said, "Nothing in the way of what killed him. Not yet, anyway. We talked to a security officer from the courthouse who saw the officer park his car and hurry up to the apartment. He wasn't chasing anyone as far as the witness could tell. Interestingly, the security officer recognized Gomez as someone who had been there before. He thought the officer lived there or had a girlfriend there or something."

Captain Walker held my gaze for a long moment but didn't reply. He looked at Josie, who sat thumbing through the personnel file. Walker said, "Twenty-nine years old, seven years on the job. Single, never married, had a deduction on his paychecks for child support. No further details about that. Officer Gomez was a first generation American, a native Californian who grew up in Watts. He graduated from Jordan High School in 2008 and joined the Army. There was a juvenile record that is sealed and coincides with his entry into the armed services. Probably one of those *join up or go to jail* options that some juvie courts still believe in."

"What did he do in the Army?" I asked.

The captain indicated the personnel file that Josie now perused. "It says there he was a combat engineer, trained at Fort Leonard Wood, Missouri, and was stationed at Fort Hood. Had a deployment to Iraq and got out after four years as a corporal. No indication of disciplinary action, no reported injuries."

Josie looked up. "Can we get copies of this file?"

He nodded. "I'll have it copied for you before you leave."

"Who are his friends and partners here, people who would know the most about him?"

The captain leaned back in his chair. "I'll ask his shift sergeant. I honestly don't know much about him. He's only been here six months and was on nights until a month or so ago."

"Where was he before he transferred to Newhall?" Josie asked.

"East Los Angeles."

"So still, no connection to Compton," I said.

The captain shook his head. "It's a complete mystery to us why he would have been there. I had my lieutenant check with Dispatch and we also pulled his activity logs for the month he's been on days. I'll get you copies of all of it. But the bottom line is, he shouldn't have been there. I don't know what he was doing, but he was AWOL from his reporting district, and there is never an excuse for that. The executives are coming unglued, worried there's going to be a major scandal resulting from all of this."

"Like what?" Josie asked.

Her tone was somewhat defensive, and I wondered if she took the captain's comment to be accusatory.

"I don't know," he said. "Nothing surprises me anymore. I've got seven months until I retire, and I can assure you the types of officers we see now are far different from those of my generation—your generation too. It's these millennials coming onto the job lately. Hell, half of them still live with their parents, come to work with backpacks like they're headed to school. If they thought they could get away with it, they'd probably skateboard to work. And there's always some kind of drama involving male and female officers. It's like running a daycare now, and I can't wait to be done with it."

Josie nodded slowly as a way of acknowledging his point, but not necessarily agreeing.

"Has his locker been cleaned out?" I asked.

The captain shook his head. "We didn't know what you guys would want done, so we left it the way it was. Your call."

I considered that for a moment. "Well, we don't even know if we have a homicide investigation at this point, but I'd like to go through his belongings nonetheless, if you have no objection. Also, I assume he has a POV here. If his keys are in the locker, we'd like to go through his personal vehicle, just to be thorough."

"When do you think you'll know about cause of death?" he asked.

I shrugged. "Unfortunately, we have no way to know when the autopsy will be scheduled. My guess is, it will be either tomorrow or the next day. But I could also be wrong. We'll let you know as soon as we hear something. Did you want to attend?"

"I'll have one of our investigators join up with you. We have a few who have attended autopsies before and don't mind. I don't need the baggage."

The three of us stood and paused a moment. The captain said, "Anything you need, you've got. Anything you find out, I'd appreciate first notice, especially if this goes bad."

I nodded.

Josie held up the file. "Copies, sir?"

"Come on," he said, "We'll drop that with the secretary and go have a look at his locker."

7

It was the lunch hour when Josie and I left the CHP office and pulled onto The Old Road, heading south. Josie asked about lunch. I told her I wasn't hungry and got the appraising look in response. Anticipating the subject of what might be wrong with me, I pulled out my notebook and started flipping through it, avoiding trivial conversation. I had just filled several pages while going through Officer Gomez's locker and personal vehicle, and while talking to a female CHP officer named Becky Shaw who had worked alongside him for the last month on dayshift.

"So according to Officer Shaw, our boy didn't have a girlfriend and didn't have many friends. He was sort of a loner and really didn't get along with other officers."

"Well," Josie corrected, "he didn't seem to enjoy the company of other officers. That's a little bit different than not getting along with them."

"Why wouldn't a cop get along with other cops?"

Josie checked her sideview mirror and changed lanes, positioning us for the southbound Golden State. Once in her lane, she looked over at me through her shades. "What are you saying?"

"What?"

"You're already wondering if he was dirty."

"I didn't say that."

She accelerated up the on-ramp. "You didn't have to say it; I know what you're thinking."

I let it go and flipped another page in my notebook. "You have his address?"

Josie picked up her phone. "Already programmed on the map. We're fifteen minutes out."

"See, that's another thing. San Fernando. Why would a cop live in San Fernando? He could easily afford to live somewhere nicer."

"Maybe his family is there."

"He grew up in South L.A., not far outside Firestone's area, and he went to Jordan High. Don't you think he'd want to live somewhere nicer, now that he could? San Fernando's just another gang-infested barrio."

Josie didn't respond. The atmosphere in the car felt heavy, and I wondered why. Was she mad at me for some reason, or just being defensive about the officer? Maybe she felt I was stereotyping him due to his race, culture, and background. Well, I probably was. Profiling was not the dirty word politicians and activists portrayed it to be, and for cops, it was instinctive to do so. A cop would be a fool to ignore the training and experience that guided his intuitions. Josie knew that. She was no different than me or any other cop when it came to that. We were believers of the duck theory: if it walks like a duck, and quacks like a duck…

I said, "And the female cop said he had a roommate, right?"

"Officer Shaw. Yes, she said he had a roommate, but she didn't know anything about him—or her. He had only mentioned to her once that he had one."

Her tone still had an edge.

"Well, why don't we handle this, then grab lunch," I said, trying my best to sound like nothing was bothering either of us—though clearly something was.

"Sure," she said, driving home the point.

We arrived a short time later at the address we had obtained from the personnel file of Officer Gomez, which was the same address indicated on his driver's license and vehicle registration. It was a small, older home, yellow with white shutters, a red brick chimney, and a single-car garage. The walkway to the front door was uneven and had large cracks with weeds jutting up from the ground below. The lawn was a mixture of dirt and crabgrass, and the tracks of car tires revealed the small patch of ground was mostly used for auxiliary parking.

There were no cars at the home, and the small garage door couldn't be opened for all of the debris that was stacked in front of it: miscellaneous car parts including an old truck fender and a large chrome bumper, a milk crate filled with smaller parts, several oil containers, shop rags, and cardboard flats stained by various automotive fluids. A few wrenches were scattered about as well, and a floor jack sat near a pair of jack stands in front of it all.

"Looks like he does his own mechanic work," I said, as we carefully stepped around the debris on our way to the front.

"Or his roommate does."

There she went, defending him again. For some reason, I'd heard enough. "Yeah, I'm sure your boy Gomez never stood out in the driveway drinking beer and turning wrenches until midnight with his buddies. He probably got up on his days off and went to the gym, grabbed a latte on the way home and spent the rest of the day pruning those dead rose bushes and tidying up inside. Jesus Christ, Josie, what the hell is your problem?"

She had turned to stare at me while I finished, and now she took her sunglasses off and stepped into my comfort zone, face-to-face. She pointed her finger at my chest and said, "You're the one in the foul mood today, taking everything personal and acting like someone pissed in your oatmeal. Whatever's going on with you and Emily, get over it. We've got a dead cop, a missing old lady and her little girl, and you're more worried about this guy's lifestyle than what happened to him. So what if he lives in the barrio and works on greasy cars at night? That doesn't mean he was a dirty cop, or that he deserved to die, or that his lifestyle contributed to his death."

She turned and stomped to the front door.

I said, "It doesn't mean it didn't, either."

Josie stood to one side of the door and rapped on it with her knuckles before I had positioned myself to the other side. Her jaw was tight, her body rigid. I wished I hadn't made the last comment. I should have let it go. I didn't want to fight with Josie, yet it seemed we were at each other's throats today.

She stared at the door, waiting for a response from within, and also avoiding looking at or talking to me. After a long moment, she knocked again. There were no sounds from inside that would indicate someone was home. We waited another moment before Josie turned to walk away, huffing as she did.

I called out to her. "You don't want to go in?"

When she turned back to face me, I held a set of keys up for her to see. "We have his keys."

She continued to look at me but still didn't respond.

I continued, "Exigent circumstances. Maybe the roommate is injured or dead inside."

Josie remained unresponsive.

"We should at least clear the house, make sure there're no additional crimes here before we leave. No harm, no foul. We lock it up and go about our business, leave a card in the door for the roommate to call us—if he isn't dead on the bathroom floor."

Without saying anything, Josie tracked back toward the door, grabbing the keys from my hand as she passed me. At the door, she tried several keys until the lock turned open. She glanced at me as she lifted her pistol out of its holster. I pulled mine as well. She nodded—because now we had a situation that required communication, regardless of our mutual irritation.

We moved through the home in a practiced fashion, covering one another and watching for threats from unchecked areas as we progressed with only an occasional nod for direction or affirmation. At the back of the house, we came to the last bedroom and saw that it, too, was unoccupied. I was relieved that we hadn't stumbled onto a secondary crime scene.

Josie was holstering her gun as I began flipping through clothes in the closet, the last area I had checked to make sure we were alone. She said, "Well, we've cleared it. Now you want to go through his underwear drawer?"

I had started to respond, having had several retorts pop into my head that would have done nothing more than fuel the fire. I could have said it was she that was the one more likely to go through his underwear drawer, or I could have reminded her that being thorough was Rule Five of homicide work, followed by Rule Six—which might have been more suitably five-point-five—that commands that one take his/her time at a scene, to never be in a hurry, to not allow outside influences to alter the course of an investigation. I could have cited Rule Seven: Trust your instincts, and I could have elaborated that *my* instincts on this case indicated that something was seriously wrong, and that *that something* centered around our victim.

But I didn't say any of those things, nor did I cite to her any of the rules, many of which she had heard from me on previous occasions, probably out of order and maybe even completely differently each time they were cited. The truth was, there was no rule book, per se. Though there were general practices and procedures and guideposts and lessons learned from those who had paved the way ahead of us, chronicling their successes and failures in order to advance the art of death investigation. From the back of the closet, I pulled out a clothes hanger with a black leather vest. A large patch on the back depicted a motorcycle wheel with wings and a bloody dagger. Below it was the rocker patch: San Fernando, and to the side of it, an M/C patch, signifying membership in a motorcycle club. I displayed it for a moment, and then turned it around so she could see the other side.

Josie said, "How do we know it's his?"

We entered the garage through an interior door and found two bikes parked in the center, shining beneath florescent lights. There were large rollaway toolboxes, an arc welder, cabinets containing parts and tools, a refrigerator with biker-related stickers plastered to its door, and a workbench with tools, a vise, a large portable radio, and an assortment of opened and mostly consumed bottles of beer.

Both bikes were custom, not the bought-off-the-showroom-floor types that most cops rode. One was a shovelhead, so called due to the design of its rocker covers shaped like shovels. It was an eighties-era Harley with shotgun pipes and ape-hanger handlebars with long leather tassels hanging from their handgrips. The other was a much older bike, maybe from the fifties or sixties, the style known as a hardtail or rigid-frame due to its lack of suspension for the rear tire. These types of bikes were considered hardcore, reserved for the toughest of motorcyclist enthusiasts, and were almost always equipped with solo seats with large springs to compensate for the terrible ride they offered. Its panhead motor was typical for this type of bike, the name derived from the appearance of the rocker covers that appear as upside-down cooking pans, made of chrome or polished aluminum. Panheads were coveted by bikers everywhere, but you had to be a fair mechanic to own one. They weren't practical for cross country rides, but they were eye catchers on the boulevard and around town.

"Nice scooters," I said.

Josie hadn't spoken to me since I'd pulled the biker vest from the bedroom closet. She still didn't. She moved around the cluttered area, careful to not touch anything dirty or greasy, which was no easy feat. Finally, she turned to face me. "Okay, he liked motorcycles. Lots of cops do. Are we done here?"

I smiled. "Josie, this isn't your typical cop who buys a Harley and a leather jacket. I've been around bikers a lot, and this—" I turned slightly and panned the room with my hand "—this is hardcore shit. This is why Gomez didn't hang around other cops. *This* is what I've been expecting to discover—not this, per se, but something like this. Something about this guy that separates him from your average, run-of-the-mill copper. This guy had some shit going on, and now we need to figure out what it was."

She looked away, scanned the garage interior once more as I waited, and then met my gaze with the soft brown eyes I had come to know and love, her anger seemingly subsided. "Yeah, maybe."

I nodded toward the door behind her, and she turned to walk out, high-stepping across an oil-stained strip of carpet that led the way. I followed, shutting off the lights behind me. When we locked the front door and started for the car, Josie said, "Let's talk to his neighbors, then you can buy me lunch."

8

ON THE WAY TO LUNCH I CALLED DWIGHT CAMPBELL, A SERGEANT WHO supervised the surveillance teams that had been assigned to watch the Acacia Avenue apartment. There was nothing to report, he said, as far as activity at the apartment went. However, he wanted me to know there was a security officer at the parking structure across the street, a Mexican named Gustavo, who told Campbell that I was like the cops in Tijuana, the way I had bullied him into letting me park for free.

I said, "Whatever," and Dwight just laughed. He wanted to know how long we were planning to have them watch the place, and I told him I didn't know. I said, "Boss, until we figure out if we have a murder, until we figure out what happened to the woman and child who lived there, I think we just have to sit tight."

Josie and I were nearly downtown, sailing along in light traffic and discussing where we should eat, when it occurred to me that we needed to get some information about the child support that was being garnished from Gomez's wages. I asked Josie if she knew how that worked. She didn't, she said, but she assured me there would be plenty of guys at the office who would know. I couldn't disagree with that.

She said, "Or just run his name through civil court records, see what we come up with. There has to be a case if his wages are garnished."

I suggested we swing by East L.A. station and get on a computer before we went to lunch. She asked if I were on a diet or if I had a bug or if I was simply trying to torture her through malnutrition. Rather than answering, I pointed out a perfect place for her to park as we pulled into the rear parking lot of Fort Apache, as the legendary station was often called.

A steady stream of radio cars came and went, deputies coming in with arrestees and rushing back into the field for an assistance request or hot call. This pattern repeated itself a couple of times during the one hour we were there to run the biker chippie through some databases, and it made me miss the days of working patrol. The seemingly non-stop action at stations like East L.A., Firestone—where I spent my time in patrol—and other stations in high crime, gang-infested neighborhoods, attracted a certain type of cop. Some cops were drawn to the profession to help people, regardless of how cliché it sounded, and others were attracted by the steady pay and benefits. Then there were people like me who had predator in their blood and were only content when on the hunt. Homicide allowed me to hunt the worst of mankind, and that was satisfying, but it was a slower, more methodical hunt, very different than rolling down your windows and cruising the streets looking for bad guys. The thrill of that was an addiction for which there is no cure.

Josie tore a length of paper from a printer and came toward me, jarring me from my reverie. I nodded as she approached. "What'd you find?"

"We have a name. Monica Hernandez."

Hernandez was part of the missing tenant's name, but it was also a common one. I said, "Mo-nee-ka," drawing it out and putting a tune to it.

Josie frowned, puzzled by my response.

"Inside joke," I said. "So did you find an address for this Mo-nee-ka?"

"I did."

I waited, but Josie didn't continue. She stood in front of me, clutching a computer printout in one hand and her notebook and pen in the other, a smirk on her face.

"Well," I said, "do you care to share it with the class?"

"She's not far from here."

"Okay, good. *Not far.* You're driving, so I guess I'll know where we're going when we get there. Perfect. Nice job, partner. Great communication."

Josie turned and started for the door that would lead us out of the detective bureau and to the back door where we had come in. Watching her black hair bounce on her shoulders, I said, "Hopefully, she'll be there when we arrive."

"Oh, she'll be there, all right."

I was silent during the drive, still somewhat irritated at my partner. It was one of those days, and I was fairly certain I was to blame. How could a day following a night like last night *not* be a disaster? I should have called in sick and stayed in bed, or lain around on the couch all day watching daytime television the way half of our fellow residents did, or so it seemed. Or dusted off my clubs and headed to the local course to play 18 holes and try to match it with beers.

I flipped through my notebook to refresh my memory on the players as we headed to this interview: Antonio Carrera Gomez was our dead biker chippie, and presumably he is the father of Monica's baby or babies. The apartment was rented to a Maria Guadalupe Gomez Hernandez. Gomez and Hernandez. I looked out my window as we drove west on 3rd Street, crossing under the Long Beach Freeway and heading toward the city, thinking about how the names were connecting dots. Now we were on 4th Street, still traveling west toward Boyle Heights, the Aliso Village housing projects, or beyond it to downtown Los Angeles.

She'll be there all right.

It hit me. We were headed to Bauchet Street. "I'll bet you lunch I know where baby mama's living."

"You're buying lunch."

"It's going to be dinner by the time we stop to eat, at this rate."

"Okay, deal. Where are we going?"

I smiled. "Four-fifty Bauchet Street, Twin Towers."

Josie glanced over after completing her turn onto Soto Street. She didn't have to say anything now. We would soon be turning left onto Cesar Chavez—a street I still fondly remembered as Brooklyn Avenue, as the street had been for a century before being renamed in the honor of the hard-left labor leader with communist ideology—and from there it would be a straight shot onto the street known by every cop and criminal in Los Angeles County, Bauchet Street.

441 Bauchet Street was the location of Men's Central Jail, the largest jail in the world. During the eighties and nineties, the half-century-old jail housed roughly 10,000 inmates, though it was built to house half of that. In 1997, Twin Towers Correctional Facility was built across the street, and it housed both men and women prisoners. The Metrolink's Central Maintenance Facility—Metro CMF—and a bail bond storefront, were the only other properties with addresses on the infamous Los Angeles street.

Josie said, "You're still buying lunch. That was a con."

"No pun intended, I hope."

The parking structure sits at the far north end of Bauchet Street, leaving a long walk to the towers. Josie was forced to maintain a fast gait to keep up with me, as I was in no mood for a casual stroll among the hundreds of brand-new deputies in their crisp uniforms who sauntered along the sidewalks, in no hurry to make their p.m. shift reliefs, which traditionally began at two o'clock. Most of them didn't appear old enough to have driven themselves to work, walking in with backpacks slung over their shoulders like they were on their way to school. They certainly didn't look like they should be out past ten, the time of night they'd be set free from custody to run amok. When I had been new on the department and assigned to work here, the end of p.m. shift signified the beginning of social hour. Deputies would rush for their vehicles and head to local watering holes or to nightclubs in Hollywood or other locales throughout the southland. An old sergeant once said, while watching as the throngs of robust young deputies rushed through the security gate at the end of a Friday night shift, "It's a frightening thing to release all of that testosterone into the city at once."

We secured our weapons in the gun lockers, exchanged our department identifications for visitor passes, and were escorted to an interview room where we waited for ten minutes. It felt more like an hour in the isolation of the windowless concrete room. The absence of levity between Josie and me contributed to the punitive feel of it.

Finally, a woman wearing an orange jumpsuit and plastic sandals was escorted in, unhandcuffed. Her dark hair had streaks of gold but was oily and unkempt and hung recklessly over her face. The pair of deputies who had escorted her directed her to a seat across a small metal table from us. I asked her name as Josie checked her wristband, a habit built early in our careers while working at custody facilities. It wasn't uncommon to have the wrong inmate brought to an interview, sent to the clinic or the attorney room or to visiting, or, on rarer occasions, released from custody. You always checked their wristbands while asking them to identify themselves.

"Monica Hernandez. What's this about?"

I nodded to Josie, signaling for her to take the lead.

"Hi Monica, I'm Josie. This is my partner, Richard. We're with the sheriff's department."

On television they would say their names were Detectives Sanchez and Jones, but I've never seen "Detective" on a birth certificate. Josie had learned to follow my lead, to downplay the authoritative approach, to allow the people we spoke with the opportunity to be on our level. It had always worked well for me. With hardcore criminals I might go by last names but still drop the title. Everyone we ever needed to speak with knew we were detectives, we didn't have to remind them. I also liked that she didn't mention our assignment. We were "with the sheriff's department." Nothing raises the intensity of an interview more than letting them know we were the murder police.

Monica looked from Josie to me, and back, expectantly.

Josie continued. "You're not in any trouble. We just have a few questions for you."

"Okay," she said, cautiously.

"First, can you tell us what you're in for?"

Of course, we already knew. Ms. Monica had picked up a possession beef when LAPD responded to a disturbance call and found her walking down the center of Pacoima Boulevard with a half-emptied bottle of Cuervo in her hand. She was detained, arrested for being drunk in public, and then, during a booking search, a female officer found two ounces of meth stashed in her panties. Possession of a controlled substance was now only a misdemeanor in California, but Monica was held in county jail due to a probation violation out of Las Vegas for the same charge. In Nevada, it was still a felony to possess a controlled substance.

Monica said, "They said some kind of bullshit warrant out of Nevada. I never even been in Nevada."

Now we had a baseline. We knew she was going to lie to us whenever it was expedient to do so.

"So you'll have to go face charges there?"

"My attorney said we'll fight extradition, but I'm ready to waive it and get on. This place is fucked up."

"Are you married?" Josie asked.

Monica clucked her tongue. "Ah, hell no. Why do you want to know that, anyway?" She looked at me again. "What's this all about, Detective?"

I shrugged, forcing her to stay with Josie.

Josie said, "Kids?"

"Okay, what the fuck, eh? Why are you asking me about all this shit? Has something happened to my daughter? What's going on here?"

"So you have a daughter?"

Monica leaned back in her chair. "I'm not saying another goddamn thing until you tell me why you're here asking me about my family."

She turned her gaze toward me and held it, the two of us locked on with a sudden intensity that changed the tone and pace of the interview. Nice hadn't worked with her. I wasn't sure Josie had caught it, so I decided now was as good a time as any to lay down some cards and get to the point.

"Your daughter lives with your mother in Compton. You either lost custody of her or walked away to chase a high or be with some loser old man."

"Who the f—"

I slammed my palm on the table. Monica jolted and I came out of my chair and leaned across the table toward her. "I'll tell you who we are— we're the murder police. We're here investigating a death—"

Her eyes widened and she released a heavy breath.

"—and it may involve some members of your family. And now your mama is missing, and your little girl might be missing too. How's that? Feel like talking now?"

Her gaze darted away, looking to Josie now. Drawing her knees to her chest and holding herself, she began to shake, and her eyes became soft and moist.

I knew better than to let her off the ropes. "We have no idea where they are, whether they were taken, or whether they ran away. You're the only person we know of who might be able to help us."

She looked at me again, her expression now soft, willing—almost pleading. "My baby daddy's a CHP, works in Newhall and lives in San Fernando. I can give you all of his information. Maybe she's with him."

I looked at Josie who turned her gaze toward Monica. "Monica, there's no easy way to tell you this... Antonio is dead."

WE DECIDED ON CHINESE SINCE WE WERE DOWNTOWN ANYWAY, AND OVER a late lunch or early dinner, we discussed the direction of the case.

"First, we need a cause of death. We might be spinning our wheels," I said.

"At the very least we have two missing persons," Josie reminded me.

I pondered it a moment, and said, "But we don't work Missing Persons."

"So if Gomez wasn't killed, we're done? We walk away from the little girl? You know something happened there. The chippie didn't abandon his post and drive from Newhall to Compton just to check in. Something happened there, and he was square in the middle of it."

I finished a beer and nodded at the waiter. "I get that. But they'll pull us off if it isn't a murder. If Gomez died of a heart attack, we're finished. Metro handles kidnappings, not Homicide."

Josie pushed back from her plate. "Are we done working?"

She was referring to me ordering another beer. Technically, drinking while on duty was against department policy. *Technically*. Vice cops, undercover cops, and homicide detectives were unofficially exempted. Vice cops because part of their jobs was to go into bars and fit in with the patrons. Undercover cops had to fit in with dopers, bikers—whoever. And homicide detectives, well, we had to handle the deaths of babies, kids, and cops, stand over them in their final poses and again as a medical examiner dissected them. We had to knock on doors and tell their loved ones that they were dead and try to explain what had happened to them. Then we had to go home to our own families and act as if it had been just another day at the office. We stored all of these images and their attendant odors in our tormented minds, and at various times of the day and night, we randomly recalled these sights and senses. Unexpectantly. Uncontrollably. But we carried our own water and didn't allow others to see the pain. So yeah, sometimes homicide dicks drank, and they didn't always wait until they were off the clock.

"Are we ever?"

"Good point," she said, revealing a half smile for the first time today.

I held her gaze for a moment, seeing a question in her eyes. I knew what was coming, but the waiter saved me. He set my beer down and walked away, and I quickly changed the subject.

"We're going to need Monica's help, but we're in a jam with that Nevada warrant. Any ideas?"

Josie looked around the small dining area. It was empty other than the two of us and what I presumed to be a husband/wife pair, the owners. Her gaze returned to me and she said, "Yeah, as a matter of fact, I do have an idea."

I took a drink of my cold beer and set it down. "Let's hear it."

"Farris."

I raised my brows. "Farris?"

"His daughter is a prosecutor in Clark County, Nevada. Maybe she can help us out."

"It's a probation violation with extradition; I doubt a deputy DA is going to be able to make that disappear. Also, how did you know that about Rich? I didn't even know that."

"You don't talk to your colleagues about personal matters. You're 'Dickie all-business-all-the-time Jones'. All we need is for someone to pull the file and see if the original charge is really that big of a deal. If not, maybe the probation violation can be withdrawn—with a little influence— and the probation could be reinstated. Then we could get her out of custody and have her work with us to find her little girl."

I thought about it for a long moment, then took another swig of beer. "I like the idea of it. She didn't seem as if she was going to be all that helpful from inside."

"She was definitely interested in using the situation to get out of jail."

I nodded. "Big surprise there, right?"

Josie shook her head, showing disgust. "Mother of the year."

9

RICH FARRIS HAD BEEN A STANDOUT SHORTSTOP AT WOODROW WILSON High School in Long Beach, California, making second team all-conference his senior year. A right-hander, he dug his cleats into the clay at the shortstop position where he had gained a reputation as a golden glove prospect with a powerful arm. There were only six shortstops in California to receive a higher scout rating than Farris, and it was his bad luck that a crosstown rival, Rico Coletti, who was considered the Number Two high school shortstop prospect in the nation, happened to be one of them. So Farris walked on at Cerritos Junior College, a school known for producing players that made it to the big leagues. In his first year, during a non-conference game, Farris drew the attention of a coach from Cal State Fullerton, a national powerhouse that had won two college world series championships by that time, and which would go on to win a third a decade after Farris had hung up his cleats. It was a promising start.

Cal State Fullerton offered Farris a full-ride scholarship the next year, but he would move to third base. Farris's old rival, Rico Coletti, had gone to Fullerton straight out of high school and had sewn up the shortstop position. Farris adapted and even excelled at third, but he struggled to hit the hard-breaking stuff of right-handed pitchers at that level. Yet in spite of Farris's bat, he was scouted by the Chicago Cubs and offered a job playing in their short-season single-A team, the Geneva Cubs.

Geneva, New York, a three-day bus trip from Los Angeles, California, is where Rich Farris began his professional baseball career.

He arrived at McDonough Park late one afternoon and carried his bags into the office, dreaming about the day he would make it to the big leagues. At *The Show* he would no longer carry his own bags nor ride buses to the games. He would play beneath brilliant lights and to the roar of thousands of fans in sold out stadiums. It was the start of a dream come true. Farris found the manager in his office, a lanky man in his fifties with black hair that was slicked back and likely dyed, and who had a strong accent Farris figured to be that of a New Yorker. Farris had never been to the east coast. The manager didn't bother with greetings or introductions. He told his assistant—a heavyset black man who sat slouched in a chair, his uniform disheveled, well-worn Birkenstocks on his feet and a wad of chewing tobacco stretching out one cheek, to show Farris to his locker and give him the schedule. The assistant did as he was asked, introducing himself as Babe McFarland as the two baseball men shuffled through the locker room. "No relation to Mr. Ruth," he had said.

Two days later, Farris came into the locker room with his head hung low. He had been exposed, a term used in the sport to describe the phenomenon of stepping to the plate against an elite field of talented, professional baseball players. Even at its lowest level, these athletes who played America's greatest sport were of an entirely different caliber. Farris had never reached first base during his eight at-bats through eighteen innings of play. He had struck out six times, grounded out to the pitcher, and popped up to a bubble-blowing second baseman during his last at-bat of his professional baseball career.

The next day he arrived at the park to find an envelope taped to his locker. There was no note inside, only a bus ticket back to L.A. and a fifty-dollar check for travel expenses. He spotted Babe McFarland on his way out, but the old baseball man just looked away.

Farris reflected on those days as he sat in the low light of a local bar, a game overhead on the television and two beer-guzzling baseball *experts* seated near him. The two fans—neither of whom appeared to have done a single sit-up since junior high—chastised an "overpaid" second baseman for striking out with two men on base when their team was down by one in the eighth. This man, who year after year would hit twenty dingers and drive in a hundred runs for their team, was "a bum" who had no idea how to hit the goddamn ball. How hard could it be?

His cell phone vibrated, jarring him from the internal dialogue he was having with his fellow patrons. He looked at the screen for a long moment while deciding whether or not to answer it. At the last moment, he clicked on. "What's up, Dickie?"

AFTER I PAID THE TAB FOR LUNCH, JOSIE AND I HEADED BACK TO THE office. On the way, I called Rich Farris to see if he was still around. I thought it best for us to talk to him in person and explain the entire situation before asking for his help.

The phone rang four or five times, and I was about to disconnect when I heard him answer. "What's up, Dickie?"

I could hear loud voices and a TV in the background, and guessed he was out to lunch himself. "Hey man, where're you at?"

"What's that? I can't hear you."

I repeated myself, and Rich said, "Hang on, man, I've got to go outside, before I smack somebody in the mouth."

I looked over at Josie and smiled while waiting for Farris's end of the line to clear up. She scrunched her brows and nodded, as if to ask what was so funny.

"I think he's in a bar, and it sounds like he's about to kick someone's ass."

A moment later it was quiet, and Rich's voice came through clearly. "Dickie, you still there?"

"I'm here, Rich."

"What were you sayin', man?"

"Well, I was asking where you were, wondering if you were at the office. But it sounds like you might be done for the day."

"Yeah, man, I am. What's up?"

"Josie and I wanted to talk to you, maybe see about getting a little help on something. But it can wait. You coming in tomorrow?"

"I don't know, man, I might just take the rest of the week off. I need some time away right now."

I thought about his partner, Lizzy Marchesano, and her current battle with cancer. I wondered if that had anything to do with his disposition and figured it might. Then I thought about his level of irritation, wherever he was. That wasn't something he needed either. I said, "Are you anywhere near Sierra Madre, by chance?"

"I can be," he said.

Josie glanced over from behind the wheel. "Sierra Madre?"

I pointed in the direction of the office, and mouthed, "Let's go pick up my car." Then, into the phone, I said, "Rich, meet us at the Buccaneer in an hour."

An hour later Josie and I walked in through the back door of the Buccaneer and paused as our eyes adjusted to the dark interior. Once I could see, I quickly scanned the place looking for Farris, and checking to make sure there was nobody else I knew. The last time I had been here, it was with Katherine. But I doubted she had ever returned on her own. I didn't think she ever really appreciated the place the way I did, which actually spoke to our differences and helped explain the demise of our relationship.

Rich Farris had beat us here and was bellied up to the end of the bar where he would see the front door and could just turn his head slightly to glance at the back door too. It was a cop thing. There were patrons at the bar hoisting grog, others scattered about at tables, and a few were gathered at the dartboard, beers in hand, cheering or jeering one another as a competition was clearly underway. Josie slid onto a stool next to Rich, and I stood to the other side of her, propping myself up with an elbow on the bar.

The bartender, whom some called Moby because he closely resembled the American songwriter/singer with his bald head and black-framed glasses, made his way toward us. I glanced at Rich's beer and saw that it had just been poured or else he was nursing it along. My guess would have been he had just received it. Moby arrived and wiped the bar as he asked what we were drinking. I ordered a beer and Josie said she'd have a glass of water, a wedge of lemon if it wasn't too much trouble.

"We're definitely off duty now," I said.

"I'm cleansing, currently."

Moby set our drinks in front of us. I raised my frosted mug of Coors Light as a toast and said, "Me too."

Farris partly turned on his stool so that he was facing us and leaned in to be heard over the crescendo of a Queen song playing on the jukebox. He said, "Dickie, how the hell did you find a place like this, pirate shit and naked women all over the walls?"

"Isn't it cool?" I smiled, took a swig of my beer and set it down. "A couple of good friends of mine turned me onto it. Tom and Rosie, both LAPD. They live just a few blocks from here. You don't like it?"

Rich glanced around and rubbed a hand over his hair. "It's different. I'm not sure a brother's going to find much action in a place like this."

Josie put her hand on his forearm. "Rich, you've got to hide in a place like this just to take a break, all the action you get."

He chuckled.

"Thanks for meeting us, Rich," I said.

He raised his glass. "My pleasure, man. What can I do for two of my favorite colleagues—the new Mod Squad."

I grinned. "It's been a while since I've seen that one, Rich, but if my memory serves me correctly, we'd need you to partner with us to be the Mod Squad. And you'd have to grow a fro."

He rubbed his head again. "Those days are long behind me, brother."

I lifted my fedora and rubbed a hand across my bald head. "Yeah, same. Anyway, Josie wanted to ask a favor of you."

Josie frowned at me and then turned to face Farris. "Rich, you mentioned to me once that your daughter is a prosecutor in Vegas, right?"

He nodded. "Yeah, Clark County. Why?"

She glanced at me. "Where do I start?"

"With the dead chippie."

Farris said, "Dead chippie? You've got my attention."

Josie gave him the details, starting with the suspicious death of Officer Gomez, and ending with our interview of Monica Hernandez at Twin Towers just a few hours earlier.

Farris, his brows set low, said, "And you want her out of jail to help you find the kid?"

I shared his obvious concern. It was a gamble knowing she was an addict who had mostly abandoned her daughter for drugs. How could we expect her to help us find her daughter now? If she had been taken—along with her grandmother—how would someone who had been locked up have any ideas about what might have happened to them? Those were good questions, questions I had asked myself, and that Rich Farris likely had asked himself also.

"I think she knows what happened, Rich. Or she at least knows why it happened. You could look into her eyes and see the wheels spinning, turning with secrets and knowledge but also opportunity, a way to get out of jail."

Rich nodded slowly, processing the information. "And how does her being out of jail help you find Grandma and the kid?"

"Fair question, Rich. She claims she would be able to find out what it's about if she could get on the street and hook up with her connections. She confirmed that our victim is her daughter's dad and suggested that he might have been involved in some things that caused it."

"You're talking about the chippie?" Rich asked, skeptically.

Josie said, "I don't trust her."

"The dude's a biker and kind of a misfit at his office," I said, "so who knows. Maybe he was into dope also."

Josie shook her head.

Farris said, "When you say biker, what do you mean? He owned a Harley? Shit, half the cops on our department own Harleys now."

Now I was the one shaking my head. "Not like this. Guys on our department walk into dealerships and walk out with a bike payment, a 'Harley Owners Group' leather jacket, a flyer advertising the next rider safety course, and a maintenance schedule because they have no idea how to change the oil on one. This guy, Gomez, had two bikes in the garage, a panhead and a shovel, and from the tools and debris around the place, I'd say he likely built one or both of them himself. He's a real biker."

"Okay, but still," Farris argued, "that doesn't mean he's an outlaw."

"No, I'm not saying he's a one-percenter—"

"Yes, you are," Josie said.

"—but he was more biker than cop. Trust me."

Farris smiled. "Well, I mean, chippie, so…"

Josie pushed off of her stool and said she had to use the ladies' room.

Before she walked away, she looked at Farris and said, "Dickie's had a hard-on for this guy from the onset. There's no real evidence that he was dirty."

As she walked away, I said, "Watch, his labs will come back with coke or meth."

She dismissed it with a wave of her hand, not bothering to look back.

Farris watched her walk away before looking back at me with a grin. "She's really something, isn't she?"

"She's on my jock today, buddy, I'll tell you that."

He smiled and finished a beer. I signaled for Moby, but Farris waved him off. "I'm good, man, gotta be able to drive home."

"Well to finish up what I was saying, I think she plans to use us to get the whole story about what went down and who's responsible. I don't think she necessarily plans on being truthful with us about what she learns, but if we know that going in, we'll use her to gather some intelligence and then dump her back into the slammer."

He nodded, standing up from his stool now. Josie reappeared and stood next to him. It was time to go, apparently.

I said, "The bottom line is, we need some love in Vegas to make this extradition go away. No way we're getting her out of jail here with an out-of-state detainer on her head."

"I'll see what I can do," he said. "Send me all of the information you have on her and the case in Nevada, and I'll talk to my daughter. You ready?"

I looked at my mug that was still half full. "I'm going to just finish this one. You guys go ahead."

I watched my two friends walk out the front door and waited for it to close behind them. Then I signaled for Moby.

"One more?" he asked.

"And a scotch on the rocks. Make it a double."

10

THE NEXT MORNING, I WOKE WITH A DRY MOUTH AND A BURGEONING headache. It was 7:30, so Emily should have left for work by now. But to be certain, I lay still and listened for signs of life from the apartment next door. I didn't want to see her or talk to her just yet. Apparently, the feeling was mutual, as neither of us had called or even texted the other since *our talk*. Nothing was ever easy when it came to women.

Finally, I got up, shuffled into the kitchen and started the coffee. I looked through the window and then went to the front and peeked out. I couldn't see her car, but that didn't mean she was gone. The majority of the carport was out of view from my apartment. I tried to remember where her car had been parked when I came home last night, but I couldn't think of it. I must not have noticed. I remember being focused on her windows and relieved that the lights were out. It was the primary reason I'd stayed for another drink, or two.

I started the shower and checked my phone while letting the water heat up. No messages from Emily. Nothing from Josie. I was relieved but also somewhat disappointed. I'd try calling Josie on the way into the office, see where she was at with me today. I wasn't sure what to do about Emily, but I couldn't avoid her forever since we were literally next-door neighbors.

A half hour later, I was sitting in traffic on the I-5 sipping black coffee and taking gulps of bottled water in an effort to rebalance my electrolytes. I shook my head at the radio news of an overturned vehicle at the East L.A. interchange. How did they do it? How could they be driving along on a flat, dry surface, and flip their car? The idea of it baffled me, yet it happened more than every once in a while. I began planning an exit strategy for the next off ramp, Los Feliz Boulevard—the happy road, apparently—so that I could take my happy ass to work via surface streets. Sometimes L.A. could wear you down.

Before calling Josie, I wanted to get an update from the surveillance team to see if there had been any activity at the apartment. I called Dwight Campbell, who said there had been no activity at all. Then he asked how long we wanted them to sit on it, letting me know that his team was nearly out of hours and that they would need Homicide to pay the overtime if they continued. Being on a 40-hour flex schedule, they could burn through their regular hours in two days, allowing the rest of their week to be a long weekend or a money-making extravaganza. I took the liberty of telling them Homicide would pay the overtime. One day my captain was going to kill me.

When Josie answered, I could hear the sounds of a Wednesday morning in the squad room. It was the one day everyone assigned to Homicide was supposed to be there. At nine, we'd have a bureau meeting where the captain would drone on with administrative bullshit, and then investigators would brief their cases. I wasn't looking forward to briefing this one, because I wasn't sure what I'd say about it. *We think a chippie died as the result of something happening at an apartment in Compton, but we don't know what that something was, and we aren't even sure how the chippie died.* I could only imagine the heckling that would follow any such briefing. Homicide was no place for the thin-skinned, as it could be a very rough crowd.

As I was winding through Elysian Park, snaking my way down Stadium Way in order to circumvent the East L.A. interchange with its upside down Angeleno and the ensuing cluster of emergency vehicles and civilian looky-loos, a call came in from the desk. This could be just what I needed—an autopsy! Besides crime scenes and court, autopsies were the only other legitimate excuse for missing a bureau meeting.

I answered the call and my hunch was correct: the desk had received the "two-hour notice" from the coroner's office that the post of Antonio Gomez was beginning in half an hour. Silvia, a civilian assigned to the front desk at Homicide, said she had already spoken with Josie, who had asked her to let me know she'd see me at the coroner's office.

The postmortem examination of Officer Gomez had been treated in the same manner as any of the other 10,000 cases the coroner's office processed each year. From the scene, his remains had been transported downtown and wheeled into the service floor where he was weighed, tagged, and then photographed in the condition in which he arrived. After photographs, the coroner's investigator had obtained samples of his hair and fingernails. Then his clothing had been removed, his body washed, x-rayed, and wrapped in plastic and stored in the cooler.

If it had been an obvious murder, the autopsy would have been handled differently, given the fact that Gomez was a law enforcement officer who died on duty. However, Coroner's Investigator Nick Stewart had written it up as unknown causes, a possible natural. I hadn't argued, as the very small abrasion to his head was superficial and there were no other signs of trauma or foul play. A tipped-over end table was the only possible sign that violence had occurred, but it was as likely that the table had been upended as the victim fell. He may have even hit his head on it as a result of the fall, causing the small abrasion.

Josie had waited for me outside. We pulled on our respirators before entering the back door, the sour smell of death a miasma hanging over the loading dock. Inside, we signed in, greeted the paradoxically cheerful receptionist, and made our way through two hallways lined with gurneys holding corpses, some wrapped in white sheets, others naked to the world. Before descending to the service room, we slipped into something more appropriate for the occasion, meaning we went into the supply room and covered ourselves in blue paper gowns, booties, and gloves. Josie donned a matching blue hairnet while I stayed with my style, today a smart Dobbs fedora, natural straw with a black, red, and silver band. No feather.

There are two rooms where autopsies are performed on the service floor of the coroner's office. Both are at the end of a hallway, one on either side. Each has a set of double doors with small windows and multiple scars from the constant ramming of gurneys. Sometimes you could find your "table" by spotting the work in progress from the window. But if your victim happened to be a male of average weight, you might have to make a closer inspection of several tables to find your guy. Extraordinary sizes would help you home right in on where you needed to be, either the morbidly obese or a child. Of the dozen autopsies taking place on any given day, the vast majority were adult males.

It was common to arrive shortly after the notice that a post was scheduled, only to find that the medical examiner had begun about three minutes after the "two-hour notification" was received advising that the autopsy would begin in thirty minutes. We pushed through the heavy doors and walked into the ghoul factory where the remains of human beings were sliced, chopped, sawed, examined, washed, drained, and hastily reassembled with heavy sewing thread and a needle the size of a shark hook, before being wrapped in plastic and moved into cold storage, pending final placement. And people wondered why we drank.

Gomez's examination was half finished. A giant Y had been cut into his chest, the top of the Y extending from each shoulder and meeting below the breastbone, where a single incision continued to the pubic bone. The rib plate had been removed, and the organs had already been examined, weighed, and samples had been taken.

I knew the head would be next. A scalpel would be used to make an incision from behind one ear, across the forehead to the other ear, and back around. The cut would then be divided, and the scalp pulled away in two flaps. The front flap would be peeled forward over the face, and the back flap would be peeled backward over the back of his neck. An electric saw would then be used to cut through the skull, and the cap would be pried and popped off, exposing the brain. It was this part of the procedure that interested me most on this particular case. How significant was that injury to his forehead? Could the strike or blow to the forehead have caused traumatic brain injury and resulted in his death? Hopefully, we would soon know.

I reached over and placed my business card on the doctor's rollaway workstation. I had added Josie's name to the front of the card above mine. This made it easy for the doctor to later note in the coroner's protocol who had witnessed the procedure.

Dr. William Langley looked up from his work, his eyes scanning us through a clear face shield, and uttered something unintelligible because of his respirator.

I leaned in, "What's that, Doc?"

He straightened from his hunched position, lifted his face shield, and pulled the respirator an inch from his mouth. He indicated the card, and said, "I said, 'Thank you.'"

I nodded. "Any significant findings yet, Doc?"

He leaned toward me and lifted his respirator again. "Sudden cardiac death."

I glanced at Josie and shook my head.

Her eyes shifted toward the doctor, and she, too, lifted her respirator from her mouth. "Doctor, are you saying this is a natural?"

He nodded. "Looks that way."

I couldn't believe it. A natural? I shook my head again. "What about the injury to his head?"

"It appears to be superficial, but we'll have a look here in a minute."

The doctor moved to the end of the table where a scale swung from a chain and hung over the stainless-steel sink that ran the length of the wall. He reached up and removed a heart from the pile of organs and walked back with it cupped in his hands. Displaying it for us to see, he rotated it one way and then the other as he showed us the signs of the deadly disease.

Josie said, "He was so young, and he appeared healthy."

"Usually, in a case like this," Doctor Langley began, "the condition has been caused by genetic mutations. In other words, inherited cardiac conditions—a bad ticker passed down from the father. To be honest, the results of the case won't be back for a while. We'll have a cardio expert dissect the heart and break it all down for us. But as I see it now, absent significant brain trauma, this is most likely a natural."

Josie leaned over and lifted her respirator. "Sort of changes everything, doesn't it?"

I thought about it for a moment. Did it? I didn't know. Something had happened in that apartment. I said, "Hey Doc, question for you."

He looked up from the heart.

"If something happened to trigger the cardiac episode, say an altercation, would you be inclined to call it a homicide?"

He glanced at the heart in his hands, at the other remains on the table, flaps of skin exposing the empty torso cavity, and then his gaze came back to me. "It depends."

"On?"

"Had there not been an altercation—presuming that one did occur, and that you can prove it—how do I know that he wouldn't have dropped dead at lunch, or while writing a ticket later that morning? See, it becomes rather speculative."

"Well if a dude with a bad ticker gets shot the morning his ticker was set to stop working, it's still a murder. See? I mean, we can *what if* it all day. But my question is straightforward: if this chippie had an altercation at about the time of his death, would you be able to say, with some degree of certainty, that the altercation did in fact trigger the cardiac arrest? Regardless of whether or not he was living on borrowed time."

He seemed to consider it as he retreated to the end of the table where he replaced the bad ticker. The doctor came back to the head of the table and picked up his electric saw, apparently still pondering it. Finally, he said, "In my opinion, an altercation would have substantial contributory elements to the sudden cardiac death."

I looked at Josie and smiled.

She said, "What a clusterfuck."

11

THE BUREAU MEETING HAD FINISHED LONG BEFORE JOSIE AND I ARRIVED at the office. Half the detectives were gone, judging by the parking lot. The post-meeting mass exodus usually resembled Dodger stadium at the end of the seventh inning, no matter the score. Josie pulled into a spot next to the back door of the office, and I backed into a space a few spots down. By the time I had exited my car and started for the door, she was nowhere in sight.

I set my briefcase down next to my desk and started out on my usual circle: the restroom, the kitchen for coffee, then the front desk where I would check my mail slot and look at the board to see what types of cases had gone out, before returning to my desk. Hopefully, there hadn't been any cases in which the bodies of an elderly woman and a ten-year-old girl had been discovered. I cringed at the thought of it.

Floyd found me at the coffee urn on the second stop in my circle. "Hey, Dickie, you still work here?"

"You're running out of material, pal," I said, handing him the coffee I had just poured.

"Speaking of material," he said, "I'm kind of digging that tie. The fed buy it for you? I know you don't have that good of taste."

I put the pot back on the burner and turned, cup in hand, and moved to a nearby table. I had intended for the coffee to be just a quick stop—a coffee to go, so to speak—but I hadn't seen my old partner for several days and thought it'd be good to catch up. I smoothed my tie after taking a seat, and said, "No, actually. I bought this one all on my own at The Rack."

Floyd pulled up a seat across from me. "What'd you guys end up with in Compton? I heard you had a murdered chippie, then I heard it was a natural, and now I'm hearing that you and Josie aren't getting along."

I flinched at the accusation. "Who told you that?"

"Which part, Dickie?"

"That me and Josie aren't getting along. And as far as Compton, cause of death is pending. I don't know what we have."

"I'm messing with you. I ran into Josie coming in a few minutes ago, and I asked her where the hell her idiot partner was. She said she didn't know and didn't care, and she was all pissy about it. Fucking broads, man."

It suddenly felt warm in the office. I lifted my hat and wiped my forehead, then set it loosely on the top of my head. I unbuttoned my shirt sleeves and turned them up, saying to Floyd, "I have no idea what their problems are."

"So basically, what you're telling me is, Josie's pissed off at you *and* you're having trouble with the fed. Right?"

"That about sums it up," I said.

"Your track record with broads is nothing to boast about, Dickie, I'm not going to lie."

I nodded, took a sip of my coffee. "The funny thing is, Josie is only pissed off at me because she thinks I'm pissed off at Emily. Isn't that crazy? They barely know each other but they're thick as thieves already."

Floyd leaned back, crossed one leg over the other, and grinned. "Dickie, there's a reason they never go to the head alone. They're all in it together. It's a pack. They all know the secrets that we'll never know, and all of them are smarter than we think."

"The secrets?"

"Yeah, the secrets. The code. They learn it early in life. I haven't been able to prove it yet—because, Jesus, you can never get any of them to break and spill the beans—but I'm convinced it started in junior high."

"Really," I said, my tone one of disbelief. It sounded to me like another twisted Floyd philosophy was coming my way.

He continued, "Yeah, junior high. You know how on rainy days our gym classes were moved inside, and we'd play dodgeball or do gymnastics?"

I nodded, taking another gulp of the high-test.

"Well, where the hell were the girls?"

I set my cup down and thought about it. Maybe he had something here.

He said, "That has always bothered me. I mean, they weren't out in the rain, for Christ's sake, so why weren't they inside doing gymnastics with us? Well, I eventually figured it out. That was when the girls would go to a secret location, be sworn to silence, and indoctrinated to stand together against the opposite sex. It's still going on, Dickie, I'm convinced of it. I can't believe nobody else has figured it out."

"What do you suppose they were teaching them?" I asked, skeptical.

"Jesus, Dickie, isn't it obvious? They taught them to stick together no matter what. They showed them how to drive us crazy and make us do anything to have them. I mean, think about it, what percentage of the men in prison do you think are there because of a woman?"

I shrugged.

"Well, let me tell you—almost all of them. One way or another, there's a woman behind the failure or death of just about every man walking the planet. It started with Adam and Eve, and nothing's changed.

"Take a guy that does bank jobs. You know there's some trampy broad back at the pad waiting to help him count the money. Oh yeah, and she'll be turned on, too, because all of them like a bad boy. Without a woman, he'd have no need to rob a bank. He'd be happy with what he had, and he'd have nothing to prove. But the broad, you see, she wants to ride around in style, wear designer clothes and drink fine wines, go out on the town for two-hundred-dollar dinners. How's the average guy going to provide all of that without robbing a bank? And if he doesn't have the balls to do it, she'll find someone who does."

"We will do some stupid stuff for women, that's for sure."

"Hell yeah, Dickie, just look at some of the idiots around here. These dudes on their third and fourth marriages, paying alimony and dividing their retirements among all the plaintiffs in their lives, yet they're still out there on the hunt. Still looking for Mrs. Right."

Davey Lopes popped his head through the doorway and said, "Hey, what are you two gay boys doing?" Then he laughed and disappeared, flipping the bird at us before he left.

I chuckled and made a mental note to stop by Unsolveds and bullshit with him later. Lopes was always good to bounce ideas off of, get some other perspectives. I'd tell him about the chippie and maybe mention Emily. For sure the chippie. Probably not Emily, now that I considered it for a moment.

Floyd was saying, "Now, in your case, you don't keep them around long enough to worry about all of that. Which is a little unusual, and it makes me wonder if Lopes doesn't have a point about you."

"Bite me," I said.

"Anyway, how did you screw this one up?"

"Emily?"

He nodded.

"I didn't. That's what's funny. Josie thinks Emily and I are on the outs, but that's not the case. I'm just dealing with some stuff she threw at me."

"Like?"

Josie appeared at the door. "Hey, partner, when you and your sister get done gossiping, the lieutenant wants to meet with us."

Floyd stood up. "Think about it, Dickie." He began walking out, and as he passed Josie in the doorway, he said, "Your partner's driving me crazy."

Josie started to turn from the doorway. I called out to her, "Hey, wait."

She stopped and turned to face me.

I got up and went to her, tossing my coffee cup in the trash along the way. "What's the LT want?"

"He asked why we missed the meeting, and I told him we had the autopsy. Then he asked how that went, and I said, 'It's a long story. Let me find my partner.'"

"And here you are."

"Right," she said, and turned again.

I put my hand on her arm. "Wait—"

She looked at my hand, and I pulled it back.

"Josie, I don't know what's going on. You've been mad at me since yesterday morning. It seems like you're mad at me because—"

"I'm not mad at you, I'm disappointed. As a single woman, I find it frustrating to watch you start things you're not willing to finish when it comes to relationships. Floyd is right, you find a way to screw things up any time you get a good woman at your side. And I happen to really like Emily."

"Floyd told you that?"

"He's said it to you in my presence!"

"Oh," I said, deflated.

"But I'm your partner, not your mother or your sister, so I need to not worry about it. Just do me a favor and don't introduce me to anyone you're seeing in the future." She turned and started down the hallway, saying over her shoulder, "Let's get this over with."

I stood still for a moment watching her walk away. Wishing she understood what was going on. Wishing I could tell her. Why couldn't I? Why hadn't I told her yesterday when she came up with the idea that Emily and I were fighting? I could have straightened that out right then and saved all of this drama. But hell, I didn't even have the balls to tell Floyd what was going on between us. Eventually I would have to own up to it. I'd have to first admit it to myself and then share it with those who were close to me. I couldn't keep it a secret forever.

1 2

THE MEETING WITH LIEUTENANT BLACK BECAME A CONFERENCE WITH HIM and Captain Stover, and those never seemed to go well for me. Black was in my corner; Stover was his usual obstinate self: "We have enough real murders that need to be worked. By the way, are all of your cases solved?"

That was it. He shut us down. A direct order. "Close it out and solve some murders."

In the parking lot afterwards, Josie said, "I guess we better let Rich Farris know that we're done with Gomez. Hoochie mama can stay in jail."

We were leaned up against the hood of her Charger, which was parked in the shade of the building. Still, it had to have been ninety degrees where we stood. I could feel the sweat dribbling down my back, and my head was damp beneath my hat. A cool room with cold beer sounded good right now, but I glanced at my watch and it wasn't even three. Not that anyone kept track of our hours at Homicide. How could they? Though we were a centralized unit, our assignments took us throughout the county, an area encompassing nearly 5,000 square miles. When you caught a murder in the north county, sometimes you wouldn't be in L.A. for a week. Your lieutenant might call and ask if you had any overtime that needed to be submitted, but other than that, they left you alone. Nonetheless, I had a lot on my mind and plenty of work that needed to be done.

I said, "I'm going to research some case law about this."

Josie smiled. "Of course you are."

"Years ago, I handled a murder case where an older man got into a fight with a thirty-something, the result of a road rage incident. The older guy had a heart attack and died at the scene. The other guy split, but we were able to eventually ID him. The DA only charged manslaughter, but still... You know what I mean? We still worked it like a murder—a homicide investigation. What's the difference?"

"The difference is we don't know that anything happened in that apartment," she said.

It was a good point. "But if it did..."

"If it did, that's different. But until we know otherwise—"

"That's my point," I said. "If we don't work on it, how will we ever know? The captain's wrong on this; we should be working it until we know for certain that no crime occurred. We need to at least take it to the point where we find out what happened inside that apartment."

"They've given the missing persons case back to station detectives, and Major Crimes is going to monitor it in case there's been a kidnapping, or it ties into human trafficking. When they find Grandma and the kid, then we'll find out what happened. It's not as if the case isn't being investigated."

I stared across the parking lot without really seeing the assortment of unmarked sedans that sat with rays of sunlight reflecting off their windshields and shiny hoods. I pictured the scene that morning, Gomez's radio car hastily parked outside of the apartment, his body just inside the door, no clues left behind. I tried to imagine him running inside, and what—tripping over his own two feet, hitting his head on that table and having a heart attack as a finishing touch? No, that didn't make sense to me. But if he ran into the apartment and his adrenaline was pumping, his heart pounding, and a physical altercation occurred, then he might have had a heart attack, fallen, and hit his head on the way down. Or he was struck in the head when he ran through the door, maybe interrupting a kidnapping in progress.

Why would anyone kidnap an old lady and a kid? Assuming that it wasn't a case of human trafficking, what would be the motive? I had pondered this over the last several days and the one thing that kept coming back to me was drugs. Someone owes someone and it was a message or a threat: pay up or you'll never see them alive again. I was aware of several similar cases. The other possibility was coyotes—human smugglers. They had delivered someone but hadn't received payment, and the ante was raised.

Or, Grandma and the child fled on their own. In fear of what? Bikers? Cartels? Coyotes? Certainly not the California Highway Patrol—nobody was afraid of them.

Monica had confirmed that the missing girl, Leticia Hernandez, was in fact Gomez's daughter. The fact he had abandoned his jurisdiction and apparently rushed to the apartment, indicated to me that he had received a notice—or a warning. But from whom?

"We didn't come up with a cell phone for him, did we?"

"Gomez?" Josie questioned, shaking her head. "No, nothing on his person and, as far as we know, nothing in his patrol car. Has the crime lab finished with it?"

I wasn't sure. "We should find out. There's a reason Gomez raced from Newhall to Compton. He had to have received some type of alert or warning that something was going to happen to his daughter. That also means that he is the key. The motive for taking the kid has to be related to Gomez."

Josie thought about it a moment. "It's possible. It's also possible that Grandma told him she was leaving for Mexico and taking Leticia with her, and Gomez objected to that."

I nodded, processing it all.

Josie said, "But we're off the case."

I looked at her. "As far as the captain knows."

I caught up with Farris, who had arrived at the office late in the afternoon. He had been assigned to work the desk on the graveyard shift—Early Mornings, as it was called in our department—and he was none too happy about it.

"Why are you here already?" I asked, glancing at my watch. It was a quarter to five and the bureau was nearly empty.

Farris pulled a chair out next to my desk and plopped down into it. "I've got an interview scheduled at six, down at Century. Lizzy and I picked up a case not long before she went off on medical leave, a no-body murder case of a four-year-old boy. The mom's in custody on dope charges, and now some other broad she's housed with is trying to cut a deal, says homegirl told her the story."

"Did she murder him?"

Farris shrugged. "She had an old man who wasn't the kid's dad. I'd bet on him being the killer, and the mom is covering for him. The bottom line is, we don't have enough to charge anyone yet, and technically, we're still searching for the little boy."

Dead kids always fueled my fires, made me work long and hard and never stop until some son of a bitch paid the price for what they had done to the most vulnerable among us. I said, "What's their story, Rich?"

"Mom says her boyfriend had left two days before and went to Vegas. She claims on the day the kid went missing, he was in the living room watching cartoons. She took a shower and when she finished in the bathroom, he was gone. The door was open and there was no trace of him. She said she went around to the neighbors before calling the cops, but we haven't found any neighbors who she contacted."

"When were you guys called out?"

"That was part of the problem. We didn't get the case until three days later when Missings had run through all of the standard procedures. A case like this should be given to a team right away, in my opinion. You know there's a problem with the story."

"So was the boyfriend in Vegas?"

"They both lawyered up on us, so we don't have a starting point on that, no idea where he was supposed to have been or who he saw while he was there. We can't find any relatives or associates for him in Vegas, so who knows? The best chance we have now is mama running her mouth to the wrong person, and that's what I'm hoping for on this."

"How did this informant get in touch with you?"

"She was out at Norwalk for a pretrial hearing and told her attorney she wanted to make a deal, gave him the skinny on what she knew. The prosecutor, Preston Haynes, asked for a continuance, did a little research and found out we were handling the case. He's going to meet me at the jail and sit in on the interview."

Haynes had worked Hardcore Gangs out of Compton and Major Crimes downtown. His reputation as a tough and thorough prosecutor made him a favorite among cops. I'd had a case with him years before, and I was surprised to know he was at Norwalk now. It didn't make sense to have a lawyer of his caliber go from specialized assignments to handling cases at a branch.

"When did Preston get sent to Norwalk? Last I heard he was at Major Crimes."

"When the new DA was elected. Preston had campaigned for the opponent and made no secret about his lack of confidence in Samantha Bright. Now he's on a permanent shit list."

None of us was very happy about Samantha Bright being the new DA of Los Angeles County. She was more likely to plead a case than take it to trial because she lacked confidence in her own ability, and with good reason. When she was assigned to a branch downtown, handling preliminary hearings, she struggled to keep her facts straight on simple drug cases. Cops began referring to her simply as "Samantha who isn't," dropping the last name. But being a black female, she was assigned to a team of brilliant lawyers to prosecute a celebrity who had killed his lover during a cocaine-induced rage after a night on the red carpet in Hollywood. The celebrity defendant was acquitted, and Bright publicly criticized her office for moving forward on a case that was, in her opinion, lacking solid evidence. She became the new media darling and before long, she was insinuating that race played a factor in the hasty decision to prosecute the famous black actor for murder. When the district attorney busted her down to a filing deputy, she left the DA's office and went into private practice, sure to be the next Johnnie Cochran. Then, when the DA announced he would be retiring at the end of his term, she was among many of his underlings who threw her hat into the ring. Being a media darling came in handy, and the voting base of Los Angeles County once again failed the criminal justice system—in the view of many.

"Another reason to love Preston Haynes."

"Exactly," Farris said.

"Hey, you want me to go along for the interview?"

Farris nodded. "Yeah, sure, if you want to go. With Lizzy gone—"

"I don't mind. I need something to get my mind off the chippie case. Sometimes it's like taking a test: you can't figure something out, go on to another question and come back to it. That's what I think I need right now, a diversion. Something else to think about."

"Cool, man. Let me check my emails, make a few calls, and I'll be ready to go in about fifteen minutes."

"You got it."

13

CENTURY REGIONAL DETENTION FACILITY IS A COUNTY JAIL ATTACHED TO the Century sheriff's patrol station in Lynwood. The jail has the capacity to house 2,200 inmates, and in 2006 it was transitioned into a women's jail. At the security gate entrance, Farris showed the camera his badge and announced "Sheriff's Homicide" into the speaker. The gate slid open and we drove in, made our way past the back side of Century station to the jail facility, and parked.

We were buzzed into the secured area, where we stowed our pistols in the gun lockers before being allowed into the facility. Inside, we stepped to the counter where several deputies—male and female—worked busily on phones and computers. We again displayed our IDs, and a young woman deputy stepped over to help us. Farris indicated that he had spoken to the watch commander about interviewing an inmate. The deputy told us we were all set to go, that the inmate was waiting in the interview room along with an attorney, and that she would take us there.

Farris didn't say it, but his expression told me he hoped the "attorney" was the prosecutor, Preston Haynes, and not an attorney the inmate had retained in order to deal with us. Attorneys change the dynamics of every-thing, and seldom for the better—at least from our perspective.

It was Haynes. He sat with a wide smile, his legs crossed, comfortable on a plastic chair in his thousand-dollar suit. I hadn't seen Haynes for several years and was surprised that the thin man's full head of hair had turned mostly gray. At least he still had it. He didn't bother to stand when we walked in, though he did offer a hand, which Farris and I each shook.

"Dickie Jones," he said, lighting the room with his magnetic smile, "long time, my friend. How's the murder business?"

"I can't complain. How have you been? I hear you're at Norwalk now, you stepped on your—" I glanced at the female inmate who sat watching with interest, and quickly changed my wording "—tie."

"Yeah, I'm in the penalty box for a while. That's all right, I've outlasted better bosses than Bright."

Farris introduced himself to the inmate, and then introduced me as his partner. She said hello, but nothing more. He said, "You've met Mr. Haynes, a prosecutor for the County of Los Angeles."

She nodded.

Farris took a seat next to Haynes across from the inmate, and I leaned against the wall. I felt almost useless, like a service judge without any shuttlecocks at a badminton tournament. Then I wondered why that thought had come to mind. Because these were no players, and if detectives took badminton racquets into interviews, they would surely, at some point, use them as weapons.

My thoughts snapped back to the current situation when Preston Haynes addressed Farris: "We've gone over all of the requirements of the agreement, and she's on board. Go ahead and proceed with your interview."

Farris nodded, placed a digital recorder on the table, and said, "Let's start with who you are and what you're in for."

Her name was Teresa Livingston and she was fighting a possession for sales case. Given her record—three convictions and probation stacked on probation—she was looking at prison time. Nobody cared about dope anymore, Farris assured her, so she was the perfect candidate to use as an informant, as long as her information was truthful, helpful, and verifiable.

Livingston sat stroking the ponytail draped over her shoulder. It was tied by a strip of blue cloth, a jail-made hair tie that matched the bottom half of her outfit. Her top was bright yellow and stamped *L.A. County Jail*. I noticed her fingers were stained brown by tobacco, the nails chewed short. She was likely nervous about ratting on a fellow inmate, but she might also have been jonesing for tobacco, alcohol, or drugs—maybe all three. Before starting, she asked for a cup of coffee. I wasn't surprised. Go to an AA or NA meeting and try finding someone not drinking coffee. She'd want heavy cream and extra sugar too, if I was right about her jones.

I offered to fetch it since I had nothing else to do, an observer on the sideline. I didn't bother to ask if anyone else cared for a cup. Only the most desperate or hardcore drank inmate coffee. On my way out, I confirmed, "Cream and sugar?"

She nodded. "Please."

The same young deputy who had helped us when we arrived, greeted me as I approached her work area in search of inmate coffee. This time, I noticed her name tag: Miranda. There was a male deputy named Miranda whom I had worked with at Firestone many years before, and I wondered if she was related to him. Maybe his wife? She seemed too young to be his wife, but you never knew. I knew an ER nurse whose first name was Miranda. She was cute and sassy, but I had no idea why she came to mind. She mostly went by "Randi" anyway. Then there was Ernesto Miranda, the famous Arizona burglar whose conviction for kidnapping and rape were overturned after the ACLU argued before the United States Supreme Court that his rights had been violated. Even though Miranda had written as part of his confession: "This confession was made with full knowledge of my legal rights, understanding any statement I make may be used against me," the historic Warren Court overturned his conviction with a 5-4 vote. In 1967 Miranda was retried and convicted, although the evidence of his confession had been excluded. He was sentenced to serve 20-30 years in prison, but was paroled just eight years later. One month after his release, Miranda was stabbed to death during a bar fight in Phoenix. The police detained two men they thought to have been involved in the fight, but before any questioning, the officers carefully—perhaps enthusiastically—explained to each suspect their rights according to the Miranda decision. No one was ever charged for his murder.

I asked if I could get a cup of the inmate coffee for Ms. Livingston, and Deputy Miranda promptly provided one. I chose to not ask about any relationships to other deputies or the nurse or to the infamous Arizona outlaw, but while doctoring the coffee with cream and sugar, I thought to make small talk and asked how long she had been on the job.

"Almost a year now," she said proudly.

She was just getting started. I wasn't sure if I should pity or envy her. As a buddy of mine used to say, "You couldn't give me a million dollars to do it all over, but I wouldn't take a million for the memories either." I thanked her for the coffee and wished her the best of luck in her career.

When I returned to the interview room, Livingston was animated, no longer in a shell. Tears rolled down her cheeks as she said, "I'd give anything to be with my babies again, and this bitch gonna let her baby daddy get away with murder? I don't think so."

I handed her the coffee and returned to my position. Service judge. It seemed that everything had gone well and the would-be informant was good to go on the operation.

Farris flipped through his notebook. I could see he had filled up several pages in the short time I was out of the room. Livingston settled into silence, drinking her coffee and wiping her cheeks as she waited for another question. Farris looked up from his notes. "This is all great stuff, but I want to get her talking about it on tape. Do you think you can get her to tell it again?"

"It's all she talk about, that and getting high. When can I get out?"

"You'll be out as soon as we get what we need from her. I'll have to get a court order to proceed, so it will be a couple of days before we meet again. We'll probably subpoena you out to court to get you set up. I don't want to take a chance of meeting you here again."

Haynes said, "That won't be a problem, we'll do it at Norwalk."

As Livingston finished her coffee, relaxing and composing herself before being returned to her cell, Farris asked about her life, her family, where she was raised, school, work, babies, baby daddies—everything other than the topic of her wearing a wire and ratting on her fellow inmates. I was surprised to hear her say she had been raised in Compton and had attended Compton High. Although her dialect was consistent with black culture—or what some tried for a while to call *ebonics*—her complexion was a very light brown and her hair was straight. She was either of mixed race or a straight white girl raised in a black community.

"So you're a Tartar Baby," I said, referencing the school's mascot.

She smiled. "I guess, sorta. But I wasn't really into high school, and I never did get into sports and all that. I started using when I was fourteen, and I got pregnant during the first semester of my sophomore year. I dropped out after that."

Farris nodded, knowing the story. It was all too familiar. But my mind was elsewhere, and I had to ask. "You don't happen to know Monica Hernandez, do you? She's from Compton too, about your age, and she's locked up right now for drugs."

She thought about it for a moment. "What she look like?"

I described her general appearance, and said, "She's got a dimple on her chin and a cross tattooed on her neck."

Livingston perked up. "Yeah, I know who you talking about. Her mama stay over there across from the courthouse. She go by 'Money.'"

"That's what they call her, 'Money?'"

She nodded. "Uh-huh, Money H. I thought the H was for heroin, but I guess it can be for Hernandez too. But that's her, skanky little ho with that cross on her neck and them shifty eyes. I don't trust the bitch."

I smiled. Farris looked at me and grinned, then shrugged as if to say, "Why not?" likely knowing what I was thinking. I glanced at Haynes and then looked back at our new informant. I said, "You want to get close to her, too?"

She thought about it, turned her attention to the quiet man in the expensive suit, and said, "You gonna have to sweeten the pot."

WE STOOD OUTSIDE CRDF IN THE SHADE OF THE BUILDING, THE LATE afternoon cooler now as the summer sun faded in the west and a near-full moon appeared in the blue skies to the east, long before dark. Radio cars were coming and going from the station, deputies moving swiftly and with purpose, tires squealing as they sped from the security of the fort into the wilds of South Los Angeles. Warm nights were busy nights for law enforcement, and young cops in places like this craved the action. Old cops like me and Farris cherished the memories, gusts of warm air through open windows stirring the locker room-like odors of a radio car, the sweat of men and the stench of prisoners permeated into old vinyl, the radio squawking with one priority call after another: *211 in progress, 245 just occurred, shots fired, two victims down*... Those of us who had embraced the rush of adrenaline, the thrill of the chase, and the battles fought for the civility of these streets—however little of it was left—forevermore suffered a jones greater than any drug or drink could inspire. And there was no cure.

Two more deputies ran out the station's back door and tore away from the parking lot as if someone's life depended on them. It likely did. Watching made me want a fix.

Haynes said, "I couldn't imagine working as a cop down here."

I smiled. "I've never had more fun in my life."

We said our goodbyes with a promise to keep Haynes posted on the progress of the operation, then Farris and I drove across the parking lot to the county gas pumps. As a trustee filled the car, we discussed the possibility of using Livingston to glean information from Monica Hernandez about what may have happened to her mother and daughter. With a full tank, we pulled out of the lot onto Alameda, and Farris pointed us south.

"Where're we headed, Rich?"

He glanced over with a sly grin. "Compton, baby."

14

We turned onto Acacia from Compton Boulevard and headed south, cruising slowly with the windows down, taking in the sights and sounds of a city starting to rev up for a hot summer night. People were out on their porches and in their front yards, kids playing and adults sipping cool beverages, some enjoying a smoke. Everyone seemed to notice the salt and pepper pair with watchful eyes who crept along in an unmarked unit. There was no mistaking who we were. "Hi poh-lees," from the kids, "One time," from a couple of the younger men, a warning for all that the cops were on the prowl. "Five-O," yet another.

I pointed out the apartment where Officer Gomez had died, and we stopped a couple hundred feet before we arrived there. Farris eased over to the curb, killing the lights and coming to a stop. We locked it up and walked the rest of the way on foot, our heads on swivels in this neighborhood, still hearing the chatter behind us.

The apartment we were interested in showed no sign of life. We peeked through the window on the back side—the side that could be seen from the civic center parking structure—before going around to the front. At a glance, everything appeared as we had left it. We went around to the front and checked the door. It remained locked.

"Want to talk to the neighbors?" Farris asked.

With low expectations, I said, "Sure, let's give it a try."

Ten minutes later we were standing in front of the apartment building, gazing at the darkened window of Maria Hernandez's home as if it held a secret. Just maybe, if two accomplished interrogators stared at it long and hard, its walls would give in, crumble, throw up, tell us everything we wanted to know and beg for mercy. Sergeant Long, a good cop with a twisted sense of humor, had said I was one of the last guys he'd ever want to sit across from during an interrogation. He had said the only thing that could make me more frightening in such an environment would be if we were to go into it wearing a ghillie suit—sniper camouflage outfits. Long had said, "You could just stare at the suspect until he confessed."

The walls didn't tell us anything I didn't already know, so we ambled back to the car in silence. Sergeant Long was on my mind, his dry humor, his wry persona. He had retired, then died of a heart attack not long after, and I missed the late-night conversations we would often have. I was just thinking of mentioning one of Long's stories to Farris, a particular one I had just recalled, and which brought a smile to my face, when we arrived at the car to see the passenger window had been smashed. A softball-sized rock sat on the seat among the shards of broken glass. The street was empty, suddenly not a soul in sight.

Farris said, "Compton, baby."

We removed as much of the glass as we could, collecting it into a shopping-size paper evidence bag, and then Farris placed a blanket on the seat so that any shards that remained behind wouldn't end up in the seats of our pants. Every smart deputy kept a county blanket in the trunk of his car, along with first aid kits and emergency equipment. The blankets had a plethora of uses, though this was the first time I had used one to keep glass out of my ass.

The broken window put us both in foul moods. It would require a *damage to county vehicle* report, which was just what we needed to spend our time doing. The car would be sent to the motor pool for repair, and hopefully a loaner would be available. Most important, the street would require attention. You didn't break a cop's window and get away with it. We might not ever know who threw the rock, but everyone on the street would know we weren't happy about it. We'd talk to the local deputies and ask them to target that street for the next few nights. It would send a message that this neighborhood needed to hear.

The office was nearly empty when we arrived. I put on a pot of fresh coffee while Rich Farris started the dreaded paperwork for the broken window. It was close to midnight now, but I would stay until Farris was finished and also ready to go. We were in this together. I thought about Emily and it bothered me that I hadn't heard from her. But what did I expect? She hadn't heard from me, either. But she wasn't the one who had been blindsided by a haymaker. I had too much to process before I was ready to continue that discussion, and hopefully she understood that.

But the silence was killing me. The standoff. I knew if I didn't address it with her soon, permanent damage might be done. While the coffee brewed and I stood in the silence of an empty break room, I contemplated what I should do, and decided on a simple text:

Hi, just checking in. Still at work, putting in long hours. Also thinking about us. Just need time to sort this out in my head. Love you.

While Farris finished his reports, I took an empty file box from the secretariat and a roll of duct tape from the trunk of my car, and went outside to patch his car window.

"Good as new," I told him, when he came out to see my handy work.

"Ghetto," Rich said. "Totally ghetto, dude."

EARLY THE NEXT MORNING, BEFORE MOST PEOPLE STARTED THEIR DAY, I headed north to San Fernando to check the residence of Antonio Gomez. We had left a business card in the door, asking the roommate to call. We had no idea who it was, just that there was a roommate. I arrived at 6:30 and saw that a car was parked in the driveway. It was a late sixties model El Camino, black with chrome wheels and a Harley emblem sticker on the back window, which was tinted dark. The side windows were also blacked out, making it impossible to see inside, especially at a distance, but I copped the license number as I made my second pass, and then I parked down the street in a spot that had a view of the driveway.

I assumed the owner of the El Camino was the roommate, and that he was inside, probably sleeping. Now I had to decide what to do. Knock and talk, or wait and watch? I wanted to call the desk and have them run the license but was reluctant to do so just yet. I thought about Josie. If I called and told her what I was doing, she would be irritated that I was doing it on my own. But I could ask her to run the plate, tell her, Hey, I just ran by on my way to work to see if anything had changed. And she'd say, *On your way to work?* And remind me that San Fernando was in no way *on my way to work.* So I decided to just sit and watch for a while, see what I could learn. Whenever possible, it was always best to gather intelligence on people before speaking with them. Besides, you never knew what you would see when you spent a few minutes watching a place. I could always run the plate later when I got to the office.

A half hour later, the black El Camino backed out of the driveway and took off in the opposite direction of where I had parked. I had to make a U-turn to get behind it, and by the time I did, the Camino had turned onto Glenoaks, a heavily traveled street. I accelerated to catch up, but when I reached the boulevard, the El Camino was nowhere in sight.

I hit my steering wheel with the palm of my hand, frustrated that I had let it get away. I should have just knocked and talked, found out then who the roommate was. I turned left on Maclay, keeping my eyes peeled as I made my way to the 210. I would take the long way—but often the faster route—into the office. At least I had the license number of the vehicle, and I could run it at the office and get the registered owner's information.

Once I hit cruising speed on the freeway, I felt overwhelmed by the desire to call Emily. But her reply to my text had been fairly clear: until I was ready to finish our conversation, she didn't see a reason for idle chat. Did that mean she was angry? I didn't know. It didn't seem like she was, but I had never seen her angry, so there wasn't any way to tell. All I knew for certain was that I needed to come to terms with what she had told me and figure out what I was going to do about it. I let out a breath and focused on relaxing my muscles, feeling the tension that had built up inside me.

If the way my morning had started was any indication of how the day might turn out, I was in for a long, hard stretch. But traffic was flowing nicely—*for L.A.*—so I began to think that maybe there was hope for my future yet. What I needed was a break on the Gomez case so that I could justify seeing it through. Before I knew it, we'd be on call for murders again, and likely first up in the rotation since my captain had basically determined my last case to be a natural. It would be a battle, but I was going to prove him wrong.

When I arrived at the office, my first priority was to run the license plate from the El Camino. I wanted to secure that information before I did anything else: before coffee, before making a pit stop, before my partner or Floyd or the captain derailed me from my mission. I opened the DMV application and signed in, using the file number from Gomez's case to justify my inquiry—all databases were closely monitored nowadays. I punched in the digits as they had been recorded in my notebook, and the computer screen displayed an unpleasant message: NO RECORD ON FILE.

I checked and rechecked the license I had recorded with what I had punched in on the computer. They matched. Had I screwed up the plate when I wrote it down? That would be unusual for me. Like most cops, I had become very good at remembering license plates for short periods of time. I could glance at a plate, repeat it three times in my head, visualize it, and ten minutes or an hour later, recall it with ease. I could read license plates in my mirrors, something that took some training and practice to learn. So I was certain the plate was correctly recorded. I could still see it in my mind, yellow on black, the old California plates. And not the new plates of the old design, but this was actually an old black and yellow license plate with three letters and three numbers. Simple as could be. But there was no record on file with the California DMV.

I ran the plate through a few other databases to see if anything popped, including CalGangs. But still there was nothing. It looked like I would be making another trip to San Fernando. Maybe tonight after work or early tomorrow morning. Next time, I would knock on the door and handle my business. To hell with gathering intelligence first.

15

"JONES, IN MY OFFICE."

It was Captain Stover. I watched him walk away, shooting a stern glance over his shoulder.

What could it be now? For the most part, he and I had been getting along. Which meant I had stopped challenging him on everything and tried to avoid him. But he had changed some too, having been passed over for the commander promotion and knowing he would be retiring at the rank he now held. That being the case, he would be hard-pressed to find a better place than Homicide Bureau to run out the clock.

I decided to grab a cup of coffee on the way to see him. He hadn't said it was urgent, though his tone had implied that it was. Regardless, I needed an extra minute to think. I had to assume the reason he was calling me into his office had something to do with the Gomez case. He must have put two and two together after seeing the damaged vehicle report submitted by Farris. The location field on it would have been a hint, and with me listed as a witness, the rest is math.

I poured a cup and thought, so there it is. He'll want to know what we were doing back at that apartment, and no matter what I tell him, he'll say that if I had followed orders and walked away from the case, there wouldn't be another damaged vehicle report on his desk.

Or, could he somehow know I had been back to Gomez's home in San Fernando? How could he?

Then it hit me.

There was only one way the captain could know I had been at Gomez's, and that was if the El Camino belonged to an undercover cop. I knew from my days working Major Crimes Bureau that undercover vehicles were sometimes flagged with the DMV so that if anyone made an inquiry through their system, the identity of the person inquiring would be made known to the law enforcement agency and detail that had flagged it. The procedure was meant to protect undercover officers. If a cop had infiltrated a biker gang, and that cop's bike was checked through the DMV files by an LAPD clerk or a Riverside County deputy, then the undercover's agency would instantly know two things: the biker gang had someone inside law enforcement on their payroll, and the undercover cop had come under suspicion, and he or she was likely in danger because of it.

As I entered his office, now prepared for my response, a bigger question came to me: Why would an undercover cop be at a dead chippie's house? I had assumed it was the roommate, but I didn't really know. I hadn't seen the driver of the vehicle, and I didn't even know for certain that he had been inside the home.

I walked in and took a seat across from Stover. He didn't acknowledge my entry, his gaze fixed on his computer screen. One thing I knew for certain, there was more to the chippie case than I could have imagined.

I sat down and waited, silently watching the captain. I could see the reflection of the computer screen in his pale blue eyes. His hair, mostly light brown and carefully combed back, was thinning through the top and beginning to gray.

He clicked out of whatever he was looking at and leaned back in his chair, now facing me. He twirled a ballpoint pen between his fingers as he started: "You ran the license plate of an undercover fed."

Fed? That I hadn't expected. Caught off guard by that detail, I opted to play dumb in order to buy some time. "I did?"

He was now tapping the end of the pen on the arm of his chair. "Yes, Richard, you did. And you used the file number for the chippie case. Can you explain to me why you're still working on a natural, when you were clearly instructed to move on, and why you would be running the license number of an undercover ATF agent from San Bernardino? What the hell were you even doing out there?"

I was stunned—*an ATF agent*? And the captain has no idea why I ran the license, or where I saw the vehicle, or how it might be related to the Gomez case. What *did* he know? Apparently not much.

"San Bernardino? I haven't been out there for a long time, probably since that Pomona shooting took us out to Fontucky on a manhunt." I smiled.

He wasn't amused. Either he had heard Fontana referred to in that manner before, or he was really in a foul mood over this fed deal. It could go either way; he didn't have the best sense of humor. He watched me for a long moment before continuing. "Well, that's where the call came from, their office in San Berdoo. I guess that doesn't mean it's where he's assigned or where you saw the vehicle. Anyway, I've got this supervising agent out there asking questions and expecting answers. They need to be certain their agent hasn't been compromised. So why'd you run the plate?"

At that moment, I saw my way out of it. Nobody had any idea that this agent was somehow connected to Gomez, and nobody knew when and where I saw the vehicle or why I ran the plate. What I knew for sure was that the dude had a heavy foot, and I'd have to assume he drives like an asshole most of the time. I also knew that the concern right now was the integrity of the agent's cover, and nothing else. I could get out of this with only a lecture, if I played it right.

"The dude cut me off in traffic, driving like an asshole. It was a black El Camino with chrome wheels and a big Harley decal in the rear window. I figured the dude was a biker asshole. I copped the plate and decided to run it later for officer safety reasons. I was in my county car, so I figure the dude had to know I was a cop. Why would he cut me off?"

Stover watched me carefully as he considered my answer. After a moment, he said, "Why would you use the file number from the chippie case?"

I was ready for this one, and answered right away. "Two reasons: it's the case I was last assigned, and the notebook with its file number was handy when I sat down to run the plate. Also, I thought, what better case to use? It's a natural, so it will never be in court and I wouldn't have to worry about it coming up that I ran it."

"So you queried the DMV without having a law enforcement reason to do so. That's a violation of policy, Jones."

I considered that for a short moment. "You know boss, before they made us use file numbers to access the databases, all you had to do was indicate the reason for your search. In situations like this, I'd simply list officer safety as my reason, which is a legitimate use of any of our databases. How much shit have I been through? How long has it been since I had a contract on my life and a professional was sent to my home to fill it? I might be paranoid, but not without good reason." I pushed out of my chair, and stood in front of him, hands on my hips. "If that's not good enough for you, I'll take the days off."

He didn't reply, so I turned to walk out.

"Richard."

I stopped at the door.

"Where were you when this happened?"

Now I had to take my chances. If this agent was from San Bernardino and I saw him in San Fernando, chances are he uses the 210 Freeway just as I had to come in this morning. It was a gamble, but I went with it. "On the two-ten, on my way in this morning."

"You take the two-ten? Don't you live in Burbank still?"

"Yeah, I do. But last night I spent the night in Santa Clarita."

He frowned.

"Jesus, boss, do I have to spell it out for you? I'm a single man."

Captain Stover nodded, but none too enthusiastically. I had a feeling he knew I was full of shit. But to what degree? All that mattered was he could put the Bureau of Alcohol, Tobacco, and Firearms at ease about their undercover agent, and I felt confident Stover bought that much of the story.

I walked out, down the hallway, and was in the squad room before I let out a big breath. Josie was at her desk. I walked straight to her and said, "Come on, let's go get a cup somewhere other than here. We need to talk."

Her eyes showed concern. "Everything okay?"

"Probably," I said. "But the Gomez case just got a whole lot stranger, and the captain's got my number."

"Nothing new there," she said, as she stood and gathered her purse, keys, and phone.

We were walking out when we ran into Rich Farris, just arriving at the office.

"Hey guys," he said, as a manner of greeting us both.

"'Morning, Rich. You busy?"

"Not yet, but I'm sure I will be once I sit down and open that damn computer."

"Put it on hold," I said, "and I'll buy you a coffee. We need to chat, and you might as well be included."

He looked to Josie and then back at me. "What's up?"

"That case in Compton. I just had an interesting chat with the captain."

Farris shook his head. "Let me guess, he's pissed about the window?"

"Yeah, maybe. But he also might have forgotten all about that now. Come on, I don't want to talk about it here. Let's go for a ride. Josie can take us to one of those yuppie coffee joints."

He shrugged, and the three of us walked out together and headed for Josie's car.

16

"HERE'S THE PROBLEM," JOSIE BEGAN, IMMEDIATELY AFTER I FINISHED telling her and Rich the entire story, beginning with my check of Gomez's house in San Fernando.

I interrupted her. "The problem is we have a dead cop and two people missing, a grandma and a little girl. If they don't want me working cases, they should stop sending me out on them. Give me a case, I'm going to work it. What the hell?"

We were sitting on the patio of a coffee house in Monterey Park. There were few people inside now that the morning rush was over. Nobody else was outside, so we could speak freely. An occasional customer would walk in or out with their coffee and breakfast sandwiches or bagels, dressed in business attire and likely from one of the many nearby corporate offices.

Josie glanced at Rich Farris, who was leaned back in his seat, both hands gripping his coffee. Master of the interview, he was first and foremost a great listener. But Josie raised a brow at him, clearly asking for his input.

He took a deep breath and let it out slowly. "Here's the thing, I'm with Dickie on this. The captain is more concerned with numbers, and I get that. But we're all cops, first and foremost. A lot of our cases don't fit neatly into their little boxes. On this Compton case, the cause of death is still unknown, right? It's pending?"

I nodded. "Yeah, pending further examination of the heart and whatever information we can come up with about what happened out there that might influence their decision. Dr. Langley assured me he wouldn't make that call without speaking with us first. So for me, I'm on the clock. If there was an altercation in that room, I need to know it. That's the difference between natural and homicide on this one."

Farris continued, "Right, so even though you'd be lucky to get a manslaughter beef on the dude if that's all it was, an altercation, you might be looking at a kidnapping case to boot."

"Exactly."

"So I don't know how Stover can pull you off of it. And you've got all this other stuff going on, with the chippie being a biker, and now an undercover federal agent was at his pad. I mean, you start off with a dead cop, no obvious sign of death, and a missing family. That's enough to keep my attention. You add in the biker thing, and the ATF, man... I wouldn't put it down, either."

"Thanks, Rich," Josie said. "I'm trying to talk Dickie off the ledge and you're saying 'Jump.'"

Farris smiled. "Stop me when I'm lying, baby."

"Look," I said, "I'm not asking anyone else to stick their neck out. But I'm going to work it. I'm going to find out what happened in that apartment, what the hell's going on with the ATF, whether or not the cop was dirty, and hopefully, what happened to grandma and the kid."

"Well, I'm your partner, so we're in it together. I'm a little concerned about the potential fallout—I'm not going to lie about that—but we *are* partners, and I am going to stick with you."

"Thank you, partner."

Rich said, "I'll help you out too, Dickie. I'm slow, with Lizzy being out. I've assisted on a few cases, but honestly, I don't have anything fresh that needs my attention. Mostly, I'm trying to clear a couple of old cases out."

That reminded me. "What's the status on the Lowe case?"

Farris smiled. "That's a good one. I was able to file on both of the knuckleheads and we should have a prelim coming up soon. I don't know if we'll need you for that or not, but I'm sure we'll use you at trial."

I nodded. The Jackie Melvin Lowe murder was a case I had assisted Farris with while Josie was off on medical leave and I was without a partner. Lowe, an up-and-coming rap star, was gunned down in his own neighborhood, and we had believed it to be an "in house" murder, meaning he was killed by people he called friends and homeboys. An informant put us in the right direction, and then Farris and I had put the case together through interviews, recordings, and good old-fashioned detective work. Working with Farris was always enjoyable and usually productive.

"I look forward to it," I said. "And thanks, we very likely will need your help on this. I'm still thinking we'll need to get Monica out of jail at some point."

"I'll get in touch with my daughter and see what she thinks, tell her it's something we're thinking about."

"Thanks, Rich."

Josie was focused on her phone, her thumbs pecking away at it. When she finished, she looked up and saw that Rich and I were watching her. She said, "I've got a friend in the ATF."

I chuckled. "Of course you do."

"What's that supposed to mean?" she retorted.

I shrugged. "I'm just saying, you seem to know people everywhere. I didn't say it was a bad thing."

She shook her head and rolled her eyes. "Some of us actually talk to people when we're sent to training classes or conferences. You should try it. The lady I'm reaching out to, I met at a gang conference in Long Beach close to a decade ago. She's super cool, and we've stayed in touch."

"Be careful with that," Farris offered.

"Well, of course. I'm not planning to tell her what we're looking into. I was just thinking I'd check in, see where she's working now, maybe hook up and feel her out."

I chuckled and looked at Rich, who was smiling and shaking his head.

She said, "You guys are such pigs. Fine, I won't help."

"I was kidding. But here's the deal: we don't know who the agent is. I never even saw him. We may very well need some intel from a source like your friend there, at some point, but we also have to be careful about being inside their camp."

Josie's expression softened. She was easily riled when it came to discussions that involved her relationships. Sometimes I would tease her and feel bad about it, but then other times I figured, hey, that's what partners do. I can dish it out and I can take it.

She was sipping her coffee when I concluded by saying, "I'm just saying you don't have to sleep with her to help the case."

Rich and I laughed. Josie grinned, but just a little bit. She set her coffee down and, with both hands, flipped each of us the bird.

Farris said, "Dickie, you live on the edge, my brother."

I shrugged. "Yeah, maybe."

"I'm going to just start calling you 'Dick,'" Josie said. "Seriously, you're an ass sometimes."

I finished my coffee and walked over to the nearby trash can to get rid of the paper cup. When I stepped back over by our patio table, I remained standing, but in the shade of the building. I said, "Okay, so here are my thoughts on how we work this."

LATE THAT AFTERNOON, JOSIE LEANED OVER ME AS I SAT AT MY DESK, HER fragrant dark hair flowing over my shoulder. Her voice was soft, sultry, her breath fresh and warm as she whispered, "I talked to my lover from the ATF."

She dragged her hand across my shoulder as she continued past me to her desk. I watched as she sat down and turned to face me, a devilish grin on her face.

"You're killing me."

She shrugged. "I just figured I'd keep your little fantasy alive."

Josie turned to her desk and began working on her computer as if nothing had been said, all business again.

I said, "So what did she say?"

"Who?"

Minutes earlier, my lieutenant had served me with a written reprimand that said something about improper use of the databases, blah, something, blah, so I wadded it up and threw it at my partner.

She caught it with one hand. "She said it was good to hear from me and that we should get together." She dropped the wadded paper into a trash can that sat between us. "What was that? Nothing important I hope?"

"A letter from the captain commending my innovative detective skills."

"Ah," she said, "your written rep."

"How'd you know?"

"Lt. Black was working on it when I was at his desk to discuss the on-call schedule for next week. He told me he hated giving it to you, but…"

"What's up with next week's schedule?"

"I'm going to be out for court. They start picking a jury for Spencer's trial Monday. I don't plan on missing a single day. I asked that I be taken out of the rotation. I was going to tell you about it—"

"Great, who's he pairing me with?"

"I think Farris. With Liz out, he's been an extra in every rotation."

I leaned back and chewed on the end of a pen. "Cool. That, I can deal with. How long do they anticipate the trial will last? I almost forgot I have a subpoena for it."

She shrugged, suddenly somber. I looked around my desk for something else to throw at her, and changed my mind. I glanced at my watch. "Hey, how about happy hour tonight? I'll buy."

Josie nodded. "Yeah, we can do that. Will Emily be joining us?"

I glanced away. "No, probably not. We have to finish our discussion, and I haven't had the chance."

"You haven't made the chance. Also, you haven't told me what's going on between you two. I came out of the closet to you, the least you can do is let me know if you guys are okay."

"We're okay," I said. "Come on, let's get out of here. I'm suddenly very thirsty."

"Shall I call Stephanie, see if she wants to join us?"

"The ATF broad?"

Josie rolled her eyes. "Broad? Really? Yes, my friend who works ATF."

"Your lover."

"Maybe, someday. Working with you is going to push me over to that side."

"Touché. Make the call."

THE NEXT MORNING, I WOKE TO A KNOCK ON MY FRONT DOOR. LIGHT, polite. It was 6:30, the time Emily would usually leave for work. I stepped into a pair of jeans and answered the door with my pistol held out of view. I never opened the door without it. It was her.

"Hi."

"Here's the deal: I'm not going to allow you to keep dodging me, making excuses to avoid dealing with this. I'm going to see my mom for the weekend, and I'll be back Sunday evening. I would like you to be here so that we can talk. Otherwise, I'll be making my decision without you."

Before I could respond, she turned and walked away.

17

OUR DEPARTMENT HAD TWO DETECTIVES WHO MONITORED THE ACTIVITIES of biker gangs throughout Southern California, and both were assigned to Major Crimes Bureau and worked out of STARS Center in Whittier.

The sheriff's department's Major Crimes Bureau is a unit within Detective Division that comprises several details, including Metro, Surveillance, Prison Gangs, and Organized Crime.

Organized Crime investigated crimes related to traditional mafias such as the Italians and Russians. They also monitored casino operations throughout the county, including card clubs, and two investigators were assigned to handle outlaw motorcycle gangs. Both of them looked like typical bikers with long hair and beards, tattoos, piercings, and shitty attitudes. They were each assigned two county vehicles: some type of undercover car or truck, and Harleys.

Josie and I had set up a meeting with Anthony Brunetti, one of the two "biker gang" investigators. A guy with a name like that might seem a better fit with the Italian mafia side of Organized Crime, but Tony looked more like a peckerwood white boy with his slicked brown hair and a mustache that completely covered his mouth and half of his chin. His arms were sleeved in prison style tattoos—black ink with shades of gray—and his shoulders, chest, and arms appeared similar in size and shape to those of convicts who spent all of their free time at the weight pile. He wore a fixed blade knife on the belt of his jeans and packed a pistol in his boot when he infiltrated biker events or clubhouses. On the rare occasions when his steely eyes had invited rather than deterred trouble, his fists—the size of hams and harder than forged steel—had resolved the issues before any weapons were needed. It took a special kind of cop to work undercover, and they were oftentimes the ones whose background investigators had reluctantly given the okay to hire.

It was Stephanie Woods, Josie's "lover" from the ATF with whom we had met last night, who had suggested Tony as a source. She knew him from when she had been assigned to a task force that was investigating the Mongols for trafficking firearms in San Bernardino. At the conclusion of that case, all of the ATF agents involved were transferred out and new blood was transferred in. She had said the bureau did this as a safety precaution for the agents, and from what she understood, he was now working closely with some ATF agents in the San Fernando valley. Other than the idea of checking in with Tony, the only information I had gleaned from our meeting was that if Josie and "Steph" were to ever be a thing, I knew how the pitcher and catcher roles would shake out.

We set up a meeting with Tony at a coffee shop in Whittier, not far from STARS center. Josie and I both wore jeans for the occasion and rode in her Charger, which was far more discreet than my Crown Vic. We found Tony seated in the rear of the diner with his back to the wall, affording him a clear view of the front door and the parking lot. There were no bikes out front, so I figured he had come in his undercover vehicle, and I guessed it was the white GMC pickup with tinted windows and a sticker on the back bumper that read *Support Your Local Hell's Angels*. There were other stickers on the bumper and also on the back window: the Harley emblem, a Good Time Charlie's Tattoo sticker, a confederate flag, the POW/MIA decal, and a Jane Fonda: American Traitor Bitch sticker. I would have bet a paycheck it was Tony's county-issued ride.

He nodded as we walked toward him. I thought I had met Tony before but wasn't sure. Josie said she didn't know him but had heard of him. All of the tables near where he sat in the back were unoccupied, and I guessed that Tony had known that they would be. He probably used the location to meet with different people, avoiding headquarters as much as possible to protect his cover. Outlaw bikers were smart about gathering intelligence on undercover cops.

We slid into the opposite side of his booth, Josie first and me taking the aisle. I shook his big hand across the table, and said, "I know we've met, but—"

He grinned, though it was hard to detect behind the mustache he wore, one that Sam Elliott would envy. "You probably don't remember me, but I was a trainee at Century when you were there as a detective, working the night car. I remember you."

I wondered if that meant I had hazed him at the time. I probably had, because I had always been fond of the tradition. He must not have been that big in those days, or else I was dumber than I remembered. I returned the grin. "I'm guessing you looked different then."

"Just a little bit," he joked. "Fifty pounds later and not all of it is hair."

"Do you know my partner, Josie Sanchez?"

Now I could see his smile. "I don't believe I do." They too shook hands across the table.

He nodded and indicated with his eyes that someone was coming from behind me, but giving no indication of any concern. The waitress appeared just as I turned my head.

She looked like she had waitressed all her life, but not here—somewhere in the Midwest, maybe a place that served thick slices of bacon with eggs over easy and toast all morning and featured ice-cream floats and burgers in the afternoons, a place where teenagers hung out after school to make plans for Friday's big game and the dance after. She pulled a pencil from behind her ear and hovered it over a pad of tickets she had pulled from her greasy apron's pocket. "What would you kids like?"

I would like to be referred to as a kid by people other than a waitress whose first kiss had likely been in an old Ford coupe's rumble seat. I looked to Josie, who said, "Iced tea with lemon, please."

I told her I'd have the same, and Tony held a hand over his coffee cup and shook his head, indicating he was fine.

Tony watched her walk away before he began. "So you have some questions about bikers?"

"It's a little more complicated than that," I said. "You sure you don't want something else to drink, or eat? It's on us."

He said he might, and I started talking. I told him briefly about the chippie. I mentioned he was a loner at work, that none of his colleagues socialized with him. I slowed down and described his house in San Fernando, and then I showed him pictures of the vest from the closet that had a motorcycle club patch on the back and other decals consistent with the biker culture. As he studied the photo, I told him about the El Camino with cold plates in the driveway yesterday morning, how I got jammed up for running it through DMV because it happened to be an ATF agent's undercover vehicle, some dude who works biker gangs out in San Bernardino.

"Did you get a look at the driver?" he asked.

I shook my head.

The waitress returned with two iced teas and set them down in front of Josie and me. Tony stopped her before she could leave. "Betty, listen, you better have them grill me up a cheeseburger snack."

She said, "You bet, Tony. Onion rings or fries?"

"Onion rings."

"And do you want a milkshake to go with that?"

He thought about it a moment, looked at me and then Josie before answering. "You better bring me a beer."

I said, "Same," and slid my iced tea over in front of Josie.

It was early in the afternoon when we arrived at the office and found Farris waiting for us in the parking lot. I had sent him a text to see if he was in, giving him our ETA and letting him know we needed to have a private chat when we arrived.

As Josie backed us into a spot, Farris came across the lot. Once parked, the three of us gathered around the front of her car where you could hear the engine ticking like a time bomb beneath its hood. Farris said, "What's up?"

I suggested there had to be a cooler place to talk.

"It sounded urgent and top secret. I didn't wait out here to enjoy the weather."

I nodded toward the office. "Let's see if the conference room is open. I'm literally going to die if we stand out here five more minutes."

We gathered around a table in the cool and quiet conference room where, over the years, many plans had been laid, many debates had taken place, and many cases had been solved. There had also been plenty of these types of impromptu meetings, where two or more detectives took their conversations about cases behind closed doors.

I leaned back in a leather chair and waited for everyone to settle into their seats. I could hardly wait to see Farris's response when I told him what we had learned from Biker Tony. Even though I had suspected Gomez might have been a dirty cop, I never would have imagined that he would be involved in what Tony said the feds were investigating. I thought maybe the chippie was running dope or maybe even guns. Both were favorite activities of outlaw bikers, and I honestly wouldn't have been at all surprised to find out he was living a double life as a cop and a gunrunning outlaw biker. I probably would have just nodded to Tony and then given Josie the *I told you so* look. Which would have been gratifying and also childish. But instead, when Tony had folded his big arms across his chest, looked me in the eye, and told us about a case the feds were working that involved a chippie, I had been left speechless. Although Tony didn't know the details of the ATF's investigation, it sounded like Gomez had indeed been the target of their undercover operation. He didn't know much about it, he had said, but he sometimes worked around the ATF agents.

Farris took his seat, and said, "Well, Dickie, let's hear it."

"You're not going to believe it, Rich."

With a bored expression, he said, "Try me."

18

"OUR BOY, GOMEZ, MAY HAVE BEEN INVOLVED IN RUNNING GUNS OR DOPE to and from Mexico, according to the ATF."

Farris flicked his gaze toward Josie and then came back to me, his deep brown eyes revealing no reaction to the big news. I had often said that Farris was the last person I wanted to play poker with or be interrogated by. The room was silent for a long moment before he said, "Okay, so break that down for me."

"Tony isn't working the case involving the chippie, but he heard about it through the network of outlaw motorcycle gang investigators. Their little community is a close-knit one due to the specialized nature of their cases. They occasionally have meetings or casual gatherings where they exchange intel with one another. About six months ago, Tony heard from one of the local ATF guys that a group in San Berdoo was working a trafficking case, and that it appeared there was a chippie involved somehow. The chippie was from somewhere in L.A. County, but Tony didn't get much more information about it. He only got as much as he did because he and this other agent were working together on another case, and the guy mentioned he was going to be doing surveillance in the San Fernando valley that day.

Farris rocked in his leather chair, his gaze fixed on me. He said,

"Okay, that sounds like it's hitting close to home, but is that all there is? Is there anything to indicate Gomez is the chippie they were looking at?"

I frowned. I was a bit surprised by his reaction, or lack thereof. I had been floored when Tony dropped the same information on us at the diner. But here was Rich, showing no emotion, and thinking it through. Playing devil's advocate. I guess that's what made him the detective he was.

"Well, I think the dude in the El Camino is the link. How much warmer could we get? There's a group of ATF agents from San Bernardino investigating a trafficking ring in the San Fernando Valley, and a chippie is involved. Gomez was a biker chippie, and an undercover ATF agent was in his driveway yesterday morning. I think that puts us right on the mark, Rich."

Farris nodded.

Josie said, "It makes a lot more sense about the Hernandez woman and her granddaughter disappearing, too. That doesn't happen randomly. I wonder if Gomez screwed something up or tried to back out of a deal. Bikers don't mess around."

I looked over at her. "Yeah, it wouldn't surprise me if Grandma is dead and the kid has been turned out in Vegas, or DC."

Josie sneered. "*DC?*"

"Yeah, that place is more of a sin city than Vegas could ever dream to be. Just a different class of asshole."

She shook her head and turned back to her notebook.

"So what's your plan?" Farris asked.

"That's the question," I said. "How do we proceed from here, working a case we're not supposed to be working, based on information we aren't supposed to have and which we came up with after being ordered to put it down?"

"I say we walk away," Josie said. "Let the feds sort it out. Forward the missing person report to the ATF and say, 'We heard you might be working a gun trafficking case, so here's an FYI for you, just in case you come across anything.'"

I didn't respond. Farris shifted his gaze between the two of us. The room fell silent. After a moment, he said, "Can Tony put us in touch with those agents?"

Josie said, "We're all going to get rolled up and sent to Forgery Fraud."

I chuckled. "Rolled up" was an expression that deputies learned early in their careers while assigned to any of the several custody facilities. When an inmate was being transferred, he was told to "roll it up," which meant to roll up his bed roll and bring it with him because he wasn't coming back. And although Forgery Fraud was a serious assignment and the investigators there were smart cops, it wasn't the type of place street-oriented cops wanted to be. Forgery Fraud never found themselves in Compton in the middle of the night with yellow tape everywhere and a SWAT team nearby blowing shit up. They probably also never got shot at or even had their car windows smashed. Nonetheless, her point had merit.

"What if we told the captain we got this information over drinks with a friend? That's not even a lie. We don't have to say we were working the case. Tell him with the new information, we feel the case should be reopened."

"He'll know," Josie said.

Farris said, "I say we hook up with those agents, keep the captain on a need-to-know status. Until something breaks, the less he knows, the better. He can thank us later for a job well done."

"Like that's going to happen," I said.

Then, looking at Josie, I said, "Well?"

"Honestly, I don't like it. But I'm also going to be tied up in trial and not around to babysit you two rebels next week, so do what you think is best. You know I've got your backs."

"Call Tony," Farris said.

TONY SAID, "DUDE, I WASN'T SUPPOSED TO TELL ANYONE ABOUT THAT operation. How am I going to hook you up with it?"

"Talk to your contact, tell him—"

"Her."

"—you heard about this case we were working that might involve a dirty chippie. Don't say anything about our meeting or even that you've talked to us. Tell *her* somebody should give us a call, find out what we have. See, then your ass is covered, and my captain won't go crazy for us being involved."

There was a silence on the phone. I pulled my cell away from my ear to check the screen. The call was still live, so I waited.

Finally, he said, "Okay, man, I'll see what I can do."

"Tony—"

"Yeah?"

"Don't give them my name or number. Have them call the desk and ask about it. I owe you a keg of beer."

"A keg?"

"You don't look like a six-pack type of guy."

WHEN I WALKED BACK INTO THE OFFICE, JOSIE WAS HANGING UP HER DESK phone, and her expression had grown dark.

"What's wrong?"

"Nothing, just the case."

"Spencer?"

She nodded.

"Who was that?" I said, indicating the phone on her desk.

"The DA. He wants me in his office this evening for a pretrial meeting," she said, shuffling some papers around on her desk, apparently unnecessarily.

I watched her for a moment. "Josie, you've got nothing to worry about. You'll be fine."

She stopped what she was doing, but her stare was locked on her desktop. I knew she had been dreading the day that the former game warden Jacob Spencer would stand trial for what he did to her, and to her boyfriend at the time, Tommy Zimmerman. He faced charges of first-degree murder for the deaths of both Zimmerman and a young man named William Brown, whose murder case had taken Josie and me to the mountains near Gorman. Josie had returned with her boyfriend, Tommy, and the two of them had been run off the road. Tommy was killed, and Josie had been knocked unconscious, kidnapped, and held for several days in an old miner's shed in the woods. She had endured a lot during her years as a cop, and she had survived several deadly encounters—that one included. But being bound and held for days in the mountains would terrify the bravest person on earth, and now she would have to relive it in a public forum. And he would be there watching her, listening to her, reliving it as well, but from a very different perspective.

"I know the DA said he didn't need me to be there other than when I testify, but I will gladly be there every day with you."

She shook her head.

"I don't mind."

"You and Rich are going to be in the rotation for murders. Plus, you have your dirty biker case to work on." She forced a quick grin after she said it, her way of saying I was right about that.

"Yeah, okay, but until we get called out, I can come hang there. You know what, I'm just going to. Never mind. I'll be there."

"You don't—"

I stopped her with a hand. "I'm not going to argue. I'd want you there if I were going through it."

She looked at me and smiled, her round brown eyes a little more moist than usual, and then she gave me the slightest of nods.

"Come on," I said, "let's go get dinner and a few drinks. I'm buying."

She glanced at her watch. "I've got the meeting."

"Fine. I'll go with you, and we'll get drinks after."

19

THE CRIMINAL COURTS BUILDING ON TEMPLE STREET IN DOWNTOWN LOS
Angeles is located across the street from the Hall of Justice where the
sheriff's department is headquartered. Though the twenty-floor courthouse
was renamed in 2002 and was now called the Clara Shortridge Foltz Criminal Justice Center, most still called it the criminal courts building, or
CCB. I had never heard of Clara Shortridge Goltz—*had anyone?*—though
I would imagine there was some type of politically correct, virtue-
signaling reason for it being dedicated in her name. I parked at the Hall of
Justice and trotted across Temple Street where I went against the tide of
pedestrian traffic flooding from the elevators into the lobby and through
the front doors of the courthouse as if they had all been set free. There
were cops, reporters, lawyers, and criminals—with some crossover of the
latter two—and throngs of civilians there to fulfill their civic duties.
Black, brown, and white, some wearing suits or dresses and others in
baggy jeans or shorts, some with attaché cases and some with backpacks.
Everyone keeping to themselves, some staring at their phones, others
tuned out with the aid of earbuds. Everyone rushing toward their
weekends.

I took the elevator to the eighteenth floor and signed in with the receptionist, letting her know I was there to meet with Deputy District Attorney

Darren Fry. She asked if I knew where his office was, and I assured her I did. Fry was part of CAPOS—Crimes Against Peace Officers Section— and we at Homicide interacted with the prosecutors there frequently, primarily with deputy- or officer-involved shooting cases. The CAPOS prosecutors would review all police shooting cases in the county to determine whether or not the involved officers' actions were justified. Whenever a cop was injured or killed, this is also where we brought our cases. The prosecutors here were among the best of the thousand lawyers who made up the Los Angeles County District Attorney's Office, and Darren Fry stood out even among his peers there. He had successfully prosecuted a death penalty case that I had brought to him when he was assigned to Major Crimes, and for our combined efforts, we had put a woman on death row. During a subsequent celebration in Chinatown, I had said, "It's no wonder your mother named you Fry," which prompted the first and only expression indicating he was lost that I had ever seen on the man.

"The Fry Man. How are you, my friend?"

He grinned and stood up from his desk to shake my hand. "Detective, how have you been?" He sat back down and opened a court file on his desk. All business.

Josie, already there, sat in one of the three visitors' chairs along a wall. It was a small room with a desk, four tall metal filing cabinets, and file boxes stacked against two of the walls. There was little room for anything else. I took a seat next to Josie.

Without looking up from his work, Fry said, "How's everyone?"

"Dealing with some nerves," Josie said. She looked at me and said, "Did you call Emily?"

I nodded. "Yeah, she's not feeling well and won't be joining us for cocktails."

The fact was, I hadn't even called her when I left the office as I told Josie I would. I knew she had gone to see her mother and wouldn't be home until Sunday night. I should have just told Josie that when she asked me to invite Emily to join us for drinks after the meeting. I could have explained the situation, that Emily needed some time and had gone to see her mother, but then Josie would have more questions than I cared to answer. So now I just had to keep the lie going, as much as I wasn't comfortable doing so.

Josie, sitting next to me, said, "Is everything okay with you guys?"

Fry looked up from shuffling papers and peered over his reading glasses. "Don't tell me Dickie has settled down with a woman."

"Everything's fine," I assured Josie, before turning my gaze to the busy prosecutor with his rolled-up sleeves, his white dress shirt wrinkled and hanging on his bony frame. "They'll never completely tame me, Fry Man, you know better than that."

He smiled and moved one file to the side of his desk and opened another. After perusing it for a moment, he looked up and met my gaze again. His expression was once again serious, back to business. "I'm glad you're here, Dickie. I was going to call you earlier today and let you know I've reconsidered the order of witnesses, but then Josie let me know you'd be joining us tonight. Anyway, I'm going to put you on the stand first, right after opening arguments. You can walk us through the William Brown murder in its entirety, and then we'll go through the events of that next week when you discovered that Josie was missing. This way we start with the big picture and get the bulk of testimony through you, not Josie. I don't want her overexposed on the stand."

This was a big change from his original plan of having Josie open up with the Willie Brown murder, and then tell the jury how she had gone back up to the mountain with her boyfriend over the weekend to revisit the site, and that they were run off the road on their way back. Originally, I was going to follow Josie on the stand. Fry had said he would have me testify about the search efforts, and then describe what happened when I found her and Spencer at the miner's shed. I would describe to the jury that night when I was climbing down the side of a steep mountain and a gunshot shattered the silence. I would tell how, when I arrived at the shed, I saw Spencer with a gun in his hand and the Watkins boy dead on the floor, not far from where Josie had been tied to the ground.

I was prepared to testify to all of that, as most of it was fresh in my mind as if it had happened last week, not last year. But Brown's murder was a different story. I would have to review the transcripts of my testimony at the preliminary hearing in order to refresh my memory of my previous testimony on the case. That was more important than reviewing the murder book. Though I would have to review those several hundred pages of reports also, the trial would be much more in-depth and intensive than the preliminary hearing had been. All murder trials required a lot of preparation, and knowing what I was in for this weekend, I was relieved that Emily would be gone.

But I knew that when she returned Sunday night, there would be no further delays in our resolving the issue at hand. This was it. Sunday night we would have the conversation I had been avoiding. It wouldn't be the type of conversation that could be had in a few minutes, so the case preparation would have to be concluded by the time she got home. As long as nothing went wrong, I didn't see a problem with it.

"Okay," I promised the Fry Man, "I'll be ready to go."

MY ATTACHÉ CASE WAS WEIGHTED WITH REAMS OF TRANSCRIPTS WHEN I left Fry's office, intent on heading straight to the bureau. After a lengthy meeting and with the burden of knowing how much preparation I now had to do for the case, I had called off drinks and told Josie I was going to go straight home to crack open the files. Josie stayed behind to go over her testimony once more with Fry. For her, I had put on a good front: no problem, I'd be ready to go. I'd spend the weekend studying and when I showed up Monday morning, I'd be fresh as a daisy. But when the elevator doors slid shut, I leaned against the back wall and let out a heavy sigh. I had a lot of homework to do now.

During my drive home, I decided I would pull a late-nighter, poring over the case files and transcripts until my eyes grew heavy, then get some sleep and start again tomorrow morning with a fresh pot of coffee. Suddenly I felt the walls closing in, the pressure mounting. I was sweating, although the air conditioner was on high and the vents all pointed right at me. I had removed my hat, and I continued wiping sweat from my forehead. It was all overwhelming, as it all too often could be. Homicide was arguably the most stressful assignment in law enforcement. *No greater honor will ever be bestowed on an officer or a more profound duty imposed on him than when he is entrusted with the investigation of the death of a human being.* That was a part of the homicide investigators' creed, and those of us who were serious practitioners of the trade never arrived at nor departed a new crime scene lightly. Over time, that took its toll.

Alone in my thoughts, I cursed the chaos that seemed to shadow me.

Inside my apartment, I grabbed a beer from the fridge, changed into shorts and a t-shirt, put a ball game on the television with the volume low, and plopped down on the couch with my files. Then I made the mistake of checking email on my phone. I got halfway through the inbox before coming to a message from *BikerTrash666*. The subject simply said "Meeting," and the body of the email was brief, to the point, likely pecked out by two large greasy fingers: *Meet me at the diner tomorrow at 3*.

20

Saturday morning I hit the books again and felt I had made decent progress before it was time to drive to Whittier. As if I had nothing better to do on a day off. But when you asked others for help on cases, you didn't hesitate to go when they called. That's how I had been taught, and it's how I operated.

Tony Brunetti sat in the same booth at the back of the diner where Josie and I had met with him two days ago. He was working a fat French fry through a pool of ketchup as I slid in across from him. He nodded, worked the fry into his mouth, and then used the back of the same hand to wipe the ketchup off his imposing blond mustache.

"You hungry?" he said, still chewing.

The same waitress appeared before I had time to answer him. From the looks of the food stains on her outfit, I didn't think she had changed since the last time we saw her. "You havin' anything to eat, hon?"

I shook my head. "Just an iced tea, please."

She cocked her head and gave me a look. "Are you sure? Last time you were here, you ordered a tea, then gave it to your lady friend and switched to beer. Where is she, anyway? She sure was a cute little thing."

"Probably at the beauty salon," I said. "There's a lot of work that goes into that project."

The waitress rolled her eyes.

I said, "Yes, just an iced tea today. Thank you."

She whirled away and Tony said, "They've got great burgers."

"I'm really not hungry," I lied. "Plus, I can't be long. I have a million things to do today and it's supposed to be my day off."

Tony took a drink of some type of soda, this time wiping at his 'stache with his big hairy forearm. He grinned and said, "What time do you tee off?"

The golf thing wore on me. It was old, it was cliché, it was bullshit. I hadn't swung a club since I'd been at Homicide for six months. Once the cases started stacking up, it felt like I wore a backpack full of rocks, and the mountain I had hoped to climb suddenly seemed higher and steeper than it had from a distance. Yet all too often, detectives in other assignments—many of which allowed all sorts of time for personal pleasures—would often rib Homicide guys about playing golf. Where they got the idea, I couldn't begin to guess. I didn't know anyone at the bureau who golfed with any regularity.

I said, "I'm about ready to tee off on the next asshole who accuses me of playing golf when I'm putting in eighteen hours a day or working on my days off."

His eyes popped open; he was clearly surprised by my response, which could have been taken as a threat. Of course, I wasn't stupid enough to threaten a guy the size of Tony, but he didn't know that. So I smiled and said, "But with you, I'd use a Buick rather than a three-wood. I'm at least that smart."

He smiled, now having no reason to puff up like a fighting cock since I had made it clear with the Buick statement that I respected his size and strength. It was the establishing of the big dog/little dog relationship, a thing in which all men constantly engaged. In a testosterone-driven environment such as law enforcement in Los Angeles, you were never the biggest dog. There was always someone with a bigger bite. I had no illusions otherwise. I had worked with cops who could knock out NFL-sized men with a single punch, or they could grab an average-sized man by his collar and hurl him across the hood of a radio car. But I felt strongly about letting the bigger dogs see my teeth, even at the risk of losing them if I pushed things too far. Years before, I had worked with an accomplished and respected boxer who was also a bit of a hardhead. He and I got into an argument one night over an operation we were engaged in, just a normal disagreement that escalated to the point where it could have turned into a physical altercation. As the posturing began, I offered a succinct warning, which gave him pause. I said, "Manny, I have one distinct advantage over you. I *know* you can kick my ass." As he pondered it, I said, "Do you really think I'm going to square off with you in a fair fight? I'd break a chair over your head while you're lacing your gloves or looking around for your mouthpiece." He said he'd then get up and kick my ass. I said, "Maybe, but you'll be reluctant to turn your back to me ever again if you do."

Tony said, "Well don't be in too big of a hurry; I've got someone coming you're going to want to meet." He picked his cell phone up from the table and checked the time. "Should be here any minute."

I figured it would be one of the ATF guys, someone with direct information. I glanced at my watch—it was almost three-thirty already. But this was exactly what I had hoped for when I read Tony's email last night, that he had a hookup for me. Someone with direct information about the chippie and whatever the feds had going in the valley. If Tony only wanted to pass on some information, he would have simply called. This could be just what the chippie case needed.

"Is this the ATF agent?" I asked.

"It's the agent I told you about who had to break away to assist some of their guys from San Berdoo with the dirty cop thing. I didn't bother asking about it. I figured I'd put you two in touch and let you get what you needed directly from the source." He glanced at his phone again. "I'm too busy to play middleman on this deal."

I said, "What time do you tee off?"

He grinned and lifted his soda up to offer a toast. "Touché, brother."

Two dogs in the same yard, one bigger than the other, each with sharp teeth. Sometimes you just had to go piss on the other dog's tree to let him know you weren't afraid to come off the porch. I lifted my iced tea. "Touché."

The minutes ticked by slowly. The waitress refilled my iced tea twice before the agent arrived.

Tony, who had sat on the side of the booth that gave us a view of the front door, had gone to the restroom, so I hadn't been warned of the agent's approach. So when the tall, shapely blonde in designer jeans and a low-cut satin blouse appeared at our table, I had started to ask if I could help her.

But as she stood staring at me through expensive sunglasses, and before I finished appraising her, she said, "I know you."

This caught me off-guard. How did she know me? Was she a witness on one of my cases, or a family member of one of my victims? She might have been a deputy, I thought. Or maybe she was an attorney, a prosecutor or defense attorney. Maybe a judge. That actually made more sense, I thought, feeling the strength of this woman, her commanding presence, her unwavering gaze only slightly concealed behind her Pradas. She was the type who could send big dogs like me and Tony back up onto our porches with little more than a stern look. She was an alpha bitch.

"You do?" was the best I could come up with as a response.

She pushed Tony's dirty plate away and slid into his side of the booth. Once seated, she moved his glass of soda as well and used his napkin to clean the space in front of her, sighing as she did. Settled, she moved her sunglasses onto her head, which set her hair back away from her face and revealed a pair of green eyes I could never forget. "Yes, I do."

"Jesus," I said, "Tammy Rae Moore."

"So, you two have met," Tony said, appearing at my side of the table. "Move over, Dickie."

Tammy Rae, as she preferred to be called—never just Tammy—had been a young deputy sheriff trainee when Floyd and I were the night car detectives at Century Station. As attractive as she was—then and now— we might not have ever known her but for her emergency radio traffic broadcast one hot summer night in South Los Angeles: *Two-fifteen king one, nine-ninety-eight, Alameda and Short.*

Her call for help had gone out at the worst time possible. It would have been a busy enough night just chasing radio calls, as one hot call after another came out while swarms of residents, who had remained indoors throughout the blistering days, ventured out during the relatively cool nights, none of them having to work the next day. Tensions were high between citizens and police due to several controversial shootings throughout the country, the coverage of which had dominated the news and social media. The same tension had been present just before the Rodney King verdict had touched off the rioting in 1992, and probably during the sweltering days and nights leading up to that traffic stop at 116th Street and Avalon Boulevard in 1965. And on the night Tammy Rae Moore requested assistance, broadcasting the radio code that indicated she had been involved in a shooting, there had already been two other deputy-involved shootings within our jurisdiction.

Floyd and I—along with every other cop in the region—had rolled to each of the other two shootings that night, racing from one location to the other in an unmarked detective car, a chocolate brown Caprice with a red light on the dash and flashing amber and blue lights on the rear deck. The first shooting had left two gang members dead, sprawled among blood and broken glass on either side of a lowered Cutlass that was riddled with bullet holes, pistols near their bodies, expended cartridge casings littering the street. We had done what we could do—secured the scene and canvassed for witnesses—when a second radio broadcast of a deputy-involved shooting came over the airwaves. We raced to that one and assisted in a similar fashion: helped secure the scene, canvassed for witnesses. This one, too, had resulted in a suspect being shot, though he would live to someday be shot again.

Deputy-involved shootings that resulted in death or injury were investigated by Homicide. There wasn't much for Floyd and me—station detectives at the time—to do once the scene was secured and the bureau had been notified. But the third shooting of the night, close on the heels of the second, would be a case where nobody was struck or injured, and in which the suspect was never found, and of which Floyd and I would spend many hours trying to make sense. It was the "no hit" deputy-involved shooting of Tammy Rae Moore, and it was ours to handle.

The setting was an alley in the far north region of Century's jurisdiction, an area that was previously within Firestone's jurisdiction before Firestone and Lynwood stations were closed and the personnel combined to create Century. Floyd and I were both intimately familiar with the area, having worked there for nearly a decade. Coincidentally—or perhaps not —the other two shootings that night had occurred in the southern region of Century's jurisdiction, one in Lynwood and the other in Willowbrook. With many units tied up on the previous two shootings, and nearly all units having been drawn toward the action of them, Tammy Rae had found herself waiting for a long four minutes before the first unit arrived to assist her. Floyd and I arrived a couple minutes after that. The suspect, a black male "transient" adult, was GPA—gone prior to arrival, and never located.

But Tammy Rae had survived a harrowing, deadly encounter when she had attempted to stop the lone black male in a dark alley that ran behind an industrial complex. She had stopped her radio car, directed a spotlight onto him, and ordered him to halt and show his hands. She thought he might have been a burglar, or a metal thief—both of which had plagued the nearby businesses constantly. But the suspect had turned with a gun in his hand and fired several shots at her, striking her radio car three times. She returned fire as the suspect fled into the darkness.

When daylight came the next morning, the scene remained intact and guarded. Yellow tape had been strewn across the alley at both ends, and two deputies had remained there throughout the night. Floyd and I had spent several hours searching for evidence in the dark, while patrol deputies coordinated an intense search for the suspect that involved several canines and circling helicopters, their searchlights turning darkness to daylight. Once our scene investigation was complete, we drove back to the station where we met with, and spent the next several hours interviewing Tammy Rae.

On our way back to the scene that next morning, we had run through McDonald's and picked up breakfast sandwiches and coffee to keep us going with nearly twenty straight hours of work now behind us. We drove back to the scene, moving slowly through the empty streets that seemed calm the morning after, the daylight bringing a false sense of serenity to the area. At first, there was silence, each of us alone in our thoughts. But before we arrived back at the alley where Moore's bullet-ridden black and white sheriff's car stood waiting, secured and undisturbed at our direction, I broke the silence between us: "It's all bullshit." Floyd said, "Uh-huh."

And now she sat across from me, her green eyes fixed on me with an air of confidence I never would have expected from her after that case, and how it ended. Without breaking the stare, I said to Tony, "Yes, we've met."

21

ON MY WAY TO BURBANK, CREEPING ALONG ON THE NORTHBOUND FIVE IN Saturday afternoon traffic, I called Floyd.

"Where have you been, asshole?" was how he answered the phone.

"Me! I haven't seen you around the office for a week. I figured you and your new girlfriend, Mongo, had taken your bromance to a new level, went on a cruise together or something."

"Are you working today?" he asked.

"No, not really. I mean, we're off, but I had to go to Whittier for a meeting, and now I'm headed home. Why do you ask?"

"Because I was thinking you needed your ass kicked."

I glanced in my mirror, keeping an eye on the pickup behind me. It had a bumper that sat about even with my trunk lid and was being driven by some yuppy dude who was chatting on a cell phone and constantly looking at himself in his mirror, smiling and grooming his dark hair.

"I could probably use a good ass whippin', I'm not going to lie. But hey, guess who I just had a nice little visit with?"

"Hold on." He covered the mouthpiece and said to someone else, "Give me a minute, I'll be right there." He came back. "You there, Dickie?"

"Yeah."

"Okay, what were you boring me about?"

"You're not going to believe who I just spent the afternoon with."

"Try me," he said, his tone uninterested.

The dude in the truck was up my ass, so I hit my brakes twice and he flipped me off. I wondered if he didn't notice the amber and blue lights on the rear deck, or if the disrespect of law enforcement had come this far. I thought about moving over and allowing him to pass me, and then hitting the forward red to pull him over. But then what? I hadn't had a citation book in fifteen years, so it would be for no other reason than to further a pissing contest, one I couldn't win. So instead, I flipped him off in return.

It reminded me of an old tale, said to be true, wherein an LAPD officer went to court on a citation he had issued to a hippy who had flipped him the bird. He had charged him with disorderly conduct. The judge dismissed the case, stating there was nothing illegal about flipping someone the bird, so the officer stood up to leave and flipped off the judge on his way out. Rumor was that the judge attempted to hold the officer in contempt of court, but that the hippy's attorney spoke up for him, citing his ruling as precedence on the matter.

Glancing back and forth from the road to the bumper and grill now in my back window, I said, "Tammy Rae Moore."

"Shut the front door!" Floyd said.

"Yep. She's an ATF agent now. And I'm about to kill this asshole behind me."

"Hang on!" Floyd shouted, but the words seemed to be otherwise directed, muffled in my earpiece. "Fucking Mongo is driving me crazy. The dude is an hour past his feeding time and it's a survival situation, end-of-times shit. I'm surprised he hasn't fired up a backpacking stove on his desk or broken out the MREs. Why the hell are you meeting with her? Is she still hot?"

I jotted the truck's license number into my notebook, having read it backwards in my mirror. "She's the agent Tony Brunetti put us in touch with on this chippie case."

"Wait, what the hell are you talking about? And what's that big goon, Tony, up to? The last time I saw him we were about to go at it over another broad in a bar—it's a long story."

"Big surprise. Anyway, I guess we haven't talked. The chippie case has turned into a big piece of shit. The coroner's wanting to call it a natural, your captain ordered us to put it down, but I think the dude died as the result of a confrontation—which makes it at least a manslaughter—and I think he was a dirty cop, but I don't know what he was into, other than hanging around bikers."

Truck boy headed for an offramp and accelerated to get alongside me as he did, now leaning out his window, his face red with anger as he yelled and cussed—I was no lip reader, but I easily picked up a few words—and continually flung his middle finger at me. I waved back, thinking, karma, baby… yours is coming.

Floyd said, "Sounds to me like you should take your captain's advice for a change and move on. How the hell did Tammy Rae become an ATF agent, anyway? That bitch is scandalous."

I had no idea how she had become an ATF agent. I supposed they hadn't given her a polygraph, because she for sure would have failed it. Floyd and I were convinced she had fabricated the entire story about being shot at, but we never would have been able to prove it, and we hadn't tried. Our theory of what happened that night was that Tammy Rae knew all the other patrol cars were tied up on the murders in the south end, and that fact allowed her to safely fire shots in that desolate industrial location without another unit happening onto her staged scene. It also allowed for the delayed response times, which would reasonably allow "the suspect" to flee and never be captured. We believed she had used a throw-away gun to shoot her own patrol vehicle, and then busted caps from her duty pistol into the sky. All of this, we believed, was for attention, so she would be viewed as someone who had been in the shit. She would garner the respect of other cops at the station, who, for the most part, had only paid attention to her when they wanted something else, something that had nothing to do with police work.

But neither of us was the type to call Internal Affairs or even take our concerns to the captain. If we had been able to prove she staged it, that would have been different. But we didn't think we would be able to prove she had, and we doubted that those hacks at IA would be able to either. So why put her through it? Especially when we weren't one-hundred percent sure of what had happened. So instead, I confronted her right before I promoted to Detective Division and was sent to Special Investigations. I met her at the scene and told her to empty her pockets and take her portable radio off her belt and leave it in her car. We walked twenty yards from where we had parked, and I told her exactly how Floyd and I believed it had gone down. I finished with, "I'm headed to Special Investigations and I'm on the list to go to Homicide. I promise you I will keep an eye on you for the rest of your career, and if you're ever involved in another shooting, I'm going to be all over it with a fine-toothed comb." I also asked how she might have felt if a deputy, responding to her assistance call, had crashed and died. It wouldn't be the first time that had happened. I could see the wheels spinning, and she shrugged and looked away. Not once did she defend herself and say we were out of our minds, that it really had happened the way she said it had. I walked away that day knowing Floyd and I had it right.

I told Floyd, "And that's just one more reason for me to stay on this case. Who knows what direction this thing is going to go with Tammy Rae in the middle of it."

"Jesus," he said. "All right, well I have to feed my Mongo, and then we're off to Compton to do some interviews. Keep me posted on your girlfriend."

SUNDAY AFTERNOON I FINISHED MY REVIEW OF THE CASE AND FELT prepared to testify the next morning. Now it was time for a short nap before my evening with Emily. I didn't want to be exhausted when we finally had our time together, and figured with a nap and a shower, I'd be as good as new. But as I lay on my couch, the TV showing an afternoon ball game and my air conditioner drowning out the sounds beyond my small apartment, my thoughts returned to Tammy Rae and the chippie case. She had been coy during our meeting, not sharing much about this case that may or may not have involved a chippie, saying she needed to get permission from the agent in charge before discussing it in detail. But she was going to be my contact on it from here forward, and Tony was out. I didn't like that, and I didn't understand the reason for it. I didn't trust her one bit.

Soon my thoughts moved to Emily and the evening before us. Should I suggest we go to dinner first, order takeout, or skip food all together and open a bottle of something? Emily was different from my ex-wife, Val, and from Katherine, the shrink I had dated a short time before meeting Emily. She was different from all of the others I had dated throughout my many years of bachelorhood, and I truly believed this could actually work with her. It was as if I had finally found my soulmate, and I needed to try hard to not screw it up. It seemed I had just fallen asleep when a thud woke me. It sounded like a door closing, and it had either come from next door—Emily's—or upstairs. I checked my phone and saw it was nearly five. Damn, I guess I really had been tired. I popped out of my apartment and went to Emily's door, which now stood open. It made me wonder if she had closed it just to signal me that she was home. But an open door signified an invitation, a welcome, a cue that it was time to reunite and work things out.

She was dressed in shorts and a tank top, coiled into a corner of her couch with a book in hand. Her freckled legs were pulled up next to her as if she were warming herself, but it was ninety degrees outside, and she had her apartment opened up. Emily was always cold, and that was one problem she and I would always have to deal with. If there was to be an "always."

"Hey there."

"Hi."

"How is your mom?"

She lowered her book. "She's okay."

I noted the shortness in her tone. "Good, I'm glad to hear it. Listen, I just woke up from a long nap and need to grab a shower, brush my teeth, change my clothes. I'll be over in a few minutes, if that's okay."

A simple "okay" and a polite smile was all I received in return.

"What are you reading?" I asked.

She closed the book to see the cover for herself, as if the title had escaped her, and then held it up for me to see. "It's the biography of Eleanor Roosevelt."

I nodded. "Be right back."

As I turned away, Emily said, "What should we do about dinner?"

I stopped and looked back at her. "Anything you'd like. We can go out, order something in, eat now, eat later, whatever you want."

Her tone seemed cautious. "Okay."

I went into my apartment and closed the door behind me. I had left my air conditioner running and it felt good, like walking into a beer cooler at the market. Which gave me my first good idea. I went for the fridge, trying to remember who exactly Eleanor Roosevelt was. I knew she had been a first lady, but to which Roosevelt? There was Teddy and FDR, right? Teddy was the good one, as I recalled. Sometimes I wished I had paid attention to more than only fast cars and faster girls during school.

By the time I had showered, dressed in a decent pair of shorts and a clean polo—in case we went out—and stepped into a pair of flip-flops, I had consumed two cold beers and was feeling better. But there was a nervousness inside me that was similar to the feeling I'd get before taking the witness stand in a jury trial. I enjoyed testifying but was always nervous about it until after I was sworn, seated, and had dispensed with the obligatory introduction: *Richard Jones, J-O-N-E-S... I'm a deputy sheriff for the County of Los Angeles, assigned to Detective Division, Homicide Bureau.* The DA would ask how long I had been so employed, and if I had been so employed on the day in question, whatever day it was that some person—presumably he or she would be seated at the defense table before me—had committed whatever it was they stood trial for, usually murder. That preliminary series of inconsequential questions and answers was warmup for me, my eight preparatory pitches at the start of the game, enough to warm my shoulder and face a batter.

I tried to think of a warmup for the hitter I was about to face, knowing that one mistake and she might send me to the bench and another pitcher would be brought in from the bullpen. It could be a merciless game and you had to love it with all of your heart to want to keep taking the mound.

I grabbed another beer from the fridge, pregaming the event. As I took a long pull from the silver can, I checked my phone to see if there were any important messages. There was one, but I wouldn't call it important. It was bizarre, puzzling, the type of message that would leave me pondering its meaning for days to come. I'd consult with Floyd, see what he thought, and he would break it down and analyze every syllable in an effort to find its true meaning. Ultimately, he would likely conclude that Tammy Rae was a slut. Her message was simple but loaded: *Dickie, it was really great seeing you today. I look forward to working with you again.*

I finished my beer in another gulp, deleted the message, and walked next door.

22

Homicide Bureau at the Los Angeles County Sheriff's Department was the big leagues. Metaphorically, you no longer carried your gear to the park and you traveled on chartered planes rather than enduring long bus rides. At the bureau, each investigator was issued a take-home car, an iPhone, and a laptop computer—all of the things you would buy and maintain for yourself at most other assignments you might have worked on your way to The Show. There was no set daily schedule; you worked when and where you needed to work, and you showed up at the office when you wanted or needed to. It was the closest thing to being self-employed that a county employee could be. But as is the case with the self-employed, entrepreneurs whose successes are the direct results of their best efforts, few investigators at the bureau ever took advantage of the autonomous system in which we worked. Most of us consistently put in many more hours than we were ever compensated for, and the bosses knew it.

The downside was that you never fully escaped your job. At any time of day or night you could—and often would—receive phone calls or text messages from a host of characters: witnesses, informants, cops, and attorneys. Or from the family members, friends, and loved ones of your latest victim. Sometimes it would be the loved one of a victim whose case you had moved on from, and whom you hadn't thought about for months or years. It was another burden shared by those of us in the death business.

I had been in Emily's apartment for ten minutes when my phone began vibrating on the coffee table only a few feet away. Until then, there had been no meaningful conversation between us. I had been throwing a few warmup pitches, asking about her book, about her day at the office, about the weather—talking about anything other than the topic at hand or the text message I had received from Tammy Rae just moments before I came over. My first thought about my phone now vibrating was that the crazy bitch was texting me again. The next thought was why hadn't I silenced my phone. I tried to ignore it, but Emily's gaze set upon the pulsating device. Finally, she said, "Are you going to answer it, or check your messages? Maybe it's something important."

I could feel sweat trickling down my back. It was hot in her apartment and my phone activity pushed the mercury up another ten degrees. Emily's stare, now set on me, moved the heat index off the charts.

She said, "Why are you ignoring your phone?"

I reached for it while offering my position on the matter. "I didn't want to be distracted again. I'm sorry, I should have shut it off. It never fails…"

The phone showed missed calls from Josie, from Floyd, and from an L.A. number I didn't recognize and which obviously wasn't one of my contacts. I opened my text message app and saw that each of them had also sent one or more text messages.

From Floyd: *Dickhead, where are you? Josie is having a fit, something about your Compton case. I'm going to ride down there with her since you've probably fallen into a bottle of booze or decided to bed down with that slut, Tammy. Call me, asshole.* And the middle finger emoji.

From Josie: *They're back.* Then: *Maria and Leticia.* Next text: *The grandma and little girl. Why are you ignoring me?*—sounding like Floyd—and finally: *Hurry up, we need to get down there!* And a brown running woman emoji.

From the L.A. number: *Sir, Sergeant MacDonald Hill here, Compton Court. Yo lil Mexican family come back, I just seen um.* Then: *I got um, I'll hold onto um til you get here. Come on.* And a police car emoji.

These people and their emojis…

Emily said, "Is everything okay?"

I shook my head. "No—I mean, yes, but—"

"You have to go."

I looked up from my phone to meet her gaze. "I'm sorry. The missing family is back. There's no way I can skip out on these interviews."

She gave a half nod and looked away.

"Emily," I said, standing up from the couch, "you know I can't—"

She waved me off. "I know. I get it. Go do your job. We'll talk later."

"Are you sure? I get a pass on this, right?"

She was silent a moment. I waited, watching as she gently rocked herself, her legs drawn up tight against her chest, her arms wrapped around them. Her chin rested on her knee and her gaze was on the floor. When she looked up, her eyes were moist. She said, "I guess this is part of the discussion we'll have someday. But yes, it's what you do, it's who you are. Go."

I left without saying the things I should have said.

JOSIE HAD WAITED FOR ME IN THE LOBBY OF THE COURTHOUSE. A SECURITY officer opened the door as I approached and locked it behind me after I entered. It was after hours and the lobby was otherwise empty and quiet. Our heels clicked across the recently polished tile floor as Josie and I hastened toward the elevators.

The doors slid open at the push of a button, and we stepped inside. "So what's their story?"

"I haven't even talked to them yet," she said. "It's sort of an awkward deal with our favorite courthouse sergeant essentially taking them into custody. You know what I mean?"

"Not really. What happened?"

"I thought you talked to him."

"He sent a text, but it just said he would hold onto them. I thought he was just going to hang out with them, you know? He didn't hook them up, did he?"

She shook her head. "No, it's not that bad, but he has them up in his office and told them they weren't going anywhere until his friends from Homicide talked to them."

I shook my head and smiled. "Big Mac, making it happen. You've got to love that guy."

Josie grinned. "Yeah, he's something. Apparently, he's been coming by on his days off to check on his security guards. They have a couple here around the clock, and Mac takes his job as supervisor to the extreme. Anyway, he spotted our two missings as they were getting out of a car and walking up to the apartment. He told me he's been keeping a close eye on the place ever since we told him what happened."

The elevator clunked to a stop, settled, and its doors slid open. On our way to Sergeant Hill's office, I said, "Do they speak English?"

"Leticia does, Grandma doesn't."

"Hmmm."

She said, "Do you want to split up, you interview the girl and I'll take Grandma?"

I thought about it for a moment. "No, let's both do each of them. We'll do Grandma first. You talk, I'll take the notes. We can switch for the girl."

"Okay by me," she said, "I just figured we could get it done sooner this way. We have court in the morning, and I have a feeling this might turn into a long night."

"Well, at least I finished going over the transcripts. I'm ready to go for tomorrow, even if we work all night."

We had paused at the door to the security office while finishing our conversation. Josie said, "Oh, and your sister said to call if we need her."

"Floyd."

"Yes, Floyd. Your sister. He was insisting on coming down here with me, but I told him to chill. I don't need backup to go talk to witnesses, I don't care where it is."

"He must be bored. What's he doing in the office?"

"He and Mongo are in the barrel for PMs. I think that's why he volunteered to come with me."

"Yeah, he hates being stuck inside on the desk. They were at the office yesterday too."

Josie pushed the door open and I followed her inside.

Maria Guadalupe Gomez Hernandez and her granddaughter, Leticia, sat in chairs adjacent to the big man's desk, watching us carefully as we walked toward them. The girl was heavyset, giving her the physical attributes of a girl three or four years older. Both were clean, groomed, and modestly dressed.

MacDonald Hill looked up from his computer and stood up from his desk to greet me. "Hey there, Detective, you made it. I'm sure sorry 'bout botherin' y'all, but I didn't know if they was back for good or just droppin' by." He was dressed in khaki pants and a striped polo that was stretched tight across his chest and arms.

"You did the right thing, Sergeant. Thank you."

He nodded. "All right then, you want to talk to them right here? I can go somewheres else to write my incident report."

Josie cleared her throat. "Sergeant Hill, are there any female officers working now?"

He shook his head. "No ma'am. We got a couple of 'em assigned here, but they work the dayshift during the week. Whatcha need?"

She looked at me. "Maybe we should take them to the station where we can have a female deputy sit with one while we talk to the other."

Josie had a good point. I knew it wasn't that she didn't trust the sergeant, in fact the opposite was likely the case. However, she knew better than to place him into a situation where a simple allegation could ruin him. Our department and most others took precautions in such matters now, leaving little room for false allegations. Litigation against cops was all the rage.

"I think that's a good idea, partner." I looked at Mac and said, "Plus that way we get out of the sergeant's hair. He can write his report and be home in an hour drinking a beer, if we don't hang around here."

Mac lowered himself back into his seat and rubbed his bald head. "No worries about being in my hair, sir. But whatever you think is best."

I indicated the report on his computer screen that so far had one paragraph of words typed in all capital letters. "Can we get a copy of your report after you finish it?"

"Yessir."

"If you'd just make sure to include all the details about that car that dropped them off, and anything you can add about the driver."

"You got it, boss. I'll get it all in the report and I'll get the report over to you. You want me to fax it? I got your fax number on your card."

"That'd be perfect. Thank you."

Josie turned to face the woman and her granddaughter who still sat silently watching, captive spectators. She addressed the girl. "We're going to take you and your grandmother next door to the sheriff's station. We need to talk to you both, and it's the best place for us to do that. Okay?"

The girl nodded.

Josie looked at the grandmother and said a few words in Spanish, then turned back to the girl and said, "Okay, let's go then."

We rode the elevator down to the empty lobby and walked out into a warm summer evening, darkness just settling in. As we started across the courtyard, nearing the Monument to the Five-Year Prior, I thought about Farris's car window being smashed the last time I was here. This time, I had parked in the otherwise empty structure, as had Josie. Hopefully our cars were safe there, but I'd feel better in a few minutes with them parked next door in the secured sheriff's parking lot.

A volunteer matron was assigned to take Leticia to the break room and keep her comfortable and occupied until we were ready for her. The matron, a middle-age Hispanic woman with motherly intuition, went straight to the young girl and put her arm around her. The matron stroked Leticia's short hair and said, "*Mija*, you must be hungry."

Josie pulled a twenty from her jacket pocket and handed it to the matron. "Maybe you could get someone to go pick something up for you both."

"*Gracias*," the woman said.

We decided to use the administrative offices for our interviews. At this time of the evening, they stood empty, and the environment there was more comfortable and less intimidating than an interview room.

Maria Hernandez sat in her seat with her arms folded over a floral-print blouse that hung loosely over her brown polyester slacks and leather sandals. She didn't have a purse, wallet, or phone. She was empty handed. Josie spoke to her in Spanish, and first asked if she had identification. No, she said, she had nothing. Josie moved on, but I made a note to circle back to that question: Where was her purse, wallet, phone, ID? We hadn't found any of those items in the apartment. If she had been kidnapped, would she have been allowed to gather her belongings and take them with her?

Josie confirmed that Maria Hernandez only spoke Spanish and began the interview, first asking for her personal information. The woman gave it, and it matched the information we had obtained from the apartment. Her name was Maria Guadalupe Gomez Hernandez.

Josie continued, asking a question and receiving a response before pausing to tell me what had been asked and answered. She would then move on. The first series of questions had to do with relationships. The woman confirmed that Leticia was her granddaughter, and she said they lived by themselves in the apartment across from the courthouse. She said the girl's mother was currently in jail on drug charges, and the father, who is a cop, helps them with money for food and rent.

Josie turned to me and said, "She speaks of him as if she has no idea."

I nodded, and she continued, moving to the morning that the girl's father, the deceased CHP officer named Gomez, came to her home. I watched as Ms. Hernandez shook her head, confusion showing in her frown as she answered. Josie said to me, "She said she hasn't seen him since the first of the month when he came by with some cash."

"That would be more than two weeks ago."

Josie nodded. "She seems sincere."

"Okay, move on. We'll see what the kid has to say about that."

She nodded, then directed another question at our guest. The woman answered with a string of rapidly spoken Spanish, accentuated by active hands. Josie responded. The woman replied. It was a volley that lasted for several minutes. Finally, they stopped. Josie leaned back in her chair. The woman folded her arms again and turned her head to stare off toward an empty desk behind her.

I said, "What the hell was all that about?"

Josie let out a long, slow breath of air. "She's saying she doesn't know about anything happening at her apartment. They went to Mexico to see family and just got back this afternoon. She wants to know why we have her and her granddaughter here, and can we call the girl's father to come straighten out whatever trouble she is in."

"Okay, we'll not discuss the girl's father right now. Ask her where her purse and ID are."

Josie did, and the woman gave a short reply, which Josie related to me. "She said she was robbed in Mexico."

A half hour later we walked Maria Hernandez to the break room where Leticia sat waiting with the matron, neither of them appearing happy. A meal sat before the girl, untouched. Her chaperone sat next to her with her arms folded, frowning. Josie had a short conversation with the woman in Spanish, which she then related to me.

"The girl won't eat, she won't speak, and the matron is upset about it."

Grandma had joined them at the table, taking a seat. Josie and I stood in front of them. I said, "She seems to be more than upset. Are you sure nothing happened?"

Josie asked the matron a question in Spanish, and she answered in English. "The girl is troubled and in need of help. But she is too frightened to talk about it. I tell her, 'If you don't eat something, *mija*, you will be sick.' She tell me nothing," the matron said, waving a hand through the air dismissively.

I asked Josie to step outside the break room with me. She told the two women and the girl to wait, we'd be back. In the hallway, I said, "Grandma didn't get robbed in Mexico. She's lying. The little girl is traumatized and won't even eat. She's not going to talk to us."

"We have to try," Josie said.

I was thinking of the possibilities but not coming up with any other ideas.

Josie said, "I say we try to talk to her, and if that doesn't work, we put her with her mother."

"Put the kid in jail?" I said, surprised by the suggestion.

"Not *in* jail," Josie explained, "but we take her to see her mom. That might comfort her. Maybe she'll tell mom what happened."

I thought about it a moment. "Maybe she doesn't want to see her mom."

"I'll ask her."

"Should we wire a room and put them together, alone?"

Josie nodded. "That's an idea. We'll need a court order."

I glanced at my watch. It was nearly nine now. It would take me an hour to type an affidavit for a court order, and Josie could be finding us a judge while I did. Drive to a judge's house—hopefully someplace nearby

—get the order signed, get back here to Compton, grab the kid, and then it'd be midnight or later by the time we try to see the mom. All of that would also be contingent on being able to get someone from the tech crew over to the jail to wire a room for recording. Maybe it was too much. It was a good idea, but there were too many spokes in that wheel, and we were fighting time. Josie and I each had to be in court in the morning, and it would be nice to get some sleep since it would be a long, hard day.

I fell back against the wall and sighed, and then I checked the time again. Time always seemed to be the enemy in this job. I was trying to think of other possibilities, but not coming up with anything until a patrol deputy walked across the hallway a short distance from where we stood, oblivious to our presence.

My expression must have shown I had come up with something else. Josie said, "What? What are you thinking?"

I pushed off the wall with my shoulders, stepped over to the doorway and checked on our guests and the matron. Nothing had changed, they were all still sitting solemnly around the table without speaking. I turned back to Josie and said, "I say we do it the old-fashioned way."

Josie's brows narrowed, questioning.

"Grandma and the kid haven't had a chance to talk privately since Big Mac scooped them up. Both have to be worried about where this is all going and what might happen to them. I say we hide a recorder in the back seat of one of our cars and put them together for a while, like we used to do in the old days, throw two crooks in the back seat of a radio car with a recorder rolling, and let them get their stories straight. We can act like we're going to take them back to their apartment, and then need to chat outside the car for some reason. Give them a few minutes alone."

She was nodding. "Okay, yeah… but we'll have to stimulate the conversation."

"What are you thinking?"

Josie said, "How about we put them in my car, one in the front seat and one in the back, and I'll tell them I'm going to take them home. Then, before I leave with them, you walk up to my window—or maybe drive up next to me—and change the plan, come up with something where we are going to separate them. Maybe say we're going to take the girl into protective custody or something, or say that child services wants to take her. I'll take their side, maybe argue or question your idea, and then tell them to wait, let me see what I can do. I'll get out of the car with the windows up and the air conditioner on low. That will give them the privacy they need to talk, and the recorder should still be able to pick up anything they say."

"Why put one of them up front?"

"Because we can hide a recorder between the seat and headrest, and the one in back will lean up and the one in front will turn to face her. It will work perfectly."

"But you're going to leave the car running. What if they take off in it?"

"We'll be just outside the car, a few feet away. I don't think they're going to do anything stupid."

I had some concerns about it. This could be disastrous if something went wrong. "I don't know, Josie. It's risky. I like the idea, everything other than leaving the car running."

"It's too hot to leave them in there with the windows up unless it's running with the air on. They won't talk if the windows are down and we're outside. Plus the recording will probably suck because of all the noise outside."

I nodded.

She said, "We'll put the kid in front. She can't drive."

"Well, grandma probably can't either, but that doesn't mean she won't try."

We were silent for a moment, each of us thinking. The best I could come up with would require a little more coordination, but it would give us a buffer in case something went wrong. I said, "Okay, we'll do it your way, and we coordinate using patrol to help us."

Josie raised her brows, waiting to hear the rest.

"This time of night there's not a lot of traffic in and out of the parking lot, as long as nothing big jumps off out there. We get two units to coordinate, one coming and the other leaving right as we're ready to do this. We'll be in the parking lot, have the two radio cars stop to chat in the driveway, and that will seal it off. Nobody will be able to go in or out as long as they sit there. It will also be a deterrent, just in case one of our guests gets a wild hair and tries to rabbit with your Charger."

"I like it," Josie said, starting to smile.

"Let the matron know we're going to leave them here for about a half hour while we get this set up. Make sure she knows not to let the two of them talk."

"Why take a chance? I say we throw grandma in a holding cell and let the matron sit with the kid."

I grinned. "Great idea. That will give them something to talk about in the car."

23

OUR OPERATION WENT AS PLANNED. JOSIE AND I WERE BOTH EXCITED TO listen to the recording and see what, if anything, the two had discussed inside the apparent privacy of Josie's county-issued Dodge Charger.

There had been numerous legal battles over the last twenty years about whether the Fourth Amendment of the Constitution, which essentially affords citizens the right to be secure against unreasonable searches and seizures, had any bearing with regard to an expectation of privacy in various custodial settings. The First, Fourth, Fifth, Eighth, Tenth, and Eleventh Circuit Courts had held that a suspect does not have a reasonable expectation of privacy in conversations that take place in the rear seat of a patrol vehicle.

In this situation, we would have recorded the two together in Josie's car even if case law had ruled that a person did, in fact, have an expectation of privacy in such a setting. The only ramification would be that the recorded conversation would not be admissible as evidence in any legal action against the involved parties. It might also be argued that, under the legal premise of *fruit of the poisonous tree,* any evidence obtained as a result of knowledge gained by those recordings could not be used in court. But the truth was, the courts were on our side with this issue, and we had no belief that either the grandmother or the child was somehow involved in any criminal activity. But we did believe that they were unwilling to tell us the truth about what had happened because they feared for their personal safety. This was the case with many of the crimes we investigated that involved gangs or cartels, so you had to be creative sometimes to figure things out.

We had just dropped the two off at their apartment and we were sitting in front of the complex, each in our car, driver's door to driver's door, chatting the way cops do. There was no traffic on the street, late on this Sunday night. Even if there had been, there was room to go around us.

Josie said, "I'll listen to it on my way home, let you know what we've got."

I said, "I can take it, if you want. I have a longer drive."

"It's my recorder, and my car."

I chuckled. "Fine."

"Wait," Josie said, "what if we can't leave them here?"

"What do you mean?"

"Maybe we better listen to it now, together, in case their lives are in danger."

I nodded. "Or they're planning to split."

"Right."

Josie's face was dark, her eyes black holes in the shadows of a moonless night. I said, "Okay, let me park and I'll jump in your car. How long were they alone, ten minutes?"

"Maybe fifteen."

I checked the time and did the math in my head. It was 11:30. In a best-case scenario, I'd be home by 12:30 and might be asleep by one. If I got up at six, I could shave, shower, and be on the road before morning rush-hour traffic, maybe be at the courthouse by 7:30 or so. Grab breakfast in the cafeteria and have another hour to pore over transcripts once more.

But best-case scenarios rarely panned out for me.

I pulled to the curb and Josie whipped around and pulled in behind me. We sat in her car, both of us leaning toward the center where she played the recording on the small, digital recording device she had left running with Maria and Leticia alone in her car.

It seemed like hours before anything was said, and with every rustle or murmur, each of us leaned in closer to the device. Finally, there was conversation, and as expected, it was in Spanish. Josie listened for a minute or so before pausing the playback.

"Okay, Grandma asked the kid what she had told us. Leticia told her we never talked to her. Grandma asked what we did with her, you know, when we put Grandma in the holding cell. Leticia told her the lady watched her, but the cops never talked to her. That's all they've said, and now, as you can hear, they've stopped talking."

I indicated the recorder. "Let's see if they say anything else."

Josie resumed the playback and a long silence ensued. I pictured the setting, the two of them left alone in Josie's car while she and I stood outside, feigning an impromptu conversation about what might happen to the two of them. What we had actually discussed was my love life. Josie had said, "So what's new with Emily?" And I had said, "Really? That's what we're going to talk about?" Josie had said, "Yeah, why not?" So I told her how once again the job had interfered with Emily and me working some things out. Josie had pried, asking what we had to work out. Was it about moving in together? Or something else? Then Josie had grabbed my arm and smiled as she said, "Wait, are you guys talking about marriage? Is that it?" I hadn't answered her, and now, as we sat in the silence of her car, I was sure she would bring it up again.

I could see the lights on in the apartment across the street from where we sat and imagined the woman and young girl alone, feeling violated. That's the feeling people would describe after an intruder had been in their home, even if they were not physically harmed. Even if they hadn't been home at the time. I considered the possibility that Maria and her grand-daughter hadn't been home when the chippie—Leticia's father, as it turned out—had burst into the home during his last moments on earth. Where had Maria and Leticia been at that moment? Who else was in the apartment? What was this all about?

I looked at the recorder, hoping for answers.

But none came. There was no further conversation in the excruciating ten minutes of silence that ended when Josie had re-entered her car.

"¿Estás lista?" Josie's voice said on the recorder, asking if they were ready to go.

Josie turned the device off and looked at me with disappointment in her eyes. I said nothing. She turned and looked at the apartment. "What is this thing all about?"

I didn't know, and I wasn't sure we'd ever find out. I said, "I don't know, partner, but I know we both have a big day tomorrow. Let's get home and get some sleep."

She nodded. We said our goodbyes and parted ways, neither of us feeling we had accomplished anything.

THE NEXT MORNING, JOSIE FOUND ME IN THE CAFETERIA AND JOINED ME for a cup of coffee but declined breakfast.

"I had a Pop-Tart," she said.

"Breakfast of champions."

"I feel like I'm going to throw up."

We were seated at a table with a view of the parking lot behind the courthouse, featuring a steady flow of cars arriving and people scurrying toward the building. There were men and women all around us, some in suits, others in uniforms, others yet in casual attire. The majority of the latter group were probably there for jury duty, and none of them seemed too pleased about it.

I set the transcript down and took a sip of coffee as I studied Josie's eyes. I could see the apprehension she had about this trial. I knew she dreaded this as much as anything she had ever been through as a law enforcement officer, and she had been through a lot. Her hair was pulled back tight, topping off the black and white checked suit, a modest and conservative ensemble. She wore more makeup than usual and extra jewelry, including a silver bracelet that she fussed with nervously, turning it one way and then the other without purpose.

"Have I told you what it was like for me being shot?"

She shook her head. "Not really."

"Believe it or not, it was shameful. I was embarrassed that it happened, sort of felt like a loser, you know? Like I had done something wrong and was at fault for it happening, or that at the very least I had failed to prevent it. During that year I was off, recovering, I avoided everyone from the office other than Floyd. After a while, I stopped talking to him too. When it was time to return to work, I dreaded walking into the office that day. I felt like the new kid at school, walking in to a very large classroom with everyone staring.

"What I dreaded most were the questions I knew would be asked, what it was like getting shot, how I was feeling, how was the wife—who had left me shortly before I returned. When my return date got closer, I actually entertained the idea of not coming back to work. I could have easily taken a medical retirement and been done. But I had nothing else in my life, only the job, so coming back was the only real choice I had.

"I can still remember how I felt that morning as I drove to work for the first time in a year. I was sure I'd throw up if I tried to eat. I should've had a Pop-Tart too."

"Or a Bloody Mary."

"That would have been better. Anyway, I got to the office and I walked in the back door. It seemed like everyone had stopped what they were doing to stare at me. My heart raced and I started to sweat, nine o'clock in the morning on a cool fall day. But soon people began greeting me and welcoming me back, and I realized that I had been the only one harshly judging my actions."

"You weren't kidnapped like a helpless little bitch."

"Josie," I said, my voice stern, "I don't know how many men could have survived what you did on that mountain. You have nothing to be ashamed of. Besides, through it all, you were a cop. You fought to stay alive, and then you figured out that it was Spencer who had taken you. Now you need to hold your head high when you walk into that courtroom, and you need to know that every single person who is about to hear your story is going to view you as a remarkably strong woman, not a victim. And when you look over at Spencer sitting at the table, be proud that he is there because you're a great cop and you weren't going to let him get away with it."

She looked down and sat silent for a long moment.

I said, "Most important, you're here to send him away. So no matter what else you feel inside, you need to set your mind on going into that courtroom and facing that asshole so that he can be held to answer for what he did. What he did to you, what he did to William Brown, and what he did to Tommy."

That stirred her. Her gaze returned with a dark, distant stare that promised resolve. Several minutes went by before her expression slowly softened, and she seemed to come back from that faraway place. She looked me in the eyes and whispered, "Thanks, partner."

DURING THE NOON RECESS I CHECKED IN WITH EMILY AND TOLD HER about last night and how court had gone so far today. She was cool but not cold. I avoided the temptation of telling her I'd probably be home this evening, knowing that every time I made any such commitment, something came up. Emily said to tell Josie she was thinking about her and sending positive energy her way. Co-conspirators, all of them.

I grabbed a sandwich and a bottle of water from the cafeteria and took it up to the eighteenth floor where I could find a place to hide away from the public. The morning session had gotten off to a slow start and I had only taken the stand an hour before the recess. Which meant that so far, I had known all of the answers to the questions that had been asked of me. But after lunch, the DA would finish with his direct examination, and Spencer's attorney would be unleashed on me for cross-examination. This was where I needed to be prepared, which meant I needed more time alone to again go over my prelim transcript.

The law library was the perfect place to study, and as it turned out, I had it mostly to myself. There was one young man who would pop in, crack open a book, make a few notes, and then disappear. I assumed he was an intern doing research for a prosecutor who was enjoying his or her lunch at a nearby restaurant. But then another young man arrived and came directly to where I was seated.

I looked up from my work. "May I help you?"

"Sir, are you Detective Richard Jones?"

"I am," I said, more puzzled than curious.

"I need you to come with me, right away."

2 4

I ASSUMED THE KID WAS ANOTHER INTERN, A FLUNKY FOR SOME ATTORNEY. But his confidence left me wondering as he directed me to come with him. I sat in my chair for a moment, at a loss for words. I glanced over my shoulder, but the other intern was nowhere to be found.

"Are you talking to me?" I said. In my head, I heard a sarcastic response: *Who are you, Robert DeNiro? Yeah I'm talking to you.*

But the kid in a shirt and tie, slacks hanging off his bony frame, said, "Mr. Fry said to find you and bring you to the courtroom immediately."

"To the courtroom?" I asked, while pushing out of my chair. "The court is recessed for lunch."

But the kid had turned his back and walked to the door where he paused, waiting. I gathered my transcript, half a sandwich and my bottle of water, and followed. As I reached the door, I dropped the sandwich in a trash can.

In the hallway, I took long strides to keep up with the kid, almost needing to break into a jog. Behind him, I saw him differently than I had in the library. Yes, he was skinny, but he had wide shoulders over that tiny waist, and his narrow hips likely gave way to muscular legs. He moved like an athlete, smoothly and effortlessly like a yearling colt. I pictured him on the basketball court where his height and easy movement would be an asset, but then I wondered if he played baseball too. Maybe he wrestled. If he played football, he would be a wide receiver where he could go ten yards and bump his defender, then lose him across the middle without turning it all the way up. Oh, to be young again.

I said, "Hey, do you have any idea what this is about?"

He turned around without losing his forward momentum, walking backward while saying, "No sir, I don't. But I can tell you the DA's office emptied out when Mr. Fry got the call."

We reached the elevator and the kid summoned a car, hitting the down button four or five times as he watched the lights above its door. I checked my phone for messages, having left it on silent as I always did during court days. I didn't even want it to vibrate. There was a message from Farris, letting me know our team was now up for murders, but he and I were pulled out of the rotation until I was finished with court. There were two messages from Tammy Rae Moore, the first informing me she had some information for me, the second suggesting we meet later in the day or this evening. There was a message from my lieutenant, Joe Black, reiterating what Farris had already told me in his text. But nothing from Josie.

The elevator doors slid open, and me and the kid stepped inside, the kid turning sharply around the corner to be one-on-one with the interior panel of buttons. He punched the button to take us down to the ninth floor and then pushed and held the button to close the door. I had never pushed one of those *close* buttons in my life, because I've never seen the doors fly closed when someone else had. They would punch it repeatedly, waiting, or they would use the method the kid had chosen, push and hold. Eventually, the doors would slide closed, but never any faster than they would have anyway. It reminded me of what is said about the success of a rain dance: the way to make one work is to dance until it rains.

The elevator ground to a halt with a bump, made a slight adjustment, and a moment later, its doors slid open. There had been no stops along the way, and I assumed our direct flight down was due to the lunch hour. As we hurried through a mostly empty hallway—a rare sight at this place— my mind raced with the possibilities. Had the case taken a sudden twist, something that couldn't wait until after the recess? That didn't seem likely. Had there been some egregious violation by one side or the other that the judge felt compelled to address before court resumed? The court was scheduled to be back in session in less than a half hour now. What was it that couldn't have waited?

When we arrived, two serious bailiffs stood guard at the courtroom doors that would usually be locked during the lunch recess. One of them opened the first set of double doors and nodded for us to enter. I made eye contact with him as I passed by, but his stare told me nothing. We were supposed to be on the same team, but he stood mute, unwilling to show his hand. The second bailiff stood holding open one of the second set of doors. We were inside the courtroom now, and the bench was empty. The counsel tables were likewise unoccupied.

In most courtrooms there is a rear door that leads to a secured hallway which allows judges access to their chambers. There is also a second door that leads to the courtroom lockup. Inside the lockup are holding cells where defendants are kept while court is at recess. That door now stood open, which was very unusual for any time of the day whether or not court was in session. I could see a gathering of suits and flashes of sheriff uniforms as I pushed through the swinging partition that separates the audience from the court.

I turned to glance behind me when a commotion came from the doors I had just passed through. Two male paramedics were hustling in my direction, carrying their equipment boxes. Behind them, a woman dressed in similar fashion wheeled a stretcher. I stopped and moved out of their path, and then followed them. They came to a stop outside of the lockup as a uniformed deputy emerged from within and halted them.

He said, "We just need one of you to come in and pronounce death. We're holding it as a crime scene."

The two paramedics had a brief exchange, and then one of them set his box on the floor and proceeded into the lockup area.

The small crowd parted to allow the paramedic to pass by. Josie emerged and stepped into the courtroom, her gaze meeting mine but not connecting. It was as if she stared through me, beyond the courtroom, the courthouse, and maybe past the city and up into the mountains of Gorman, a place far away but also very close to home now.

I stood silent as she approached. She stopped in front of me, her arms at her sides, no emotion showing on her face. She said, "He hung himself."

"Spencer?" I said, the name coming out with an edge to my tone. "He's dead?"

She nodded, and then her gaze wandered about the courtroom. When she looked at me again, she said, "It's over. All of it. No trial, no testifying, no appeals. Only the memories."

"They'll go away too, eventually."

The paramedic had returned and nodded to his partner, and they joined the woman with the gurney and began reversing course through the courtroom.

A deputy approached us with his notebook in his hand. "Pronounced at thirteen-twelve hours by Paramedic Fraley, Los Angeles City Fire, Engine Company Four, Rescue Four, under the command of Chief Petrentoni, P-E-T-R-E—."

"Hold on there, partner," I said.

He looked up from his notebook.

"We're not handling this case; we're here as witnesses. You'll need to call the Homicide desk and get someone to respond."

"Yes sir." He closed his notebook and turned to leave.

"Hold on," I said, stopping the deputy in his tracks. "I'll call it in for you. This one will need an explanation and special handling."

"Yes sir," he said again.

I put my hand on Josie's arm and indicated the nearby jury box. "Why don't we have a seat, make some calls."

I called our lieutenant first and told him what had happened, assuming he would want to walk it in to the captain. Spencer's case would be considered an "in-custody" death, which is handled in the same fashion as a murder, even though in this case, it was likely a suicide. Cases like this were always questioned by the public and propagandized by the media, and oftentimes they resulted in litigation. Some two-bit attorney would see it on the news and before the end of the day he'd be knocking on the doors of grieving family members, working to convert them into hopeful clients.

After giving Lieutenant Black the basics of what we had, he began to ask questions that I didn't have answers for. I said, "I don't know anything about it, Joe. I haven't seen the body or the scene, and it would probably be best that I don't. I don't even know if he was the only inmate in the holding cell or if someone else was with him."

Josie said, "He was alone."

I told Joe Black, "Josie said he was alone in his cell."

The lieutenant said, "If you and Josie can stay put, I'll be up there with a team in a half hour."

"Thanks, Joe," I said, "I'll see you then."

"Richard?" Joe said before hanging up.

"Yeah, Joe."

"I realize this ends the trial, but I'm still going to leave Josie out of the rotation. You and Farris will go back in as soon as we sort out this suicide mess, and you guys will likely be first up by then."

"No problem, Joe. I'll see you in a few."

When I disconnected, Josie said, "But there *is* a problem."

"Huh?"

"You told Joe, 'No problem,' but there *is* a problem, and it's a big one."

I stared at her for a moment before saying, "What's the problem, partner?"

She looked away, then back at me. "The problem is, I was the last one to see him alive in his cell."

"YOU WERE WHAT?"

Rule Eight: Never become a suspect. Okay, that actually wasn't a rule, but maybe it should have been. The primary goal of a homicide investigation—*any* investigation—is to eliminate potential culprits until you've whittled the list of suspects down to one. Your initial suspect list includes the following: family, friends, coworkers, business partners, and associates. Also, the person who discovered and reported the death, and —*AND*—the last to see the victim alive. Josie, in this case.

Also in question at any homicide was the motive: Who had reason to kill him, and why might someone want him dead? Who had the most to gain from the victim's death? It could be argued that Josie would be that person as well. Josie definitely had motive to see Spencer dead.

She said, "I was the last to see him alive. I had something to say to him, and the bailiff let me back there."

I shook my head in disbelief. What had she been thinking? What had the bailiff been thinking? "That's just great," I said.

Josie pushed out of her chair and walked away, leaving me sitting in the jury box alone. I watched as she meandered behind the counsel table, running her hand over the backs of each of the empty chairs until she came to the defendant's seat. She stopped and rested her hand there, her gaze lowered to the floor.

I wondered if she was feeling guilty or relieved. Maybe both. What had she said to Spencer? Had it been the catalyst for him hanging himself? Or had he done it to further punish her? Maybe it had been as simple for him as knowing he would spend the rest of his life in prison. Cops don't fare well in the joint. He wouldn't be the first cop—or the last—to check out as a way to avoid doing time.

"Who discovered him?"

She shrugged, still facing away, her head lowered.

"You don't know?"

Josie shook her head.

Good. At least it wasn't her. One way to hold the top position on a suspect list was to be the last to see the victim alive and to also be the one who finds him dead.

It was probably just what it appeared to be, a case of suicide. But there would be doubt, questions, supposition by some. Similar to the case of the infamous and questionable death of American financier and convicted sex offender Jeffrey Epstein, if there were any doubt at all about the manner of death in the case of former game warden Jacob Spencer, there was one person who would be highlighted on the list of suspects.

The courtroom was quiet now, sealed as a potential crime scene. Jurors had been ushered into an adjacent courtroom where they were thanked for their service and dismissed without explanation. The judge had emerged from chambers dressed in slacks and shirtsleeves. He had a brief, quiet conversation with his bailiff who stood guard at the entrance to the lockup, and then he disappeared into the hallway that would take him back to his chambers. Or to an elevator that would take him to a secured parking garage beneath the courthouse, if he were planning to go home or out for a cocktail, given the sudden change to his calendar. His clerk had come into the courtroom shortly after the judge disappeared, her expression sour. She collected her belongings from her desk and tromped out in silence. Death had a way of altering moods.

Josie drifted away from the last chair the late Jacob Spencer had occupied, and walked around the table, past the clerk's station, until she stood before the imposing bench where a high-backed leather chair sat unoccupied, the court silent on all matters for the time being. She turned and faced the unoccupied chair of her abductor, the killer of both her boyfriend Tommy Zimmerman and a loser named William Brown, and she fixed a blank stare upon it. Judgingly, perhaps.

Josie suddenly turned and looked at me. "I didn't kill him."

"Of course you didn't."

She walked to the jury box and stopped in front of me the way a defense attorney might while making his final argument before the jurors. "But I told him that I would if I could. I told him if I ever had the chance to kill him and thought I could get away with it, that I would do it gleefully. The asshole gave me that creepy smile and said, 'Is that right?' Then the son of a bitch goes and kills himself after I leave. What kind of twisted shit is that? What was wrong with that man?"

I waited, giving her a moment in case there was more she needed to get off her chest. Apparently, that was all she had to say about it.

I said, "Let's just keep that between the two of us. No one else should ever hear those words. Got it?"

Her eyes moistened as she said, "But I wouldn't have. You know that."

I nodded.

"Saying it and doing it are different things," she continued. "I could never kill anyone for vengeance, in cold blood. That's not who I am. I don't know why I felt compelled to tell him I would. I guess, maybe, I just needed to stand up to him before I took the stand and recounted what he did to me, while he watched me from that goddamn chair—" she motioned behind her, toward the defense table "—with his beady goddamn eyes."

The outer set of doors opened, and I could hear the sounds of men talking. The team of investigators had arrived and would be coming through the second set of doors in the next moment. I said to Josie, "It's over now, partner. Put it behind you and never have this conversation with anyone else."

She nodded slightly.

I turned to watch the team come through the doors, Lieutenant Black along with Davey Lopes and Brenda Wells. Neither was assigned to our team. Lopes was in Unsolveds, and Brenda Wells was on Team Six, usually partnered with Lewandowski. The trio walked over, in no hurry to get to the body. Homicide detectives never rushed to see the dead guy;

there were too many important details to gather along the way. The first step at any crime scene was contacting the handling deputy or officer and obtaining the known facts of the case. We weren't the handling deputies, of course, but the three of them knew we would have some information about what had happened.

Lopes met my gaze and nodded. "What's up, Dickie. You guys whack that asshole, make it look like a suicide?" His one eye squinted as he offered a slight grin.

"Don't even joke about that," I said. "Why are you catching a case?"

"Ask your lieutenant," he said, indicating Joe Black who stood next to him—saying it as if he weren't there. "Apparently your cheesy-ass team can't carry their own water."

Lopes grinned again after saying it, just enough to take the edge off the statement that could have been either a harsh criticism or just a fun jab.

However it might have been meant, Joe took it in the best light possible, which was no surprise to me. He said, "You and Farris are the only ones on our team who haven't been called out yet. It's been really busy, Richard, so we teamed David with Brenda, who was listed as an extra for Team Six this rotation."

Nobody other than the lieutenant and Davey Lopes's mother called him David.

It wouldn't be appropriate to assign me and Farris to investigate Spencer's death since we both had been prominently involved in the investigation that resulted in his criminal charges. Obviously, Josie was out of the question. So it made sense that Joe pulled Lopes out of Unsolveds and teamed him with an extra from Team Six. Wells had only been at the bureau for a year or so, and Black wouldn't have placed an investigation with a level of importance as high as this might be in her hands. Lopes, one of the most experienced investigators in the bureau, would guide her through it and bring a level of expertise to the table that wouldn't be questioned. It should have been a simple case, but we all knew it might be anything but that.

Lopes looked at Josie. "All kidding aside, Josie, is there any reason anyone might suspect you had a hand in this asshole's suicide?"

Josie glanced at me and then back to Lopes. "Not a thing, Davey. Nothing I can think of."

He held her gaze for a long moment, but she didn't waver. Finally, he said, "Okay, let's go have a look."

Lopes led the way, followed by Brenda Wells. Josie and I tucked in behind her, along with Lieutenant Black. The bailiff, still posted at the doorway, opened the door and stepped aside. Joe thanked him as we walked in.

Inside the lockup was a short, tiled hallway with three holding cells on either side, each of them unoccupied other than the last cell on the left. It was in that cell that the lifeless body of Jacob Spencer sat on the floor. His back was against the bars, and a belt remained wrapped around his neck, the other end fastened to the gate just above his head. His butt was just off the ground an inch or so, and his legs were stretched out before him. He appeared comfortable, the way many suicide victims were found. People wanted to be relaxed when they killed themselves.

We were huddled outside the cell, each of us peering in. Lopes said, "Who's bright idea was it to leave him with his belt?"

Spencer had been allowed to change from his jail clothing into a suit for the hearings. His civilian clothing was supplied by the attorney and made available each morning when he arrived at the court. Spencer would then change back into his county-issued clothing before being returned to the jail. I had noticed during the morning session that Spencer's attire had included a belt and tie. I knew that the procedure was to remove belts, ties, and shoes with laces before an inmate is left alone in a cell; that was standard practice. But here Spencer was, hung by his own belt.

The bailiff said, "Deputy Ross secured him in his cell at the noon recess, sir. You would have to speak with him."

Lopes didn't reply. He turned to his left, and then to his right, looking at the other cells. He said, "Were any of these other cells occupied?"

"No sir," the bailiff said. "The trial was all we had on the calendar today."

Lopes nodded as he continued to look around. Wells was writing something in her notebook when Lopes bumped her arm with the back of his hand.

She said, "Thanks a lot, Dav—" and stopped when she saw he was pointing at something behind her—behind us all. We turned to look. A small camera sat in the corner of the wall just inside and above the door we had all walked through.

He said, "Well, this will be easy enough—it's all going to be on video."

Josie turned on her heel and walked out.

2 6

I FOLLOWED JOSIE THROUGH THE STILL-EMPTY COURTROOM AS SHE hastened toward the exit. I caught up to her before she reached the double doors. "Josie, you can't just leave."

She stopped and turned to face me.

"What's wrong?"

She shook her head and averted her eyes.

"Whatever that video might show, we need to tell Lopes so he knows what to expect."

She let out a breath she seemed to have been holding. "This isn't good."

"You went back and talked to him. So what? It doesn't matter what you said, there's no audio recording with those videos. So tell Lopes that you went back there. Tell him whatever you want about what you said, because it doesn't matter. Words didn't hang that son of a bitch. He hung himself from guilt, and I'm glad he did. He spared you the misery of reliving that awful week. You've done nothing wrong, Josie."

We were stopped now, arm's length apart, facing one another. Her eyes showed apprehension. She said, "You don't know that."

"I do know that," I argued. "No matter what you said to him, you're not responsible for what he did in there."

Josie looked away for a moment, then came back to me. "You don't get it. It's not what I said to him, it's what I did."

The comment stunned me like a hard jab. What could she have possibly done? I pictured her wrapping Spencer's belt around his neck and cinching him tight against the bars, holding her grip until his body went slack, and then tying the belt around the gate. But how would she have gotten him to back up against the bars? She didn't do it, I knew that in my heart and in my head. Even if I thought she was capable of murder, it would have been nearly impossible for her to get a belt around his neck and backed against the gate, all from outside the cell.

Then it occurred to me that maybe she wasn't outside the cell.

Could she have gotten the keys from the bailiff when she went in to have "a word" with Spencer? No bailiff would be that stupid. Would he? Well, you did have the pretty female factor, something that always had to be considered. Throughout the history of man, we Neanderthals could always be counted on to behave stupidly when it came to attractive women. We would lie, cheat, fight, and kill *for* them and because of them. It wasn't really a great stretch to imagine a bailiff handing his keys to a flirtatious Josie Sanchez. After all, she was a deputy. She was Homicide. What could it hurt?

I wasn't sure that I wanted to know what she had done.

It might not have risen to the realm of murder, but maybe she assisted in his suicide, helped him cinch the belt or maybe she provided it to him. Whatever it was, the idea that it was on video had drained the blood from her face.

"Do I want to know?"

She shook her head.

"Tell me you didn't kill him, and I can live with anything else. If you killed him, we're done. You're done. It ends here and now, Josie."

Again, she shook her head. "I didn't kill him, Richard. Okay? Let's get the fuck out of here."

"You don't want to get in front of it, tell Lopes what he's going to see on that video?"

She shook her head and pushed past me, continuing through the doors.

After Josie left, I went back inside the lockup and told Lopes and the others that Josie was not feeling well and needed to leave. Lopes looked me in the eye and held his gaze for a moment, knowingly. The man with his squinty eyes could see right through me at this moment, and he knew we had a problem. He would no doubt know it had everything to do with the video camera, given the timing of her change in demeanor. Lopes didn't miss much, if anything.

I said, "So if you don't need me for anything else, I'm going to head to the office."

Lopes said, "See you later."

"I'll let the desk know that me and Farris are available now for call-outs," I said to Joe Black.

"Thanks," he said. "I'll see you at the office in a while."

As I walked out, I heard Lopes say, "Call the coroner and get someone rolling. I'm going to go find out about the video camera."

Wells replied, "Sounds good."

ON THE WAY TO THE OFFICE I RETURNED PHONE CALLS, AND WHEN TRAFFIC had me at a stop, replied to text messages. I kept thinking of the situation with Josie and a dead game warden, though I tried to push it out of my mind. What had she done, and how severe would the fallout be? Hopefully, it wasn't something that would rise to the level of criminal culpability. But even shy of that, I worried whatever she might have done could cause her to lose her job or be transferred out of the bureau. I didn't want anything bad to happen to my partner, and I didn't want to lose her.

My thoughts returned to personal issues. I hoped to be home early enough to have dinner with Emily and try again to have the conversation. Being first up for murders now, I could be called out at any time, but the odds were better later at night, past midnight. The odds were even better at closing time, two o'clock. That's when the bars would empty out and drunk men would settle their differences in parking lots, alleys, and streets. My strategy was always to get to bed early, catch four or five hours of sleep while my next victim was trying to get himself killed. If all went well, the would-be victim would stagger home with a broken nose and I could wake up in my bed, not at a crime scene.

When I pulled into the lot, I scanned the rows of sedans looking for

Josie's. Though there were several Dodge Chargers, I didn't see hers, with its small cross hanging from the rearview mirror. I parked and went inside. Her desk was unoccupied. I could use a cup of coffee, so I headed toward the kitchen hoping to find her there, but knowing in my gut I wouldn't. Either way, I'd do my circle, see what's going on at the front desk, see if I could find Farris and let him know we were up for murders now, and round it off with a trip by Floyd's desk. Wait until he heard what happened with Jacob Spencer. Wait until he heard about Josie and the video. The two of us could speculate on what might be discovered therein and how it would affect both her and me.

But Floyd and Farris were in the kitchen, seated at a table along with Mongo and a sergeant named Carl Reed who was assigned to the unit within the department that tested its personnel for illegal drug use. I couldn't recall what they called that unit, because most of us just called them the piss police.

Floyd looked up and grinned. "There's Dickie. Hey partner, your number came up. I hope you haven't been smoking any weed lately."

"Are you shitting me?" I said, incredulous. It was these little irritants that could drive a guy crazy. You were living on the edge with two or three balls in the air at any given time, and they were always fireballs. You were on call. You had a trial going. Your suspect was on the move. Your partner just hung some asshole in a jail cell. Then some house fairy comes along and tells you to piss in a bottle. It was no wonder so many of us cracked up.

Reed confirmed my number had come up and asked me to follow him down the hall to the men's room. Inside, he donned a pair of gloves while directing me toward a urinal. "I have to watch," he said. He handed me a small jar.

While completing the task, I glanced over my shoulder at the piss police sergeant and said, "Carl, let me ask you something... do you actually tell your neighbors you're a policeman?"

He didn't answer.

I intentionally dribbled some down the side of the bottle before handing it back to the sergeant while proffering a smile. I washed up and went back to the kitchen where Farris was filling another cup of coffee, but Floyd and Mongo were gone.

"Where'd that asshole go?"

"Floyd?"

"Yeah, Floyd and his Mongo."

Rich Farris chuckled. "I'm not sure. What's going on with you? I heard about Spencer. I can't say I was sorry to hear he croaked."

"Me neither, Rich. The problem is—"

Reed stepped into the room. "Hey, where'd Deputy Tyler go?"

Floyd. Now I knew why they disappeared so quickly. I said, "Why didn't you get him before me? He was sitting here waiting when I showed up."

Reed shrugged. "He said he couldn't go, asked me to give him a few minutes to drink some coffee."

I shook my head. "Sergeant, you may just be at the perfect assignment for you."

His brows crowded together, contemplating the statement. Farris grinned as he turned to walk out, pushing by Reed at the door. I followed without further commentary.

We walked back to the desk to check our status on the on-call board. It showed our team had been hit hard with murders, everyone other than me and Farris having new cases written in black marker next to their names. Farris said, "Well, partner, I can't imagine we'll squeak by, not with the way this week is going."

A civilian answering phones at the desk looked up from his work. "It's been crazy."

I nodded. Sometimes there would be a murder here, a murder there. Other times it would "jump off," and bodies would be falling all over the county. Typically, it was this time of year when that happened. During the dog days of summer when people were cooped up inside and pissed off. They'd spend the days inside sweltering homes that offered little relief from the heat, and if they didn't kill each other then, it would happen after dark when the streets came alive and the booze would flow and many would be drunk or high and short-fused. That was life in the big city.

"No, Rich, I don't imagine we'll squeak by." I glanced at my watch. "Which is why I need to get out of here early today. Do you have anything going on?"

He shook his head. "Not really. You need a hand with something?"

"I have to meet with an ATF agent on the chippie case. She used to be a deputy, and she's kind of a snaky bitch, to be honest about it."

He grinned a little. "If there's one thing I'm well versed in, it's the handling of snaky women. Let's do it."

WE MET AT A DENNY'S NEAR DOWNTOWN, A PLACE WHERE COPS WITH iron stomachs could eat for half off, twenty-four seven. Many eating establishments offered police discounts because the presence of cops was good for business. It helped keep the riff-raff down to a minimum, and it gave potential customers the idea that it was not only safe to stop and eat there, but that the food was good too. What they didn't know was that most cops ate like dumpster rats, and what was palatable for us could easily kill mere mortals.

I ordered coffee. I had often said I'd never be so hungry as to eat at a Denny's. Even the coffee left something to be desired, but having spent many years drinking the stuff prepared by trustees at various patrol stations, I could handle anything.

Farris and I arrived before Tammy Rae. At the rear of the dining room, we slid into a booth that offered a view of the front door and our cars parked outside. I mostly watched two homeless people wheeling their carts around the parking lot, a man and a woman, the man leading a small dog of indeterminate heritage. They were no threat; these weren't thieves out capering, nor were they begging from others, something that many people—myself included—found annoying. It was the aggressive beggars I had the problem with, the ones who scared some people into giving them money which would be spent on alcohol or drugs. These two weren't that.

A black Crown Vic roared into the parking lot as the man crossed from one side to the other, his dog trailing laboriously behind. The driver sounded the horn, excessively, and the man shuffled a bit faster, likely as fast as he could go. He was barely out of the car's path when the driver shot past him and swung into a parking space. It was Tammy Rae. Farris and I both turned from the scene outside and minded our coffees.

I said, "There's our girl."

Farris shook his head a little and took a sip from his mug.

A minute later, Tammy Rae burst through the door and paused, taking the place in. I turned and waved to get her attention. She seemed to frown when her gaze met mine, and then she started toward us. I wondered if she was disappointed that I had brought someone with me, or disappointed by who it was.

"Do you know this broad?" I asked Rich Farris before she arrived at the table.

He shook his head, and then nodded to let me know she was now behind me.

I was going to get up to greet her, but she slid in next to me before I could move. I scooted over to accommodate her.

"Hi," she said, staring at Farris. "I'm Special Agent Tammy Rae Morris with the Bureau of Alcohol, Tobacco, and Firearms, former Los Angeles County deputy sheriff."

Farris said, "I'm Rich."

"Are you?" she said with a coy grin. "Would you happen to be single too?"

He didn't answer nor smile, so she turned her gaze to me. "Did you guys order?"

I told her we hadn't, lying that we had eaten a late lunch and were going to stick with coffee. She shrugged, *no big deal*. A waitress approached and asked what she would have. Tammy Rae regarded her for a long moment, perhaps a beat too long before saying, "Diet Coke, hon," and turned her long fake lashes back toward me. The waitress walked off without comment, though I had the feeling she would have liked to have said something to her. Maybe while dragging Tammy Rae from the booth by her hair.

Tammy Rae ran her hand through her wavy blonde hair and then let it fall into place on her shoulders. She said, "So, you want to hear the scoop on your boy, Gomez?"

27

THE WAITRESS RETURNED WITH A SODA AND PLACED IT IN FRONT OF Tammy Rae, who behaved as if she hadn't noticed. I said, "Thank you," as the waitress retreated.

Tammy Rae took a long sip and plopped the glass back onto the table, leaving bright red lipstick on the straw. She breathed an "ahhh" sound, indicating its refreshing value. It was overdone. But everything about Tammy Rae seemed overdone. Her hand moved from the glass and found its next resting place on my forearm, which sat on the table. Her long red nails closely matched her lipstick and accentuated the gold jewelry she wore: rings on two fingers and her thumb, and a small rope bracelet with dainty charms spaced evenly around it. She left her hand there, and said, "What I'm about to tell you stays between us. It can't go in your file, not even in your notebook. Got it?"

I pulled my arm from under her hand, lifted my hat and reset it, then folded my arms across my chest. The act accomplished three things: it freed me from her coy embrace, it likely sent a message about my receptiveness to it, and it gave me a moment to consider my words.

I said, "Tammy Rae, that's not a reasonable request. We have a dead chippie who may have been involved in any number of illegal activities, one or more of which might have led to his death. We know your agency was close to him—or I assume it was—since an undercover ATF agent has been to his house since his death. I don't know if the UC lived there with Gomez, or if he was just visiting, but clearly the ATF has something going on that could shed some light on this case. I can't really go forward until I figure out why he abandoned his post and drove forty-some miles to Compton to the home of his daughter and her grandmother—who had just happened to disappear that same morning but came back home last night."

"Wait," she said, "they did?"

"Yes. They're home, though I have no idea if they're safe and sound or still in harm's way. Do you understand why we need to have the whole picture here? This isn't just about Gomez's death; it's also about the lives of two innocent people."

She rolled her eyes. "Maybe one."

I let that hang there a moment.

Farris said, "So Grandma's dirty, too, huh?"

Tammy Rae flicked him a glance but otherwise ignored him. Looking at me again, she said, "They're safe. You can trust me on that."

"How do you know?" I asked. "How can you say that with certainty?"

She smacked her lips. "Just can. Anyway, do we have a deal, or are you two going to camp out in the dark?"

Her cockiness hadn't come out during my last meeting with her in the presence of Tony Brunetti, where she had been mostly tolerable. But this was the Tammy Rae Moore I had so disliked, distrusted, and thought to be a scandalous liar. These same thoughts gave me pause in dealing with her now. What did she want? Why was she making this more difficult than it should have been? It was as if some type of national security were hanging in the balance, the implied cliché that if she told us, she'd have to kill us.

I could see in the always-appraising eyes of Rich Farris that he didn't like it and wasn't impressed by her. In fact, he was anything but. If I was picking up his vibe correctly, he was telling me to fold my hand and leave the table; the game was rigged against us. I had a similar feeling. It seemed that was often the case when dealing with feds. They felt superior to us "local" cops, even though the majority of them could never survive one shift on the streets we patrolled night and day. Most of them had been recruited from campuses across the states, some Ivy League, others just lowly state colleges, and very few were from the streets. Few had been in the trenches where the foundation of being a good cop was constructed. You didn't know how to be an investigator by attending training classes—those were to refine the skills you brought with you from the streets where you learned the hustle, the score, and the rules of a subculture that no college kid understood. Without an intimate understanding of each of those things, you would never be complete. You could get by—as most of them did—but as the saying went, you don't know what you don't know.

I knew Farris's vibe was right on the mark. Sometimes you have to walk away and leave your chips on the table. I said, "Can you let me up, please?"

Her expression showed confusion and curiosity as she slid out, her tight designer jeans over high-heeled shoes squeaking across the vinyl. She stepped back to allow me to exit the booth, and then sat back down. She must have thought I needed a restroom break, but that was because she didn't know the score. Farris was now sliding out too, because he was the scorekeeper and he knew my play.

I said, "I don't play games with feds, Tammy Rae. You know how to get in touch with me. If you want to give me the scoop, fine. If not, you and the ATF can go fuck yourselves. And don't go crying to my captain when I out your operation once I figure out what you've done. And I *will* figure it out, just like I figured out your caper in the alley that night."

She was speechless as I turned and walked away.

As we crossed the lot to our cars, Farris said, "Good for you, Dickie. That bitch is poison."

"Yes, she is, Rich. And she's been trying to play me since the day Tony put us together. I hadn't thought about it before, but I think she's held a grudge toward me."

We stopped at the back of my car, ready to split up and go our separate ways until which time we would reunite at some crime scene, some other place with a new story of life and death in the merciless city. He said, "Why would she have a grudge against you?"

The homeless man with his dog was coming our way. The woman was nowhere to be seen. I said, "It's a long story. I'll tell you about it while we're working our next case."

He nodded.

I indicated the man coming up behind him, and Farris turned and greeted him. "How we doin', boss?"

The man wiped at his mouth with a soiled shirtsleeve, and said with a gravelly voice, "I ain't gunna complain, officer, 'cause it don't do no good."

It didn't surprise me that he knew we were cops even though our suit jackets concealed our guns and badges. We were two grown men in suits in the parking lot of a questionable food establishment, a salt-and-pepper team, both with piercing gazes that no one from the streets could escape or ignore.

As he started past us, his dog bringing up the rear with a wagging tail, I said, "You watch out for that woman in the black sedan when she comes out. The bitch is crazy."

The old man stopped and looked back at us. "Show me one who ain't."

MY PHONE RANG AT 2:28 A.M.

It could only be the office or one of four people calling: Josie, Floyd, Lopes or Farris. Each was programmed into my phone as Favorites, which meant their calls would bypass the Do Not Disturb feature on my iPhone that silenced all notifications for text messages and calls between 11 p.m. and 6 a.m. My phone was thus configured for the last six months as part of my own little experiment. There were many informants, witnesses, and the family members of victims who would call at any hour of the day or night —though almost always at night, far past the hours working class people kept. We called it "Crook Time." The majority of people we handed our business cards to were permanently on it and I had tired of losing sleep to answer stupid questions. When I ask patrol deputies or gang cops to assist on a case, to look for a certain person of interest or witness I needed to talk to, I made sure they understood the need to go through my office to get ahold of me after hours.

Emily was on the Favorites list also, but it couldn't have been her calling. She was curled up next to me, fast asleep, her radiating warmth causing me to perspire on this hot summer night. But it felt good to be back in her bed. *Our bed*, as she had called it after we had had The Talk.

My feet hit the floor as I grabbed my phone and hurried into the bath-room to answer it. The screen showed *187*, confirming it was the office calling. The caller was a civilian employee named Hughes who had immi-grated to the states from Wales and spoke in a thick Welsh accent that seemed to make women swoon but drove me crazy. I couldn't understand half of anything he said even when I was standing next to him, wide awake.

"Marcello," I interrupted, "slow it down. I haven't understood a goddamn thing you've said."

In the next minute, Marcello Hughes—I called him Baby Hughie due to his permanent boyish smile and his rosy red, chubby cheeks—spat out a number of phrases I had come to understand over the years working around this *bloke*. Two men were *on the piss* and had been *chopsing* over one thing or another, when one *barmy bloke* pulled his knife and gutted the other poor bastard like a fish.

"So, two drunk idiots argued and one got stabbed."

"Jolly right," he said, maybe playing it up a bit. "Cheerio."

He said the scene was a bar in East Los Angeles but the victim had been transported to White Memorial. I asked him to text me the particu-lars: file number, location, coroner's case number, victim's name, and whatever else he might have. I then asked if the suspect was in custody. "Of course," he said, "the sheriff don't fuck around."

When I came out of the bathroom, Emily was no longer in bed. I could hear her in the kitchen, and I saw that the lights were on in the rest of the apartment. Both of these observations were made possible by the compact floor plan of a small apartment built in the sixties. I turned on the bedroom light and began dressing for work, thinking about the things Emily had said she dreamed of for us: a roomy house with a large master, a walk-in closet, a bathroom with two sinks and a tub we could fit in together, or where she could soak in warm, bubbly water and get lost in a good book on those long nights when her man was out on the streets protecting women and orphans.

She came into the bathroom wearing a t-shirt that didn't quite cover her naked bottom. I was looking in the mirror, running my tie through its loop, but my gaze traveled downward to a better reflection than I could ever produce. Emily stepped in close and took over, pulling the knot tight and then adjusting it just right. She smoothed my collar and kissed me on the cheek. "There. Now you're fit for the dead. Who got killed, anyway?"

I picked up my phone and checked the text. "Trinidad Flores, Hispanic, male, fifty-two."

"Hmmm."

"In a bar in East L.A., so I would have to guess alcohol was a factor. That and likely a *señorita* or two."

"Always a woman's fault, right?" she said.

"They usually factor in, one way or another. You better get back to bed, get some sleep."

"I will." She stepped in closer and put her head on my chest. "I wish you didn't have to go."

But that was part of the deal, and she knew it. We had covered that during The Talk last night. I wasn't going to take a desk job anytime soon, and she could do whatever she wanted with her career too. We would make accommodations as necessary, but neither would sacrifice their career nor ask the other to do so. That would be Rule One in the forthcoming rule book: *Domesticating Dickie.* Or maybe, *Settling Down after Forty.* How about, *Living with Women,* or *Living with Women and Learning to Love It.* It didn't matter, the rule book would only be published in my mind and shared with a select few. Those on my Favorites list. Those other than Emily and Josie.

"Hey, it's overtime, and it looks like we're going to need it."

She kissed me again and walked away, headed toward the bed. I followed her into the bedroom, enjoying the view. Standing next to the bed, I cinched my belt tight and took my gun from the nightstand and slid it into the holster on my hip. I clipped my six-point star to my belt, just ahead of the gun. I inserted two extra magazines in a leather pouch located on my other hip, as I gazed into the prettiest hazel eyes I had ever seen. I leaned over and kissed her goodbye, slipped my hand beneath her shirt and gently trailed my fingers across her stomach. "I love you."

On my way out I grabbed my suit jacket and hat, then I stepped into the warm, moonlit night. I closed the door softly behind me, checking twice to make sure it had locked. A few minutes later, I was sailing down the I-5 doing eighty, the traffic almost non-existent now after three in the morning. I called Farris and we agreed to meet at the scene, the *Guadala-*

jara de Noche on Beverly Boulevard. When I disconnected, my mind went back to Emily, to The Talk, to our future plans, and there it stayed for the rest of the drive. Normally, I would have been thinking of all the possibilities that awaited me on the given case. Not tonight. Tonight, my mind raced with the thoughts of a future with a great woman.

I pulled up to the scene to see that Farris had gotten there before me, and so had Josie. She wasn't in the rotation and I knew she hadn't been called out on this case. The last time I saw her and spoke with her she feared for her future, worried about a video tape in the courtroom lockup. But then she had disappeared, and I was glad to see her here.

I pulled up near the curb and parked just outside the yellow tape, a short distance from the front door of the bar. Josie approached me as I exited my car.

"Hey," was all she said, somewhat melancholy.

"Hey," I replied. I glanced around to see if anything of interest was outside. There appeared to be a rear parking lot, but it had not been secured by radio cars or crime scene tape. The sidewalk and entryway were taped off, and a uniformed deputy stood guard at the edge of that area. I said, "What brings you here?"

"I was bored. Besides, with the trial now off the table, why should I be out of the rotation? We're still partners, aren't we?"

I nodded. "Of course. But how did you get the information on the callout?"

She smiled a little. "Marcello. I called the desk a few hours ago and asked if he would notify me if you were called out."

"Good old Marcello." I waited a beat, wondering if I should ask. Rich Farris had ducked under the tape and walked inside the front door, inspecting the ground before each step with the beam of his flashlight leading the way. I met Josie's gaze and said, "So, did you hear anything about the video?"

"There was no recording."

I held her gaze for a long moment, thinking about the possible implications of that statement. Was there really no recording, or did Lopes make it go away? I had known him since my early patrol days, and I knew him to be a great cop and investigator. He might slap a gangster when the asshole had it coming, but he wouldn't destroy evidence in a criminal matter.

Would he destroy evidence in a case of suicide, if by doing so he saved a good cop's career? Maybe.

I decided not to ask any questions. Some things were better left unanswered. Either there never was a recording, or it had disappeared. Maybe the surveillance camera was only for live monitoring of the inmates. Either way, it was over. I knew in my heart that Josie didn't kill Jacob Spencer, so whatever else might have happened, I could probably live with.

I broke eye contact and looked around again. "Anything worth seeing out here?"

She shook her head. "Not really. A little blood on the sidewalk, but everything else is inside."

"Well, let's go have a look."

28

INSIDE, FARRIS DIRECTED MY ATTENTION TO A CORNER OF THE BAR WHERE a bloodstained knife sat near a package of cigarettes, an ashtray, and a bottle of beer.

"Is this where it happened?" I asked, shining my flashlight on the barstool and the floor beneath it, but not seeing any other bloodstains or evidence of a killing.

"Nope, out on the sidewalk according to our witness. The suspect and our dead guy stepped outside to settle something—"

"Did it involve a woman, by any chance?"

Josie hit my arm with the back of her hand.

Farris said, "As a matter of fact... But anyway, our victim, Trinidad Flores, took a blade to the gut before they even had a chance to get at it. That took the fight out of him, and he walked away. Those few drops of blood out on the sidewalk are about all we have. After the stabbing, the suspect walked back inside and took a seat—" Farris shined his light on the bar top, highlighting the knife and a few drops of blood "—set his knife on the bar and went back to his drink."

I pictured the man sitting there, sipping on his *Modelo Especial*, unconcerned about the act of violence he had just committed. He was likely from Mexico or somewhere in South America where violence and

267

death were viewed with far less disapproval than they were here in the States—at least in most of our communities. The image I had was that of a big man, heavyset, dressed in double-knit slacks, a silk shirt, handmade-in-Mexico leather boots and belt, the ensemble topped by a Stetson hat that covered a head of thick black hair. I pictured him with a grin that spread his thin mustache across his face, showing a silver and gold smile.

"How'd they catch him?"

Farris said, "That's the best part. He was still sitting here drinking when the cops showed up. They took him into custody without incident."

"Easiest murder arrest they'll ever make."

"Exactly," Farris said. "Hopefully, he'll talk to us."

Josie said, "Who's the witness?"

"The bartender," Farris said.

"That's it, huh? Everyone else in the bathroom?"

Everyone was always in the bathroom when someone got killed. Bars, parties, weddings too. Cops would joke that the venues in L.A. boasted the biggest bathrooms in the country, a hundred guests and all but the killer and a dead guy were in the bathroom when it went down.

Farris said, "I don't know about all that, but nobody other than the killer waited for the cops to show up."

"So how did the woman factor in?"

"According to the bartender, the fight was over a B-girl. The killer had danced with her and bought her drinks, and then our dead guy had the audacity to do the same. Apparently, Fernando is the jealous type."

"Is that our suspect, Fernando?" I asked.

Farris opened his notebook and flipped through a couple pages. "Fernando Belmontes. That's what the deputies gave me. Male Hispanic, forty-six. It's all I know. That, and he was booked at East L.A."

"I say we let Josie do the interview."

Farris shrugged. "Okay by me."

Josie said, "Are you assuming he speaks Spanish?"

"I'm assuming he will want to talk to you more than he'd want to talk to me or Rich. This man kills for a woman's attention," I said, and smiled.

"He has a point," Rich Farris said.

The bartender had also been transported to the station and was awaiting our arrival. In high-crime communities, patrol deputies still got away with the questionable process of gathering witnesses and holding them for Homicide. They would be driven to the station where they would be provided with a cup of coffee or access to the vending machines and were then *asked* to wait until they could be interviewed. Most of them didn't protest, but you got the feeling that few believed they were free to leave. It was decided we would all go to the station together, and that Josie and I would interview the suspect. Which meant Josie would do all the talking—so long as it went as we hoped it would—and I would keep the notes. Meanwhile, Farris would get a recorded statement from the bartender who would no doubt change his story if he ever had to appear in court.

But first, we would all drive over to White Memorial and take a look at the victim. When a victim was transported to an emergency room rather than being pronounced dead at the scene, most investigators would generally process the crime scene first and then view the deceased at the hospital after. Even though the dead guy wouldn't be going anywhere anytime soon, we wanted to view the remains as part of the initial investigation rather than waiting for the autopsy. Sometimes it could be days before the coroner got around to your case, and in the meantime, you would be taking statements from witnesses and suspects. It was one thing to talk to your witnesses without having viewed the deceased, but it was not advisable to do so when it came to suspect interviews. You could always go back to your witnesses for clarifications, but you rarely got a second chance to interview a suspect.

Josie and I dropped our cars at East L.A. station and rode with Farris to White Memorial. We were escorted to the hospital's morgue where Trinidad Flores rested on a gurney beneath a white sheet. Farris gloved up and removed the sheet. There were all the signs of life-saving efforts: intubation apparatus, EKG pads on his chest, discoloration of his skin from iodine, and blood smeared on his stomach, chest, hands, and arms. There were several puncture wounds to his abdominal area and one higher up over the rib cage. I imagined that this wound might have penetrated a lung, which can eventually become fatal.

"Where was our victim picked up?"

Farris looked at me. "We have to get that from the paramedics; I'm not sure."

I nodded. "I'm just wondering how far he walked before collapsing. I bet he's got a punctured lung."

Josie leaned over for a better look, studied the victim for a long moment and then retreated. "Our suspect is left-handed."

The wounds were all right of center, which would definitely be consistent with a left-handed killer. "I think you're right," I said.

Farris looked up. "Anyone want to get a selfie with him before we say goodnight?"

"I'm good," Josie said.

I shook my head. "Maybe just get a head shot for identification."

He pulled the sheet up around the neck, stood on his tiptoes, and snapped a couple of pictures with his phone. It wasn't that long ago we'd use a Polaroid camera for this. Farris covered the victim's head and said, "Okay, let's roll."

Back at the station, Farris spoke with the bartender/sole witness while Josie and I went into an interview room where Fernando Belmontes sat waiting. I couldn't have been any further off on my image of the man. He was a small man with narrow shoulders, wearing shorts and a tight-fitting t-shirt, red with a pocket on the chest. His eyes were soft—not the eyes of a killer—and he greeted us pleasantly, and in perfect English. "How are you?" he said.

He was seated at the end of a table that was pushed against the wall. Josie sat near him, just across the corner of the table from him where she could easily touch him if she so desired, which was an often-effective strategy during interviews. The deputies had left him handcuffed so I wedged myself behind him and told him to lean forward. I removed the cuffs and said, "Okay, lean back." He did.

I noted the time and date in my notebook, along with the location of the interview—East L.A. Station—and that Josie was with me. She began with the basics: name, address, phone number... "Have you been arrested before?"

I looked up from my notes. Fernando was rubbing his wrists, one and then the other, looking Josie in the eyes. "No ma'am, never."

There was no denying he was in custody now and that he was not free to leave. With formalities behind us, Josie produced a card as she asked, "Are you familiar with your rights?"

He nodded, but she placed the card before him anyway and began reciting it while pointing her pen at the sentences as she read: "You have the right to remain silent. Anything you say—"

"I'm not sorry if I killed him."

This was a spontaneous statement, not a response to a question about the case. All Josie asked to this point were questions about his identity, whether or not he had ever been arrested, and if he was familiar with his rights. These questions were simply part of a process that included establishing one's level of intelligence and understanding. His spontaneous statement would be admissible in court, even though Josie had not finished advising him of his rights. It would have been admissible had she not even begun.

Josie reached over and lightly touched his arm. "Okay, Fernando, that's not a problem. But before you tell me more about that, let's get these formalities out of the way." She continued with the rights without waiting for a response. "You have the right to an attorney—"

"That would be best, I think. May I call him?"

Josie stopped, and the room stood silent for a long moment. That statement ended the interview. There was nothing else that needed to be said and we were unable to ask any other questions without the suspect having an attorney present. It wasn't like television or the movies where you could talk them out of it, get them to change their mind about wanting a lawyer. At least you couldn't do that *and* expect to gain anything from it. His statement would not be admissible, and anything that he might tell us that would lead to other evidence against him would be *fruits of the poisonous tree.*

I closed my notebook and pushed out of my chair, the metal legs screeching against the tile floor. Josie followed suit, slowly rising from her chair. As we each started for the door, the small killer said, "Thank you, detectives. I appreciate your time."

Outside the interview room I handed a waiting deputy the pair of cuffs I had taken off the suspect's wrists. "He's all yours."

Farris was still with the bartender in an adjacent room. Josie and I walked back to the detective bureau, which was empty. I started a pot of coffee. We were guests here at East L.A., but as was the case at every sheriff's station in the county, homicide detectives were treated with great respect, and usually the personnel there went out of their way to accommodate us. Josie put a couple of dollars beneath the coffee can as a contribution to the detective's coffee fund. Most station detective bureaus collected a monthly contribution from each assigned detective so that coffee was always available to them and their guests. They would never ask for outside donations, but it was a nice gesture nonetheless.

We sat down with our coffee and discussed the case for a few minutes, both agreeing that with or without a good statement from the bartender, we had more than enough evidence to charge the suspect with murder. We had his statement, and as long as a forensic examination of the knife produced both the victim's DNA and the suspect's fingerprints, it would be a straightforward prosecution. Even so, it was the type of case that the district attorney's office would likely try to resolve with a plea bargain. It would probably be filed as a murder and pled to a manslaughter since there didn't seem to be premeditation, and since the victim willingly accompanied the suspect outside to physically settle their differences. Such a negotiation would be a better strategy than allowing a defense attorney to paint his client as a frightened and weak man who acted in self-defense, something that in this case would be a reasonable sell to a jury given the physical stature and demeanor of the suspect.

I started working on a statement of probable cause, something we would use to charge the suspect within the allotted seventy-two hours. Josie began assembling a filing package that would accompany the statement when we presented our case to the district attorney.

We worked silently, side by side, the sounds of keyboards pecking with a background of faraway voices and police radios squawking. The silence between us was awkward, and it reminded me of the strange day that had preceded this one. It wasn't even twenty-four hours ago that Jacob Spencer had hung himself in a cell at the courthouse under questionable circumstances that involved Josie's presence. It was something I had to put behind me and move on from unless I planned to confront her about it. I was still mostly inclined to drop it, though my curious nature sat in conflict with that idea.

Josie eventually broke the silence. "So, you seem relieved."

I looked up from my work, puzzled by the statement. Relieved about what? That there was no video recording of lockup? That was my first thought. Or was it something else? Relieved that we had a suspect in custody, an easy "solved" case for the stats?

She said, "You've worked things out with Emily."

It was a statement, not a question. Had she talked to Emily? Or was this part of her woman's intuition?

"We're fine," I said, not sure how much I was willing to say.

Josie said, "And?"

I leaned back in my chair and watched her for a moment. Her brows were up, questioning, her expression letting me know she expected an answer. Or she knew the answer and was waiting to hear it from me. Using her interrogation skills on her partner. Sometimes I hated the cops.

I said, "We're getting married."

FARRIS WALKED IN SAYING, "THIS DIPSHIT—WAIT, WHAT ARE YOU TWO grinning about?"

"No, please, tell us about the dipshit," I insisted.

Rich Farris slapped his notebook down on the table next to the coffee pot and began helping himself to a cup, saying, "At the scene, dude tells the deputies he saw the suspect go outside with our dead guy after exchanging heated words inside. Not a minute goes by, the suspect comes in and sets a knife on the bar, starts finishing his beer. The victim doesn't come back in. Then, this dude—the bartender—notices blood on the knife. He slides into his office and calls nine-one-one, but now, all of a sudden, he *don't know nothin'*."

Josie said, "What did he say on the nine-one-one?"

Farris came over with his coffee and sat near us. "I don't know yet, but I hope it's good. What'd you guys get?"

"Dickie got engaged."

"Get the fuck outta here!" Farris said, smiling widely as he reached over and patted my back. "Congratulations, man. Seriously, that's cool, brother... Emily's a good woman. Good for you!"

"Thanks, Rich." I looked at Josie and said, "Thanks for being the town crier, partner." She had no idea that she only knew half of the story.

"Sorry, I think I'm just caught up in the excitement. I can't wait. I *am* invited to the wedding, right?"

"Possibly."

She slapped my shoulder. "Emily will invite me."

I looked at Rich who was still smiling, pleased with the news and enjoying the banter. I said, "But to answer your question, Rich, we got a spontaneous statement that is pretty incriminating: 'I'm not sorry if I killed him.' But then he lawyered up on us."

Josie said, "Unless something else comes up, a witness who heard the suspect threaten to kill our victim, or something similar, this is going to be a tough case to prove as a murder."

"Right, it'll go manslaughter at best," I said.

"Or self-defense," Farris added. He gazed into the distance for a moment. "Okay, man, I'll get a copy of the nine-one-one before I go. Are you guys about ready, or are y'all still working on something?"

"I'm writing up a statement of probable cause. Josie's working on the filing package. Might as well get as much of this done as we can tonight, while we're on overtime."

He grinned. "Okay, cool, man. Well, let's talk bachelor parties then."

When all else was finished, we walked up to the front desk together and Farris asked the watch deputy for a copy of the 9-1-1 call. As we waited, Josie told me she had to go back to the courthouse this morning, that the DA wanted her to be there when the judge went on record to formally dismiss the Spencer case. "Just in case anything comes up," she said.

I put my hand on her shoulder and looked into her dark, apprehensive eyes. "I'll go with you."

She turned toward me, and I dropped my hand. Josie surprised me by suddenly stepping into my purple circle and throwing her arms around my neck to hug me. "You're a great partner, Dickie. You know that? I'm really happy for you."

Farris and the watch deputy were looking at us. I shrugged.

Josie backed away but held my gaze, her damp eyes contrasting her smile. She said, "I'll see you there."

I walked outside to see the sky had turned pale blue in the early hours of dawn, the air already thick and stale as the summer heat persisted. I made the short drive to the office on side streets which allowed me to dodge the worst of the morning traffic, and I used the time to plot my day. A couple of hours in the office to update the dead sheet and fill out some overtime slips, and then I'd grab a cup of coffee and head downtown for court. If all went well at the hearing, and if there were no other pressing matters that arose between now and when we finished at court, I would go home to catch a few hours of sleep before Josie and I had to be back at nine tonight for our turn in the barrel. On a hot summer night in L.A., anything could happen.

As I arrived at the bureau, I received a text from Emily. *Hope you're having a great day! Love and miss you!* Smiling face and heart emojis followed. After backing into a spot, I replied: *Love you too! See you this evening.* I considered an emoji but decided on X's and O's instead. Then I headed into the office where I promptly lost my smile.

"Jones, my office."

I glanced at my watch as I trailed along behind Captain Stover. I didn't have time for distractions if I was going to be at the courthouse by nine. Besides, why was Stover here so early? There were others here too, more than usual for seven in the morning. I wondered how many cases had gone out overnight, and was glad we caught the case we had. It was a solved, and a relatively easy one to wrap up. Stover rounded the corner and stepped into his office. I followed and assumed my usual chair across the desk from him. It was a place that held mostly bad memories, the wood-shed of the office where I'd received more than a few lashes. What was up now? You never knew, and Stover had given me no indication of the direction this was going.

Stover sat in his oversized chair and leaned back in it, appraising me. After a moment, he said, "Where's your partner?"

"She's at East L.A. We picked up a murder there last night and she's finishing up and heading back to court from there."

He waited a moment. "I thought that was a done deal after the prick hung himself."

Yes, Jacob Spencer was a prick, and he had indeed hanged himself. I didn't need to see a video to be certain of it. The captain's statement put me at ease, because there seemed to be no question about it from him, either. "They just have to go back on the record and formally dismiss the case. The DA wanted her there for it, most likely in case there are any questions about what happened."

"Why would they need to be on record for anything after the idiot croaked himself? No defendant, no case."

At times I wondered how Stover had risen to the rank of captain, while also understanding clearly why that was where he remained. In the end, with all of the battles he and I had fought, I had to credit him with being more like the troops than the administrators. I glanced at my watch. "Not to rush you, but they want me there too."

He nodded. "Okay, I'll get to it. We now know why Farris's window was smashed down there in Compton."

This caught me by surprise. I had half a dozen ideas in my head about why I had been called into the skipper's office, and if I had been given a hundred guesses, I wouldn't have gotten it right. Now I was just relieved that I wasn't there for an ass chewing, for a change. I said, "Because that street is full of assholes?"

Stover leaned forward. "Maybe, but I can't say I blame them for this one."

He had my attention. I felt my brows crowding my eyes, and I didn't bother prodding him for more. It was coming, and I was back on familiar ground, knowing I'd not like what he had to say.

"Did you or your partner happen to run over a dog down there and not bother mentioning it to anyone?"

I leaned back in my chair, distancing myself from him. What the hell was this? "No... Hell no!"

"Well, that's what someone told Captain Ruiz at Compton. It came up at one of her community relations meetings, and apparently several people swore to it. They said that a few nights before the window smash, someone in a detective car ran over a dog and kept going."

I couldn't believe it. "That's bullshit, unless it was someone else. Why are they putting that on us? Compton has all kinds of slick cars: DB, Gangs..."

"But Compton DB and Gangs weren't at that apartment building where your chippie died."

I looked away, fixed my gaze on one of the few blank spots on the wall behind him where no awards or photographs with executives were displayed. Our callout on the Compton case happened on a Monday morning, and we didn't go back there at night until two days later. It was Wednesday night when Farris and I went to Century to interview the informant, and after that we had driven to the apartment. That was when Farris's window was smashed. If Josie had checked it at night on her own, she would have told me. This didn't make any sense to me.

"Look, Captain, you've got my word on this, none of us was at the apartment at nighttime before the night Farris's window was smashed. I have no idea who ran over a dog. I have no idea who would even do something like that without stopping to see if they could help it. How do we know it wasn't some civilian in a Crown Vic? Hell, you see them all over the place down there, old cop cars that have had their decals removed and sold at auctions."

Stover swiveled in his chair while biting at the end of a pen and studying me as I defended myself and my partners. I said, "Put me on a poly."

"Compton's started an I.A. on it, so you just may get your chance."

"Is that all, boss?" I glanced at my watch again to drive home my point.

"That's all for now."

JOSIE AND I TOOK SEATS IN THE FRONT ROW OF THE AUDIENCE. THERE were reporters all around us and their camera crews lined the back wall. Word must have traveled that there had been an extraordinary conclusion to the case. Spencer's attorney sat at the defense table holding his head in his hand and staring at the uncluttered table before him, a table that would normally be littered with case files and notepads. The prosecutor—Fry Man—stood at the podium with a pen hovered over a notepad. He was probably rehearsing how he planned to address the court when he asked that the case against Jacob Spencer be dismissed. The court clerk had her gaze set upon the computer screen at her desk, and the bailiff, the one who had likely allowed Josie to visit with Spencer just before he killed himself, sat long-faced at his desk too, his gaze darting around the room with a renewed sense for courtroom security.

I leaned toward Josie and whispered, "Wait until you hear what the captain is all fired up about now."

She turned toward me and pushed her hair behind her ear. "Let's hear it."

I glanced behind us to make sure no reporters could pick up my voice. "Compton has an I.A. going because someone ran over a dog and left it to die on the street, right there near the apartment."

She frowned. "Near what apartment, our chippie case apartment?"

I nodded. "The word is, that is why Farris's window was smashed a couple nights later."

Josie didn't whisper when she defended herself. "Neither of us ran over any goddamn dog."

I looked at the nearest reporter, a tweed-clad nerdy fellow who sat one row behind us and just a few feet away. He stared at me, unflinchingly, prepared for an unexpected new scoop to run with. *Defendant allegedly hangs himself in lockup and the detectives murdered a dog on the way to court.* Still locked on with the eyes of Nerd Boy, I just shook my head and clearly pronounced, "No, we didn't."

The judge entered from the back hallway and the bailiff asked that we all rise. As he took his seat at the bench, the judge said, "Please be seated."

Josie leaned over and said, "That property manager dude you liked so well, he drives an old sedan, could easily be mistaken as a detective car."

I whispered back that I had also noticed Moe's car at his office that night, but I didn't think anyone would mistake it as a cop car. "It had whitewalls, for the love of Pete."

From the bench: "We are on the record regarding People versus Jacob Spencer, is there anything we need to address before I dismiss the case?"

Spencer's attorney rose, and started, "Your Honor, in light of..."

Josie said, "Probably someone from Compton then, trying to put it on us."

I shook my head. The judge was saying something about the attorney's objection being noted and overruled. "That's what I thought," I told her, "but Stover doesn't think so. I told him half the moes in Compton got cars from the police auction."

She elbowed me in the ribs for the "moes" comment, knowing it was a cop term that was short for *mojados*, which, of course, was a derivative of wetbacks. I silenced a grunt. Josie said, "How would you like it if you were a moe?"

I chuckled and she elbowed me again. Holding my side, I leaned over closer to whisper as the reporter seemed more interested in our conversation than the proceedings on which he came to report. "Anyway, I'm not worried about it, but I am a little puzzled at how that could come back on us."

The judge began, "In the matter of Jacob Spencer..."

AFTER COURT, I MADE MY WAY THROUGH THE CROWDED STREETS OF Chinatown where parked cars lined the sidewalks and others sat waiting for their spots, oblivious to yet more drivers who leaned on their horns in protest. Crushes of pedestrians moved like ants along sidewalks and cross-walks, oblivious to it all. Halfway through, but now committed, I wished I had taken the Hollywood Freeway instead. But soon enough, I was through Chinatown and merging onto the Harbor Freeway. I jockeyed over to the left lane where I would transition onto the Golden State, and, once settled, I called Farris.

"What's up, Dickie?"

"Hey, Rich, you sleepin'?"

"Nah, man, I'm up. I got a few hours and now I'm hangin' around the crib, being lazy. What's up with you?"

Traffic had come to a stop, a line of brake lights ahead of me on the transition, traffic to our right whizzing by. "I'm trying to get home now, stuck in traffic near the stadium. I was wondering if there was a day game today, but I don't think the Dodgers have too many of those on weekdays, do they?"

"Brother, I'm an Angels fan. You can have your Dodgers and Chavez

Ravine and the gangsters that go with it. Plus, I don't like Puig, that goofy brotha that licks his bat and does all that other stupid shit."

I chuckled. "Puig's Cuban, and he's gone now anyway."

"Yeah, well, still… So what's up, anyway, you didn't call to talk about Cubans."

I told Rich Farris about the dog that was run over and the internal affairs investigation they'd started as a result of it. I told him about being pulled into Stover's office and what he had said about the window smash being the reason for it. Farris said, "Shee-it, man, nobody ran over no dogs down there—not any of us, anyway."

"That's what I told 'im, Rich. And then Josie and I were talking about it at court here a few minutes ago—"

"What happened with that?"

"Court?"

"For the Spencer case, right?"

"Yeah, not much to it, Rich. They dismissed it and the defense attorney made a few arguments for the record, probably building the case for a civil suit. Anyway, nothing really to it—"

"Good deal, man."

"—but we were talking about it and wondering how Compton put it on us. How do we know it wasn't one of their gang detectives, or someone else from there?"

"This complaint, they say who was in the car? They get a look at anyone? What's the make and color of the ride these dog slayers supposed to be drivin'?"

"Dark sedan is all they've said."

"Well, that fits mine and a thousand others on the department, half of LAPD, the feds—who knows, maybe it was that crazy bitch from the ATF we met with, she drove a black Crown Vic."

The car in front of me suddenly stopped, like all of the cars ahead of it, forcing me to slam on my brakes. My thoughts were swirling after Farris's comment about Tammy Rae driving a black Crown Vic, and it had slowed my reaction. My car settled and I heard Farris saying, "…they can look all they want, swab the undercarriage for doggie DNA, all I care. What was it anyway, a pit bull or a chihuahua?

"Rich, you may have just unraveled something here."

"What's that, Dickie?"

"You saw how Tammy Rae flew into the parking lot with no regard for that homeless man and his dog. I could see her running over someone's dog and not even slowing down. But what would she have been doing there? That bitch is up to something."

"You ain't lyin', my friend."

After hanging up with Farris, I contemplated the possibility of Tammy Rae's involvement for the rest of the drive home. What if she had been at that apartment after Officer Gomez was found dead there? Had she known what had happened to him? We didn't tell her about it until after Farris's window was smashed. Had she already known? Had she known about the missing kid and her grandmother? Suddenly there were a lot of questions I had for Miss Tammy Rae. But the real question was, would she answer any of them if asked.

One thing I knew for certain, I thought, coming into Burbank on the northbound I-5, anything Tammy Rae was involved with had the potential of being scandalous. Maybe we were looking at this from the wrong direction.

———

AFTER GETTING SOME MUCH-NEEDED SLEEP AND SPENDING A NICE EVENING with my fiancée, I showered and shaved and dressed for early mornings on the desk, which consisted of slacks and a shirt but no tie or jacket. I'd have those things with me in the event I had to respond to something that warranted a sharply-dressed detective.

The only thing on my mind was Tammy Rae Moore, and not in the way she likely assumed men often thought of her. My thoughts were unpleasant ones, the type usually reserved for the killers I faced in the course of my duty. I didn't think Tammy Rae was a killer, but I knew she had a hole in her, a dark place in her soul that affected her moral compass and allowed her to lose her way. That intuition Floyd and I had shared about her staged shooting back in our days at Century station had resurfaced, having washed over me the moment Farris suggested it was she who had run over the dog. I had no proof that she had been at the apartment since Officer Gomez was found dead there—or even before—but my instincts about her were strong again, warning me that something wasn't right with the hand she was playing. I needed to figure out what she was up to. It had to be something, because, well, it was Tammy Rae.

But how would I figure it out?

After relieving the PM shift at the desk and settling in with fresh coffee in the quiet of night, the homicide bureau peaceful for the time being, I ran it by Josie. I'm not sure what I expected from her in the way of a response, but I did expect *something*. Her dark eyes bore through me, unblinking and far away. Several moments passed in the silence before I said, "Well, what are your thoughts about that?"

Finally, she blinked, and now she felt close again, back from wherever she had gone in her mind. Josie said, "You didn't tell me it was Tammy Rae Moore who Tony hooked you up with, and who you and Farris met with."

I shrugged. "Didn't think to mention the name. Apparently, I should have. You know her, I take it."

"When I was at Compton gangs, she was working patrol there. I think she actually trained at Century—"

"She did," I said, wondering if my story would trump what I was about to hear.

The desk line rang, and Josie snatched the phone before I could lean forward in my chair. "Homicide Bureau, Sergeant Sanchez." She readied her pen over a scratch pad on the desk. "Okay, and your name again?"

Someone had died. How would it affect us? I hoped it was a natural with a doctor to sign. That would only require the field deputy to notify us. If not a natural, I hoped it was a murder, not a suicide. For a murder, all we would have to do is fill out the Dead Sheet, send out the next team in the rotation, and make a few notifications. A suicide meant one of us would be responding to handle it from the office while the other manned the phones. I didn't know about Josie, but I wasn't in the mood to handle a suicide. With my luck, it would be up in Palmdale, an hour drive from the office.

Josie, still on the phone, said, "What is she wearing?"

That was an interesting question. I leaned up and glanced at Josie's notepad to see she had written exactly three words: *927D* (the radio code for a death investigation)*, Newhall,* and *Lung/SCT.* I assumed someone had died in Newhall, and Deputy Lung of Santa Clarita station is who had called it in. Josie was saying, "Uh-huh, yes, I want you to describe for me exactly what she has on... yes, even if you have to pull the bedding down... no, you won't be disturbing a crime scene—if it's a natural, there is no crime, right?"

I leaned back in my chair and thought of Tammy Rae again. Where had Josie and I left off? Josie knew her from Compton station. I wondered how well they knew each other and what stories I might hear as soon as Josie finished her conversation with Deputy Lung. I doubted the two were friends, but were they enemies? You heard tales of serious drama taking place in the ladies' locker rooms throughout the various stations. Almost always, it had to do with men. Though sometimes, it had to do with other women, in the same carnal sense. And once in a while, it might involve both. Not that there weren't problems among male deputies, but usually those problems were settled in ancient form, which greatly reduced the drama aspects that the fairer sex seemed to endure.

Josie looked at me with the phone tucked under her chin. "Seventy-nine-year-old female, lives alone, found dead in her bed, the result of a 'Check the Welfare' call. Hopefully, it's a natural. Sounds like it is."

"You don't trust the deputy," I said, a statement not a question.

She shook her head. "I've heard Farris's story."

Rich Farris had a deputy report a natural that turned out to be a homicide. The deputy, uncomfortable in the presence of death, had stopped at the threshold of the bedroom, observed what appeared to be a dead person in her bed, backed out and called it a natural. His reasoning had been that he knew the person was elderly, and that she had died in bed. Naturally. But beneath the covers lay the naked, battered body of an elderly woman who had died at the hands of her so-called caretaker. Farris would tell the story to all newcomers and suggest they always ask for a detailed description of the body, its position, clothing, et cetera. When in doubt, drive out to the scene yourself.

A moment later, Josie had the phone back in front of her mouth, saying, "Uh-huh, okay, great. And no signs of any trauma or foul play, right?... Okay, good, yeah... Do you have a doctor who is willing to sign the death certificate? You can usually find a name on some prescription meds around the house. Check the bathroom... okay, you bet."

She tucked the phone again. "This kid must be brand new. Probably went six months on training up there and never handled a dead body."

I waited as Josie ended the call, saying, "Great, call him and as long as he will sign the certificate, we're done. Have a relative choose a mortuary and they'll take care of the rest." She hung up and leaned back in her chair, looked at me and shook her head.

I said, "You want to drive to Santa Clarita?"

"No, I think we're okay on this one."

"I hope so. Now finish telling me about Tammy Rae."

JOSIE FINISHED TELLING ME ABOUT TAMMY RAE AND HER PENCHANT FOR "dating" married deputies, and how one such deputy happened to be married to another deputy who worked at Century station, and how that deputy and Tammy Rae ended up in a fistfight one night in the Compton station parking lot. But two cops exchanging blows as a way to sort out adulterous affairs neither fazed me nor held my interest. I said, "So Tammy worked at Compton after leaving Century and before going to the ATF."

Josie shrugged. "Yeah, apparently."

I pictured the parking lot where the two women had likely pulled one another's hair while swinging wildly with fists of painted nails. It was the same parking lot where Josie and I had allowed Leticia Hernandez and her grandmother a moment of privacy in Josie's wired car, hoping to learn more about their disappearance and the inexplicable circumstances that led to Leticia's father, Officer Gomez, being found dead in their home. Afterwards, we had dropped the two of them off at their apartment, which is located around the corner and just a few hundred feet from the station.

Was it a coincidence that Tammy Rae, who happened to be involved in a trafficking investigation of which Officer Gomez might have been a part, had previously worked at Compton station, a Tiger Woods nine iron shot from our crime scene? Was it a coincidence that a dark-colored detective car, similar to the one in which Tammy Rae had nearly mown down a homeless man and his dog, had been to the apartment since the chippie's death and had, in fact, run over a dog on its way out? It didn't make sense that it had been a Compton station detective, as surely any of them would have stopped. Hitting a dog is easily explained; running one over and continuing on is inexcusable. Whoever it had been that took out the neighbor's dog had not wanted to have their presence there documented.

Were these things all coincidental? I didn't think so. Rule Nine was there were no coincidences in death.

At the least, Tammy Rae Moore and her ATF colleagues had information about the Gomez family and what might have happened that Monday morning in the apartment. Worst-case scenario, they were somehow involved in it. Like many of my colleagues, I had learned not to trust the feds. They had a practice of lying and denying when things went bad, and racing to the cameras to take credit when something went right. Either way, they were never team players when it came to joint operations with local cops.

Josie said, "What are you thinking?"

I pushed out of my chair. "I think someone should take a look at that natural in Santa Clarita. I'll go."

She raised her brows. "You wouldn't be planning a stop in San Fernando, would you?"

I shrugged. "Not a bad idea, is it? Just take a drive by Gomez's house and see what's going on. We never did find or even identify the roommate. Maybe I'll get lucky and catch someone home, late in the evening. Maybe I'll swing through Compton on my way back."

The phone rang and Josie picked it up. Covering the mouthpiece, she said, "Compton isn't on your way back." Then, into the phone, "Sheriff's Homicide Bureau, Sergeant Sanchez."

I stood at my desk, donning a tie and thinking about my upcoming excursion. I would get to Santa Clarita first and handle my business there. If it was, in fact, a natural death, I could be in and out in ten minutes and on my way to Gomez's home. I pictured the squalid home with its oil-stained driveway and decrepit wooden garage door that you would pull open against its heavy springs if there weren't auto parts stacked up in front of it. I pictured the cold-plated El Camino that had sat in the driveway the last time I visited, and I envisioned the fed who drove it as a burly man with tattoos and a beard, a Tony Brunetti type from whom mothers sheltered their children, having no clue the man wore a badge. But I didn't truly know that he appeared that way at all, as I hadn't got a look at him the morning he left there, concealed by the dark-tinted windows all around. He could have been a scrawny black man for all I knew, but profiling came naturally to me and I didn't think that would be the case. But why had he been there early that morning? That was a question I had yet to answer. It was my feeling that the roommate was, in fact, a fed. Did Gomez know that to be the case? Or was that part of the operation that Tammy Rae and company were involved in?

I picked up my attaché case and started for the back door, where I would find my Crown Vic parked alongside Josie's Charger under the lights in an otherwise empty parking lot.

Josie called out from the front desk. "Hey, be careful."

I paused and looked across the squad room. She was leaning against the doorway that led to the front desk area, looking tall and trim in her black on black ensemble. "What could go wrong?" I said.

She rolled her eyes and went back to the desk.

In the solitude of my car, I pondered the case of the deceased CHP officer, the part that Tammy Rae and her crew might have played in it, and how I would proceed. The long drives from one end of the county to the other could offer excellent opportunities for contemplation. I would often jot notes as I thought of things that needed to be done on a case, or theories that might help solve it. Lately, I had been dictating these notions using my iPhone's Notes application, doing my best to keep up with technology. A failed relationship with Siri had led me to this new process. Siri would chastise me for my language at times, and then we would argue. It was a relationship that just wasn't meant to be, so I fired her and added her to the scroll of the living dead, a list reserved for my former counterparts of failed relationships. As I cruised along the I-5 heading north to Santa Clarita, I had an idea, so I thumbed open my Notes application, pushed the record button, and said, "See if Ty can triangulate that bitch's phone, seventy-two hours before and after the time of death." Notes didn't argue or suggest that such language wasn't necessary. I loved Notes.

A few minutes later, I decided it couldn't wait until I saw Ty in the office, so I called Josie at the desk and asked her to text me his cell phone number. She said, "What's up?" I told her my idea and she said, "You think he's going to be able to get phone records from a fed without a court order?"

She had a point, but I wasn't deterred. "That asshole does all sorts of shady shit. He can probably do it on the sly."

"But it won't have any value—*if* he can get it done," she argued.

True, we wouldn't be able to use any such data against her in a court of law, but I didn't necessarily think Tammy Rae and the feds—*wouldn't that be a catchy name for a band*—had actually committed any crimes, at least not any crimes that I would be interested in. I'll put it this way, I didn't think they killed Gomez or kidnapped the girl. So if I didn't expect to someday present my findings to a prosecutor or in a court of law, this was merely intelligence gathering, trying to see where the ass meets the saddle, so to speak. I said, "I'm going to see what he can do."

A few minutes later, I left a message for Ty Couture to call me, assuring him I would be up all night.

The scene at Santa Clarita was no scene at all. The deputy had departed, having finished what needed to be done, and a small gathering of people I assumed to be family and friends sat gloomily in the living room while a man and a woman from a mortuary attended to the deceased in the adjacent room. I briefly introduced myself to the family—forgoing any mention of Homicide Bureau—and made my way into the room, where I saw the remains of a frail woman who had likely lived through the Great Depression, two world wars, Korea, the assassination of President Kennedy, Vietnam, Watergate, and the revelation that even men who occupied our nation's highest office were not above committing lewd and lascivious acts. Then, she departed in her sleep, just shy of a century old and with a car in the driveway and no walker near the bed. That was a win in my book. I took a couple notes and headed south.

When I exited the interstate and started through the city of San Fernando, I prepared myself for what I might find at the former residence of Officer Gomez. Those images ranged from dark and empty, to a biker party with topless women dancing on Harleys, to a lone El Camino sitting ominously in the driveway with no other signs of life. What I actually found when I arrived was a vacant home with a "For Rent" sign in the front yard. I walked to the front and shone my light through several windows to confirm that it was, in fact, vacant. I made a note of the phone number on the sign and continued my journey south.

All the way to Compton, I contemplated the vacant rental and what it had meant. Did Gomez have the lease and his roommate had to move out following Gomez's death? Or did the roommate bail out for other reasons? I had dictated a reminder to call the landlord of the San Fernando home to see if I could learn the roommate's identity and find out if a forwarding address had been supplied.

I passed the Monument to the Five-Year Prior and pulled to the curb in front of the Acacia Avenue apartment. My gaze homed in on the two darkened windows of Maria Hernandez's unit, and an emptiness that might only be rivaled by the interior of that home swept over me. It only took a moment to realize the window coverings were gone, and finally I noticed the *For Rent* sign that hung on the wall. I slammed the shifter into park, killed the ignition, and popped open my door. As I stepped out and turned to walk around the rear of my car, I was startled by the sight of a man standing on the sidewalk nearby. I held his gaze as I walked in my intended direction that would have me passing just feet from where he stood. "How are you tonight, sir?"

He said, "You the one ran over my dog?"

3 2

I STOPPED AND FACED HIM. "NO SIR, AND I'M SORRY TO HEAR THAT happened to you."

His gaze drifted to the ground and he held it there for a long moment. When he looked back up, his eyes were moist. He took a step backward and regarded my Crown Vic. "Yeah, I don't suppose it was you. The car I seen hit Barack was darker'n this one."

"Barack?"

He nodded. "First black President, first black dog. I guess he was hard to see at night."

I pictured the former President for a moment and then thought about the dog. "What kind of dog was he?"

"*She* was a rock-wiler."

I nodded. A black female Rottweiler named Barack. "And you saw it happen?"

He turned and indicated some place to the north of us with a sweep of his hand, the direction I had just come. "Yup, it happened right there"—he turned and gestured toward a house behind us with his other hand—"and I was sitting right over there on that porch. She'd just gone out in the yard to do her bidness, and when the cop car come by, she run after it. Mother-fucker hit my girl and kept on going."

I shook my head, a vision of Tammy Rae in her black Crown Vic in my mind. "I truly am sorry, sir. That's an awful thing to have happen, and I honestly hope they find out who did it and she pays for it."

"It was a woman poh-lees?"

I shrugged. "I don't know, maybe. You didn't get a look at all?"

"Nah, man, 'cause the other car had gone on ahead of it and was racing away. I was watching it and thinking, that cop gonna get yo dumb ass, nigga, and then bam, baby girl let out a yelp and I seen her go down."

I let a moment pass. "What kind of car was the other one?"

"El Camino, black jus' like the cop car."

"HE SAID IT HAPPENED TUESDAY NIGHT, LATE. THAT WOULD HAVE BEEN after Gomez was killed and before I went back there with Farris."

Josie, on the phone, said, "Assuming he was killed."

I shook my head and rolled my eyes. Josie seemed to have sensed my response. She said, "Well, anyway, would you mind picking up a salad from Jack-in-the-Crack on your way back? We can talk more about the former dog owner when you get here."

Former dog owner. Josie and I had been watching the news one slow night in the barrel when a reporter interviewed a carjacking victim. The caption had read: *Former car owner,* and both of us had been amused by the classification.

"Sure, dear. What type of dressing would you like?"

"Ranch, please. Oh, and can you grab me an iced tea, too? You're the best."

I hung up and continued across Compton Boulevard to Atlantic, where I turned north so I could pick up the Long Beach Freeway off of Rosecrans. Memories of many murders I had investigated crowded my thoughts as I traveled the short distance. Most of my Compton cases had been gang-related, and many of them remained unsolved. There was a triple murder at Compton and White, a drive by at Pixley and Lime, and "Waybo" had been shot in his apartment at McMillan and Fraley, but I had no idea why. It was the one murder that hadn't been directly gang related, so far as I could tell. I did have a good idea about who it was that had whacked Waybo, though there were no witnesses nor evidence to tie the man to the murder. There were fingerprints, yes, but he was a friend of the deceased and he admitted frequenting the apartment, smoking crack and throwing back malt liquors with his *former friend*, Waybo. I interviewed this person of interest twice, once that day at the scene, and again a few months later after he had been picked up on a burglary case. That was an in-custody interview that lasted nearly three hours, and wherein I had him on the ropes a couple of times but could never finish him. I was certain he was at the scene when Waybo got whacked, but I didn't think he was necessarily the killer. Either way, he wouldn't give me what I needed, and the case remained unsolved, much to my chagrin.

I hit the northbound onramp and shifted my thoughts back to Gomez because it did no good in this business to dwell on cases to which you had given your best effort yet had come up empty. The culture made it next to impossible to solve murders in Compton, and the best you could hope for —once you'd exhausted all leads—was that someone would eventually talk. A gangster with two strikes and a gun under his seat might use his knowledge of one or more murders as a bargaining chip to avoid spending the rest of his life in prison.

The line for the drive-thru at Jack's stretched around the building, everyone needing emergency tacos and fries. At this time of night, the choices for food in the area were slim and almost non-existent for anything healthy. At least Jack offered salads that weren't too bad and were better for you than mystery-meat tacos and fries, all of it prepared in vats of grease. I ordered two salads and two iced teas, the latter of which came in a cardboard carrying case which I held onto as if it were "the football"—the nuclear suitcase—as I negotiated the remaining few blocks to the office.

I settled in at the front desk and gave Josie her food. "So the guy's dog gets hit by a cop car but dude is watching this El Camino speed away ahead of it. Coincidence about the El Camino? I think not."

"You're thinking it's the same car that was in Gomez's driveway."

I nodded without looking up as I emptied a container of ranch dressing onto my salad, working it in circles from inside to the outer perimeter and back. "You don't see a lot of those on the road anymore, especially in Compton."

"And what do you think they might have been doing there, if it was indeed the slut and whoever drives the truck?"

I regarded her while I finished chewing, took a sip of my iced tea and thought, *not bad.* "I don't know that I'd call an El Camino a truck. Kind of a combo—half car, half truck. I mean, you won't see anyone hauling gravel in one, but you can't load the kids up and head to the beach either."

She waited. I smiled and said, "But to answer your question, I don't know. Looking for something, maybe?"

Josie picked through the Styrofoam container of salad. "Or someone."

That is what I had wondered too. Had they been checking to see if grandma and the kid had returned? Or was it something else? If they were investigating Gomez, they would have known about the relatives, and they likely would have known by the time they went down there and flattened Barack on the way out, that Gomez had died in the apartment. What had Gomez gone there for, and where did Tammy Rae and company fit in to all of it?

It reminded me I needed to get word to Livingston, the informant I had asked to see what she could learn from the kid's mom, Monica Hernandez. It seemed now that we wouldn't need either of them, and I was happy for it. Monica was the type who would become a permanent headache, always needing a favor, always working an angle. And Livingston had her get-out-of-jail card punched already for the work she had done with Farris.

The phone rang and I grabbed it before Josie had a chance. "Homicide, Jones... yessir, hold on." I pecked the pound sign and then four digits to transfer the call.

Josie indicated the phone. "Who was that?"

"Eddie Roberts, said he needed to leave a voicemail for his lieutenant."

She nodded. "So you were saying that the apartment is vacant now."

"For Rent sign out front. We need to call Mr. Moe tomorrow." I lifted my phone and read from my Notes app. "Call Moe, get in touch with Ty about Tammy's phone, and call on the San Fernando pad."

The phone rang again, and this time Josie beat me to the punch. "Sheriff's Homicide Bureau, Sergeant Sanchez."

I pushed out of my seat and passed behind her, the iced tea sending me down the hall. On my way back to the front desk, I heard several lines ringing at once. I jogged back and grabbed a phone, glancing at the Dead Sheet my partner was filling out as I spoke into the phone, "Homicide, Jones." The few lines she had written told me what I needed to know: there had been a deputy-involved shooting in Hacienda Heights.

On the phone, the lieutenant of Team Two said, "Dickie, Jordan here. You guys have something for us?"

I read over Josie's shoulder as she continued collecting information and recording it on the Dead Sheet. "Yeah, boss, looks like you guys have a DIS out in Industry, suspect dead, no deputies injured."

The lieutenant told me who to send and said he would be on scene in half an hour. I hung up and began calling the two investigators who would be assigned to handle the case, and two more who would be assigned to assist. Then I called the coroner's office to notify them and to obtain a coroner's case number. By the time I finished with the notifications, Josie was off the phone. "Did you get everyone rolling?" she asked.

"Yes, but I haven't notified the captain yet. Have at it."

She frowned. Nobody liked calling the captain at two in the morning, but he was to be notified for all deputy- and officer-involved shootings. Josie put a finger on the roster where the captain's cell phone number was listed, and punched it into her phone. I turned to my computer with another train of thought, something that had nothing to do with the deputy-involved shooting in Industry, but had everything to do with a deputy-involved shooting in Firestone, more than a decade ago.

AS THE MORNING SKY TURNED A PINKISH-ORANGE AND RESIDENTS CAME TO life in Southern California, Josie and I pulled to the curb in her Dodge Charger, several houses away from the one we planned to watch for an hour or two this morning. We sat low in the seats behind tinted glass in order to avoid detection by early walkers and joggers, each of us sipping coffee in an effort to stay alert after a long night on the desk.

Josie said, "Your captain's going to kill us."

"Only if he catches us."

She twisted in her seat to face me. "He told us a week ago to put it down. Now we're doing surveillance on an ATF agent whose address you obtained with the use of databases that are strictly monitored and forbidden for personal use. Richard, we could get fired for this—or at least kicked out of the bureau."

I raised a small pair of binoculars to my face. "Again, only if he catches us. Hold on, I just saw movement through the kitchen window. She's up and moving around. There, lights are on."

"If something goes bad here—"

"It won't," I insisted. "I just need to get some intel on Moore, see what she's up to. I know she's up to something, regardless of how the Gomez case shakes out. Floyd and I let her slide once. I'm not going to do it again."

"So that's what this is about?"

I lowered my glasses and looked at her. "What?"

"You feel like she was dirty on that caper back in the day, the shooting she was involved in, and you let her slide. Now you're feeling guilty about it."

I turned my focus back to Tammy Rae's home, and took my time replying to my partner. The first words that had come to me weren't the appropriate ones to use in response. I needed to let my emotion on the matter subside, and address the allegation at hand. I took a deep breath and returned my attention to Josie. "Yes, that's probably it. We should have turned her over to I.A. back then, but that was never my style. I mean, if there had been no doubt that her shooting was contrived, I might have felt differently. But because I couldn't prove it, I wasn't about to ruin a career by running to Internal Affairs with it. I felt like I handled it, but I hadn't taken into consideration who I was actually dealing with, and what she was capable of. Now I'm worried that she has something to do with Gomez's death, directly or indirectly, and I'm not going to let her slide again. Besides, she ran over a goddamn dog. If nothing else I have her on animal cruelty."

Josie's gaze darted toward the house. "She's on the move."

33

A SLIVER OF LIGHT GREW INTO A LARGE RECTANGULAR PATCH AS THE garage door lifted automatically. We couldn't see inside from where we had parked, but we knew instinctively that we were about to go live, and we prepared for a rolling surveillance. Josie started her car and we both buckled up, tension weighing heavily in the silence. Moments later, brake lights glowing red, the black Crown Vic backed out of the garage, down the short driveway, and onto the street, apparently heading in our direction. *Shit!* You have a fifty-fifty shot and we lost the coin toss. We would have to duck low and pray she wouldn't notice us as she passed by, and then we'd have to wait until she was out of sight before whipping a U and trying to follow her. Surveillance with only one car was never easy, and I wished we could have driven separately. But my Crown Vic was no surveillance vehicle, and Tammy Rae would spot it in an instant.

As her Crown Vic started our way, we both slouched in the seat, our heads coming together in the middle of the car. I took one final peek before ducking down and saw another vehicle was now coming out behind her. I couldn't believe it. "The El Camino!"

Josie risked a quick peek and then ducked back down. I could hear her breathing as we waited for Tammy Rae to pass by us. She whispered, "I hope they're staying together."

My gaze was fixed on the console where dual temperature controls demonstrated the stark contrast between me and my partner. Hers was set at seventy, mine sixty-two. She said, "That was her."

I lifted my head and watched through the rear window as the Crown Vic grew smaller. I turned to look back at the El Camino in time to see it going the opposite direction. "Shit!"

"Which one?"

I didn't know. My intention had been to tail Tammy Rae, but this El Camino really intrigued me. Who was driving it and what did they have to do with Tammy Rae and Officer Gomez? Whoever drove the El Camino had, just a week ago, been at the San Fernando home of Gomez in the early morning hours, which led me to believe it was Gomez's roommate. Then the plates came back with no record on file, and we learned that the El Camino was an ATF undercover vehicle. So I assumed that the driver/agent was Gomez's roommate, deep undercover and working a case against the chippie for whatever it was he might have been involved in. Running guns, perhaps. Maybe dope. But now the vehicle was here in West Covina, safely secured inside Tammy Rae's garage, presumably overnight. It made me wonder if the driver lived here or only came by for conjugal visits. Either way, I needed to know who he was.

"Follow that son of a bitch in the El Camino."

Josie glanced sideways at me. "You're sure?"

I nodded, and she pulled away from the curb and stomped on the gas. I glanced back once more and saw that Tammy Rae was out of view, likely long gone by now. There was no pulling back nor changing course, the El Camino it was.

When we reached the first intersection, there were two cars between us on a solid red light. On the green, one car turned off. We continued on Pacific Avenue to Glendora, where our boy turned right, as did the car between us. We were now headed south. Traffic was light in the early morning hour, so we allowed some distance between us in order to play it safe. The last thing we needed was for an ATF agent to realize he was being tailed and call for backup.

Glendora turned into Hacienda Avenue and soon we were crossing Temple. I said, "Where was that shooting?"

"Hacienda Heights. Down south of the Pomona Freeway."

"But not too far from here."

Josie glanced from the road. "No, I guess not. Why?"

I shrugged, but she likely didn't notice. "Just thinking about where we were headed. If he stays on Hacienda, we'll go right by the sheriff's station," I said, pointing across the dash and over the hood.

Shortly after, dread grew in the pit of my stomach as the El Camino turned right onto Stafford Street, the sheriff's station in view from here. "What the—"

"He's turning into the back lot?" Josie said, dubiously.

"Don't follow," I warned. "Go straight! Keep going."

Josie continued past the driveway to the sheriff's employee parking as my gaze followed the El Camino into the lot, past the black and whites, and toward civilian parking before I lost sight of it. "What the damn hell!"

Josie hung a left on Hudson, circled behind the heliport across the street from the station, and found a place to park with a view of the station's driveway. She put the car in park and shut off the engine. "Do we go over?"

I needed a minute to think. Why would an ATF agent drive into the rear parking lot of a sheriff's station? He seemed familiar with the property, driving directly past the area designated for radio car parking and toward the employee parking area. Maybe he was part of a multi-jurisdictional task force and this is where they met.

Josie said, "I could walk through the station, see if I can figure out what he's doing there."

"We have no idea what he looks like. He could be a big black guy or a little Chinese lady."

She popped her door open. "I'm pretty sure he's going to look like a biker, or like an undercover cop trying to look like a biker. I know most of the dope guys here, so he won't be hard to pick out from the other tattooed and bearded cops."

I started to protest, but Josie was outside the car now. "Keys are in the ignition if you have to go. I can always steal a detective bureau car and catch up to you if I have to."

With that, she was gone. I watched her cross the lot, her hair bouncing as she swiveled her head to look both ways before starting across the street. A moment later she was up the driveway and out of view. I silently cursed my luck. Why couldn't I catch normal murder cases like everyone else, a dead gangster in an ominous alley and no witnesses or leads. Then I realized I was only feeling sorry for myself, because the truth of it was, the stranger the case, the more I liked it. I lifted my binoculars and scanned the portion of the parking lot I could see from my position. It appeared to be business as usual, uniformed deputies milling about and others coming and going in white t-shirts. There was no sign of Josie or the fed.

A half hour passed—I know because I checked the time on my phone every thirty seconds while hoping for a text from Josie—and my patience had run out. I locked up Josie's car and started toward the station.

Halfway up the driveway, a sedan pulled up alongside me, and the driver called out. "Dickie, whatcha doin'?"

It was Lieutenant Jordan from Team Two. "Hey boss, what's going on?"

He moved slowly to keep pace with me as he spoke. "Not much, finishing up with the DIS. What brings you out here?"

I stopped and looked around. It might have seemed like I was lost, not sure of what had brought me there. A child who had strayed from his mother, or a senile old man who had wandered off from home. Jordan waited, his arm cocked on the door, his white shirtsleeve and watch glistening beneath the early morning sun. I had come up with an answer, and was about to say I was just doing some follow-up on an old case, when Josie called out. "Hey partner."

"Just waiting on my partner," I said, forcing a smile to accompany my words. "You know how it is when a woman needs a powder break."

Josie didn't break her stride as she passed by me with a pat on my shoulder and a "'Mornin', Lieutenant," for Jordan and a "Let's go, partner," for me. I nodded to Jordan and told him I'd see him later, then turned on my heel. Josie paused at the street and glanced back, and when I caught up to her, she started across the street.

"Well?"

She looked back at me over her shoulder and said, "Really bizarre."

We were back at the car before I could ask for details. We paused in unison, looking at each other over the roof. She said, "It's your boy, Tony."

3 4

JOSIE STARTED THE CAR AND ROLLED DOWN THE WINDOWS, BUT SHE DIDN'T shift into gear and drive us to the parking lot as I had asked her to do. She questioned my plan. "What are you hoping to accomplish?"

"Look, I just want to talk to him. He didn't shoot straight with us and he is supposed to be on our team, not the feds'. He needs to answer some questions."

She lowered her eyes and shook her head, obviously uncomfortable with it. "This might blow the whole thing up."

"Right, and that's about where I'm at on this. I'm adding Tony's number when I get ahold of Ty, have him look at both his phone history and his girlfriend's."

"Why would he lead us to Tammy Rae if they had anything to do with Gomez? That doesn't even make sense. I'm not convinced we're on the right track. I think it's a mistake to go at him right now, not knowing anything else."

I looked across the street to see the action had remained the same, deputies coming and going with regularity, on- and off-duty, men and women, some with prisoners in tow. But it was Big Tony who dominated my thoughts, the image of him across from me in the diner, one of the boys, all on the same team. That's what I had thought. That's what he had presented, telling me how he knew me when he was a trainee at Century, making that connection from our past to solidify our brotherhood. But he had lied. Yeah, everybody lies—that was right there in the rule book—but you didn't expect it from your so-called brothers and sisters.

Tammy Rae had lied that night in the alley, telling us about the would-be killer who got away, describing her bravery in the face of imminent danger. Now this "brother" was lying to me on her behalf, and I didn't like it. I wouldn't stand for it, and I was going to poke the bear and see what happened. Maybe it wasn't the best idea, but it was the only idea I could come up with at the time, and a confrontation was exactly what I needed at that moment.

I turned back to Josie. "Yeah, maybe. It very well may turn out to be a mistake, but I'm going to confront him." It was Rule Ten in the book, you take the bull by the horns. Well, I was going to grab the biker by his balls and see what happened. "Now, drive me over there or I'll get out and walk."

WE PARKED NEAR THE EL CAMINO AND WAITED. JOSIE HAD ACQUIESCED but suggested that we at least not do it in the station, just in case it got ugly. It was a good suggestion, and since I hadn't seen Lieutenant Jordan leave, it made even more sense to stay outside. The time passed slowly as we waited in silence, neither of us in the mood for conversation. She may have been a little mad at me, and I wouldn't blame her for it. I knew myself well enough to know that when I set my mind on something, I could be obstinate and nearly impossible to reason with for those less persistent than myself. There were degrees of Type A personalities.

Two hours had passed and Josie was fighting to stay awake when I said, "Here he comes."

She sat up and watched but remained silent.

I studied Tony and the man who walked out with him, a smaller man, thin and clean shaven. He didn't appear to be an undercover cop, more likely an off-duty deputy leaving the station for the day. I said, "Who's the dude with him, any idea?"

Josie shook her head. "I don't know, never seen him before."

The two stopped halfway to the parking lot and appeared to be finishing a conversation. The smaller man peeled off and Tony continued toward his car. Toward us. I could feel his stare through the dark shades, and I knew instinctively he had spotted the two of us parked near the El Camino. I might have been imagining it, but it seemed he slowed his pace. Probably thinking, knowing a confrontation was coming. Suddenly there was nobody on earth but me and Tony, my mind narrowing and vision focusing on the bearded man in jeans and black biker boots, a black Harley t-shirt hanging loose. He would have a gun in his waistband beneath it, and probably a knife in his boot. Maybe another gun. Who knew what he had in the backpack? Though we were both cops, the looming confrontation put me in a combative mindset—you never knew where these things would go.

Josie said something that didn't register as I popped the door and twisted out of the car. Tony stopped ten feet from me, our gazes locked as if we were two lions starting to circle one another, each ready to fight to be king.

"Hey, Tony," I said, faking a smile, "fancy meeting you here."

He reached over and set the backpack on the hood of the El Camino, freeing his hands. He knew. I knew. This was it, the time of truth. He nodded as if to say, "What's up?"

"Where's the white pickup, the one you drove to the diner the other day?"

He glanced away for a moment, then leaned against the El Camino. The move surprised me, because it was no different than a boxer moving backwards. I instinctively came forward, seizing the momentum he foolishly allowed. Tony said, "Oh, it's in for maintenance, this'un here's just a loaner."

I was just beyond arm's reach now and knew I had won the round if not the match. He wasn't coming off the ropes, I could feel it. I said, "So ATF gave you a loaner?"

He looked at me for a moment, then glanced at the El Camino—or was it the backpack he looked at?—and nodded slowly, almost imperceptibly. "Not officially—"

I stepped into him and pointed my finger at his face. "You climbed in bed with the wrong bitch, Tony. You fucked up. Tammy Rae is a scandalous, evil bitch, and she's straight poison. Now I'm just trying to think how to keep you from going down with her when I prove the two of you were at that apartment together the morning Gomez keeled over, and again the night that crazy bitch you're sleeping with ran over the fucking dog."

"She ran over a dog?"

"That's how it came together, Tony, the goddamn dog. That dumb bitch mowed down a dog right in front of its owner when you two were leaving, and the dog's owner got a look at both of you."

He forced a smirk. "You can't see who's in this ride, man, not through those windows."

I was on the verge of losing the momentum if I left it there, and it was a big risk to bluff and be wrong. But I knew the power of the upper hand and I couldn't afford to give this bear of a man an inkling that he was taking control. I poured it on thick: "He saw you when you got back into your cars after doing who-knows-what at the apartment. Don't be fucking stupid, Tony. I don't come at another cop half-cocked." That's exactly what I had done, but so far it seemed to be working.

Tony seemed to shrink again, his arms now folded across his chest, one leg crossed over the other as he leaned against the car. It was the most submissive posture I would likely ever see from the big man, and I needed to stay inside his head. I thought back to my second meeting with Tony at the diner when he had joked about me having nothing to do but golf. It had pissed me off, and I had let him know. But before he could go macho on me, I let him know that if I had to take on a guy his size, I wouldn't fight fair. In fact, as I recalled it, I told him I'd use a Buick as a weapon if I had to. I had made my point that the biggest dog doesn't always have the hardest bite, and now that foreshadowing seemed to be paying off. Most fights were won between the ears, though sometimes you had to go straight to the bridge of the nose. I didn't want to go there with Tony, but I also didn't want him to think I wouldn't.

"And that's not the only way we can prove you two were there," Josie said. "Both times."

Tony and I each looked at Josie. She had silently watched the game and knew the score and decided that a power play was just what we needed while Tony was still on the ropes. I looked back to see that Tony kept his gaze on her, paying attention now. This was perfect, I thought, taking some of the testosterone out of the equation would allow Tony to save face when he started singing—I could hear the band warming up for the number.

He continued to look at Josie and said, "I don't have anything to do with any of the shit she's involved in. Yeah, I fucked up, did some things I wouldn't have done if—"

"You weren't sleeping with her," Josie finished for him, a smile softening the blow.

He nodded.

She said, "You married, Tony?"

His gaze dropped to the ground, and now we had everything other than a referee to count to ten and call the fight.

SEVERAL HOURS LATER, WE FINISHED UP WITH TONY. JOSIE AND I SAT IN the captain's office at Industry station while Tony remained isolated in an interview room, unarmed but also unguarded. He had given us everything in a recorded statement, and now he waited for a union rep as investigators from our Internal Criminal Investigations Bureau waited their turn at the defeated biker cop.

Stover, a guest in this captain's office, sat along one wall with our lieutenant, Joe Black. Josie and I were seated across the room alongside Farris, who had come out to assist us. His partner, Lizzy Marchesano, was not only still off duty, and not only probably not returning, but currently in very critical condition. Farris had joined us, stating he needed to keep his mind elsewhere to keep from going crazy. Captain Tippings had given us the room, glad to not be part of what was about to take place, and happy that nobody in his command was involved in it on either side. In his place, literally, sat Floyd, rocking back and forth in the captain's oversized leather chair. Floyd had been called out on the shooting in Hacienda Heights. He had come to the station to fill up his car when he saw the confrontation. I hadn't known it at the time, but Floyd had sat with his eye on us, knowing his old partner well enough to know the meeting was a heated one. He decided to stick around and help out when he considered the overtime he was making.

A man and woman in colorless business attire arrived and I knew instinctively they were feds. Introductions were curt but definitive: The woman was Assistant Special Agent in Charge Donner, from the Bureau of Alcohol, Tobacco, and Firearms, Los Angeles Field Division. The man was introduced as Special Agent Clark, and he seemed to be her assistant, carrying a binder and readying a pen and paper to take notes.

The door was closed, and Captain Stover asked me to bring everyone up to speed on the case I was working, never mentioning that I had been ordered not to.

"Ladies and gentlemen," I started, "We've got a complicated and delicate situation involving a corrupt ATF agent, a complicit deputy sheriff, and a dead CHP officer."

35

I BRIEFED THEM ON THE BASICS OF THE DEATH INVESTIGATION AS IT STOOD thus far, and made it clear that at this point, CHP Officer Antonio Carrera Gomez's death had not been ruled a homicide. "However," I cautioned, "I'll be meeting with the coroner as soon as possible and updating him with what we've recently learned about what happened that morning in the Compton apartment. Whether or not it is ever determined that the officer died at the hands of another, I now know for a fact what I've believed all along. Gomez died at that time, at that place, because of the actions of others. Had none of this happened, he may have died during a traffic stop later that same day, but that's not what happened. He died that morning because he believed his child had been taken."

The room remained silent, everyone serious, attentive, captured by the events that had brought us together and eager to hear the rest. Beyond the office walls, I could hear the sounds of a police radio, dress shoes clicking across tiled floors, phones ringing and people talking. But in this small office that had been graciously relinquished by Industry station's captain, you could almost hear the heartbeats of six men and two women as they waited to learn why Gomez's had stopped.

As I collected my thoughts, I wondered what might be in store for me regardless of what became of Tammy Rae and her boy, Tony. I had defied the captain by continuing with the case, and I doubted that he would let me slide on it. Mr. and Ms. Gray Suits were all business—serious and intense—and I had no idea of their intentions. Were they here to see that justice was swift, or would they defend their agent to the end and deny all involvement and wrongdoing? That was not unlike the feds at all—any of them. There was a reason local cops handled federal agents with the same caution they'd use in handling rattlesnakes.

I pushed out of my chair and moved to the side of the captain's desk, positioning myself next to Floyd. We had been through a lot together over the years, and I was most comfortable and confident in that familiar territory. I drew a deep breath and allowed it to leak out slowly. Relaxed now, and having the undivided attention of everyone in the room except maybe Floyd, who was probably wondering about the undergarments of the lady fed, I continued. I told them about Officer Gomez's biker lifestyle, and then I talked about how the ATF came upon Gomez.

"According to Tony, the ATF had picked up Grandma Hernandez on a wiretap they had running for their gun trafficking case. She was telling this guy on the phone that she would be making a trip to Mexico in the near future. Though they were vague about what, if anything, Grandma might be doing for the traffickers while she was there, the feds rightly assumed she might be moving product for them—who better than an old lady and a kid to bring something across the border—so they began working her. They discovered that the kid's mother was in jail for dope charges and that the father of this same kid was Officer Gomez. They dug into that and found out he's a motorcycle enthusiast, and someone at the ATF got a big woody thinking they might have a dirty cop on the hook. That someone was none other than Tammy Rae Moore."

Then I covered the relationship between Tony and Tammy Rae in an effort to give credence to the information that Tony had provided. "Tony and Tammy Rae knew one another from when she was a deputy sheriff and Tony worked patrol at Century station. Unbeknownst to the lovely Mrs. Tony Brunetti, T&T hooked up at an off-training party nearly a decade ago, and they have used each other for occasional booty calls ever since. A few years after Tammy Rae left the sheriff's department for a career with the ATF, she became part of a gun trafficking task force.

During that time, she became involved with an undercover agent known to Tony only as "Bear."

I gazed at the suits for a moment but got nothing in return. Either they didn't know who this "Bear" was, or they were excellent interrogators and poker players.

"According to Tony, Tammy Rae and Bear learned of a biker bar in the valley that Officer Gomez frequented. Tammy Rae wanted to get in close with Gomez to see if he was dirty, apparently thinking that would be an even better way to establish herself as a top investigator, netting a dirty cop in the operation. According to Tony, Bear tried to talk her out of working Gomez, telling her it was a distraction from their trafficking case. But she was determined. So she made herself known to Gomez in this bar, and soon she asked Gomez where she could get some meth. Gomez didn't know. Later, she talked to him about stealing bikes and hinted that Gomez could get in on that if he was interested. Again, Gomez seemed dismissive of the idea. Finally, Tammy Rae decided that Gomez just needed to be brought in closer, that he was overly cautious from being a cop, so she took him to a motel that night and tried softening him up the old-fashioned way.

"Following the one-nighter, Tammy Rae continued to rendezvous with Gomez while also seeing Bear and having the occasional fling with Tony." I looked at the gray suits again. "This broad might be a health risk to the bureau." Neither smiled.

I continued. "Tammy was getting nowhere with Gomez but was convinced he was a dirty cop nonetheless. Bear didn't think so. Tony didn't see any evidence to support her ideas, but said she's persistent and hard to say no to. Probably even harder when you're cheating on your wife with her and you know she's crazy enough to destroy your marriage if she doesn't get her way. That's not just my opinion, Tony said as much half an hour ago down the hall.

"So nothing is panning out for Tammy Rae and she decides they need to push him. She comes up with the idea that they—she and Bear—would confront Gomez about him being a cop, tell him straight up that they knew he worked for the CHP, while maintaining their cover as outlaw bikers. So they did, and then they told him that they needed someone like him to ride along when they were moving product, and said he'd be well compensated for very little effort.

"Gomez said let him think about it. Tammy Rae decided that they needed to keep on him while also learning more about his lifestyle. That's when she came up with the idea to put Tony in Gomez's house. Her plan was to have Tony hit up Gomez about staying at his place, saying he had been kicked out of the house. By then, the four of them were all regular drinking buddies at the bar. Tony wasn't too keen on the idea, but Tammy Rae told him the brilliance of her idea, that it would be a perfect cover story so that Tony didn't have to go home most nights. He could stay with Gomez some nights, and with her on others, and the wife would be no wiser. Well, we all know how stupid men can be.

"After a couple of weeks, Tony came to really like Gomez, and he concluded that this chippie was indeed a passionate biker, but not an outlaw. His lifestyle might not have been embraced by some of his colleagues, but in Tony's opinion, the man wasn't doing anything illegal." I looked at Josie for a long moment, a concession that she had been right about that.

The fact there had been no questions or interruptions both surprised and pleased me. I had made eye contact sparingly with my captain and the two gray suiters. My gaze mostly stayed on Josie, Lieutenant Joe Black, and Rich Farris—each unquestionably in my corner. Floyd had propped his feet on the captain's desk, and I wasn't entirely sure he hadn't fallen asleep.

"When Tony broke it down to Tammy Rae, telling her they were on the wrong path, she lost her shit on him. She was convinced that Gomez was a dirty cop, and she was hellbent to prove it. Tony told me he hadn't realized how crazy she was until that day when he could see her spinning out of control. She had become obsessed with Gomez being dirty and she couldn't be reasoned with. Meanwhile, they had heard over the wire that Grandma and the kid had left for Mexico, so Tammy Rae decided they'd put a covert camera in the apartment while they were gone. Tony reluctantly went with her to do the installation. They went in the predawn hours of Monday morning, undetected.

"Now this is where you get to the *real* Crazy Tammy stuff. She had the idea to tell Gomez that his kid has been taken. She figured if he was dirty, he'd know that Grandma and the kid had gone across the border on a run for the cartel. If he wasn't dirty, the worst that would happen is he would freak out, report it to the sheriff, and an amber alert would be issued. She told Tony he would be the one to let the sheriff's department know that the pair weren't actually taken, that through a covert investigation they knew that the pair had taken a trip to Mexico. Of course none of them had any way to know that Gomez had a bad ticker and that the news of his child being taken would trigger a massive heart attack. And it was Tammy Rae who sent Gomez the message that morning that his daughter had been taken. I'm sure we'll be able to link that with phone records."

There still were no questions, so I continued to state my case, as weak as it might have been, the foundation a jumble of hearsay.

"So apparently, once they got wind of the death, they had to go back and get the camera out of the apartment, which we apparently missed during our crime scene investigation. Tony said you wouldn't have seen it unless you knew it was there, that it had been hidden in the folded hands of Our Lady of Guadalupe, a lovely painting that hung on a living room wall. Anyway, that was the Tuesday night trip that resulted in the infamous dog slaughter on Acacia Avenue."

"Detective, to be clear, all of this information has come from *your* deputy, right?" asked Ms. Gray Suit, her narrow face suppressing a smirk.

There it was, the feds beginning to circle the wagons. I eyeballed her for a long moment before answering, and I suspect my expression revealed the contempt I had for the question—for her, for most feds in general. I said, "Yes, ma'am, Tony has provided this information freely and voluntarily knowing he will likely lose his job as a deputy sheriff because of his part of it, maybe be prosecuted too. I have no doubts about the veracity of his statement."

She began, "But it seems so far he is staying on the fringes and putting everything—"

"How well do you know Tammy Rae Moore, Miss—" I couldn't recall her name, but it didn't matter. She answered before I could finish.

"I hardly know her at all, Detective. She is one of hundreds under my command."

"Well, I know her." I turned my head and indicated Floyd with a nod. "He knows her. We go back twenty years to when she was a young patrol deputy who staged a bullshit shooting in order to be a hero. She's a liar, she's scandalous, and she's a bad cop."

Captain Stover said, "Was she fired from our department?"

I shook my head. "No, we could never prove what she did. I'm not sure how or why she left our department. Maybe she went through all the male deputies and needed a fresh batch of dick."

Ms. Gray Suit pushed out of her chair and looked Stover in the eye. "I'm not going to sit here and listen to any more of this foul-mouthed detective with his speculation about my agent and the one-sided testimony of this Tony character."

Stover and the other gray suit stood up at the same time. Stover was saying, "I agree he's out of line with the last comment, but—"

"I'll be speaking with the sheriff by the end of the day," she said. Then she turned to me and pointed a bony finger at my face. "Stay away from my agent—stay away from all of my agents. Got it, Detective?"

I didn't answer. She turned to walk out of the office and as she reached for the doorknob, I said, "I go where the case takes me, lady, and I don't answer to the fucking feds, excuse my French."

She glared at me before turning away. The room stood silent as the door closed behind Ms. Gray Suit's boy, whoever and whatever he was. Her bitch, maybe. Stover and I both stood watching the two walking away, their heels clattering hastily against the tile floor. Stover took an exaggerated breath and forced it out with a heavy huff. He turned to face me. "Richard, I've honestly had it with you. Get out of my sight, stay away from that agent, and get your ass back to the office." He glanced at Josie and then looked at Joe Black. "I'll see the three of you in my office this afternoon, say two. I'll probably need a cocktail lunch after this bullshit."

JOSIE AND I WALKED THROUGH THE BACK DOOR INTO THE PARKING LOT and drifted toward a picnic table, where we huddled under the shade of its umbrella. Farris joined us. Floyd walked past us and flipped me the bird. I figured he was beat and heading home, having been out all night on the shooting case. Perhaps he had also decided if there was a time to distance himself from me, it was now. I said, "See ya later, asshole."

I turned to Farris, curious as to what he might say now. I nodded, an obvious question in the gesture.

He said, "Well, that could have gone better."

That was true, and I regretted for a moment being foulmouthed in front of the ladies. I looked at Josie, who had taken a seat on the bench. Her disposition would be a good barometer as to how far out of bounds I had been. But her head was down as she fished in a handbag on her lap, completely disengaged at the moment. I wondered if she was looking for her phone or maybe a lipstick. Maybe a gun.

Farris pulled his cell phone out of his pocket and looked at its display. I could see he had an incoming call, the phone obviously set to silent. He turned his back to us and took the call.

I said to Josie, "Okay, let's hear it."

She brought a case out of her purse and removed her sunglasses from it before dropping it back into the bag, which she set aside. She arranged the oversized sunglasses on her face and finally looked at me, her expression indifferent, revealing nothing. "It feels like we've been doing the work of Internal Affairs rather than solving murders, and now the captain's going to have our asses for it."

I was about to agree with her, to an extent, though silently reasoning that a man had still lost his life even if it hadn't been a murder, and that we needed to focus on that as we took down a dirty cop. I focused hard on these thoughts, but stopped short when Farris turned to face us, his face suddenly slack, the dark circles beneath his eyes now black as night, his gaze distant, unblinking.

"What is it, Rich?"

He looked past me for a moment and then looked at me through glossy eyes. "Lizzy's passed away."

JOSIE AND I HAD STOOD SILENTLY AND WATCHED FARRIS WALK TO HIS CAR and drive away without looking back. We remained silent for a long time after he was gone, each of us perched on yellow plastic bench seats attached to the circular table. A helicopter circled in the distance, its chopping blades a constant beat against the background of station sounds:

police radio traffic, chatter, cars coming and going, bursts of sirens as deputies tested their equipment before heading out to the streets. Then a sudden and unexpected burst of gunfire jolted me.

I looked toward the parking lot and saw that the mobile range was open for monthly qualifications. The converted semi-trailers were moved around the county on a schedule, parking at various stations for a week or more before moving on to the next. Inside were three lighted shooting lanes with dividers and electronic controls to send targets to the far end of the trailer and then to retrieve them. A small desk with a folding chair for the range master sat in the back.

"Have you qualified this month?" I asked, finally breaking the silence between us.

Josie shook her head. I could see she was fighting back emotion, not yet ready to speak. Obviously she was upset about Lizzy but likely mad at me too, or at least frustrated with the situation we were now in, thanks to me. I said, "That might be just the thing to do right now, sling some lead downrange. Let's go shoot."

36

WE HADN'T YET MADE IT TO THE SHOOTING TRAILER WHEN FLOYD CALLED me on my cell.

"Yeah, what's up?"

He said, "I've got this dude Bear pinned down to one of two locations: that task force they're on is working out of a trailer in La Cañada behind an industrial park up off of Angeles Crest. If he's not there, the bar they hang out at is on Foothill Boulevard in Sunland, a place called The Crystal Palace, probably named that for all the crystal meth that runs through the place. Where do you want to meet? I'm on my way to La Cañada now, taking the L.A. to Canada Freeway."

The sun sparkled against Josie's shiny black hair and reflected off her sunglasses as she regarded me, her head slightly cocked. Gunfire persisted, volleys of muffled pops just feet from where we stood near the trailer. A black and white sped by, radio traffic spilling from its open windows. I watched it bounce out of the driveway, its tires chirping against the pavement. Into the phone, I said, "How the hell did you get all that, and what the hell are you up to now?"

"I've got my sources, Dickie, you know that. Now do you want this Bear asshole or not?"

He had sat and listened to Ms. Gray Suit's admonition about staying away from her agents, and yet that was the first thing on his agenda once the meeting had abruptly ended. Like me, he knew we needed someone else to roll on Tammy Rae before the feds covered everything up, someone to corroborate what Tony had told us, and the most likely person would be Bear. We both had come to the same conclusion without discussing it, and Floyd had adhered to two rules: Grab the bull by the horns, and always have your partner's back. The latter was an unwritten rule but known by all and adhered to by most. I said, "We're on our way, slick. Text me your location when you land somewhere."

THE MODEST TRAILER IN LA CAÑADA HADN'T SHOWN MUCH PROMISE WITH just one sedan parked in front; it was not the type of vehicle an undercover agent pretending to be a hardcore biker would drive, so we figured it for a supervisor or analyst's vehicle. Floyd pulled his Taurus alongside Josie's Charger, driver to driver. I lowered the air conditioner to better hear him over the rumble of her car, then leaned toward her open window to better hear my old partner, a notorious low-talker. Josie leaned away, either to give me more room or to keep everything friendly and professional.

Floyd said, "Hey asshole, are you a married man now?"

I grinned. "Almost."

Josie glanced at me and then turned her attention back to Floyd. "Don't worry, I'll keep him honest. I'm 'bout ready to kick his ass anyway, so he'd better watch himself."

"She's on Emily's team."

"They're all on the same team, Dickie. Have you learned nothing from me?"

Josie, her face expressionless, flipped him her middle finger.

"Not nice, Josie," he said. "Well, Dickie, wanna check out the biker bar?"

Josie looked at him and then turned to me. "What's he grinning about?"

"The odds of him being able to get into a fight. They're always higher in bars, higher yet in biker bars. Floyd lives for this shit."

Josie shook her head slightly, appalled. "Great. Just what we need to seal our fate." She thumbed her phone to check the time. "And we've got two hours before we go in for our ass chewing—or worse. It would be our luck to go into it banged up with bloody knuckles."

Floyd said, "Are you two lovebirds going with me or not? I'd like to get to bed at some point this week. Let's go kick Bear's ass, and then I'm calling it a day."

"Lead the way, brother."

He tore away, and Josie pulled forward to flip a U. I said, "Follow that asshole."

It was a short drive from the ATF's secret trailer to the bar on Foothill Boulevard in Sunland. But it felt like a long drive in the silence, and I could feel the tension in the air. Josie wasn't happy with many of the decisions I'd made on this case, nor with some of the directions I had taken us. But she was with me nonetheless, having her partner's back. Always.

We had our windows up. I'd turned the air conditioning to high on my side, and Josie raised hers to seventy-two. The radio was off, leaving me alone in my thoughts. Had I screwed up in the briefing? I didn't think so. Something told me that the feds were looking for a way to walk out on me from early on. Law enforcement wasn't the type of environment where harsh language was avoided around women or inside executive meetings. Perhaps when women came into law enforcement in increasing numbers, that might have been the case. But now they were mostly treated as equals —or at least most men would say that they were, and some women would disagree. But as equals or nearly so, men and women in law enforcement now worked together in radio cars and were partnered together as detectives. Sometimes they had to fight for their lives together, and oftentimes they drank together in the same way male partners always had. At these gatherings and in the confines of radio cars and while standing between two enraged adults who were married but wanted to kill each other at the moment, men and women cops often swore like sailors. It was environmental.

So no, Ms. Gray Suit hadn't gotten her panties wadded up over mere language—if she even wore any. This was all about a power play, her effort to push Stover into a corner so that he might come down on us rather than allowing the case to unfold and the truth to be discovered. We were all-in, on our way to starting a riot in the Valley, no turning back.

I looked at Josie, watching her for a moment until she allowed her gaze to shift my direction from behind the shades. "When we get there, why don't you drop me off and head to the office. I can get Floyd to take me back."

She glanced over again, and this time looked at me for longer than she probably should have, given our current speed. "What's that all about?" By her tone she was clearly irked at the suggestion.

"This needs to fall on me. There's no reason for you to take a fall too."

"We'll be fine."

"Look, you're a sergeant. They can transfer you without cause. You piss off Stover, he'll have you working early mornings as a jailer in Lancaster. He can't transfer me out of the bureau without going through the whole disciplinary process. Same with Floyd, but I don't think he'll even pull him into the equation. As long as you bail now, I think it'll just be me that Stover comes after. And I've been down that road plenty of times before."

She shook her head. "I don't bail on my partners. Now shut up about it and tell me the plan."

I thought about that for a long moment. "I don't have a plan. I guess we go into the bar and either buy this big asshole a beer and see if he'll talk, or we'll start a fight and see if we can get out of there alive. That's why Floyd's here, for Plan B."

We were on the offramp now and Josie hadn't said anything else. Floyd took a left and then a right, and we were on Foothill Boulevard heading west. The community appeared to be mostly Hispanic, which is what I had expected, but there were pockets of leather-skinned whites with callused hands and blackened lungs and livers of questionable functionality. It was pickup trucks and Harleys, ball caps and cowboy hats, tough men and tougher women, exactly the type I expected to find at the bar.

Josie turned into the patchy asphalt lot, followed Floyd past the front and parked next to him along the side of the building. "Why's he parking over here?" she asked.

"Experience," I said. "If you're lucky enough to get out the front door, you want some distance between you and whoever's coming after you so that you have time to decide whether to take a stand or start your engines. You'll also want to leave your keys in the ignition."

"In this neighborhood?"

I smiled. "Odds are nobody's going to steal our cars here."

"What are the odds we're going to have to fight our way out?"

"It's a lot more likely than our cars being stolen."

37

After parking, the three of us assembled between the two cars. I assessed the vehicles in the parking lot and figured there were no more than six or seven patrons there this morning. They would be the hardcore drinkers, which meant probably not much of a challenge, physically, but likely an easily agitated bunch. But you never knew for sure. The bikers might come here early in the day only to assemble before venturing out to commit their crimes: trafficking guns, dope, and kids, among them.

Floyd said, "Okay, here's the plan. When Dickie drops his hat, it's on like Donkey Kong."

"Let's try to do this peaceably," Josie suggested.

I said, "Yes, let's."

"The problem is," Floyd said, "this Bear dude has to protect his cover. He's not going to be very accommodating to the cops in front of a bunch of other assholes."

I nodded, looking past Floyd at a pickup pulling into the lot, a woman with stringy black hair and a cigarette dangling from her lips behind the wheel. She stared at us while wheeling into a spot, killing the engine, and getting out. She continued glancing our way as she made her way to the front door, which was beyond our view. I said, "Well, we better get to it, the town crier just went inside."

Josie said, "I say we go inside, see if we can pick this guy out from Tony's description, and then I'll go talk to him while you two watch my back."

"He can't just talk to the cops. That's the problem we have here," Floyd reiterated. "The only way he saves face is if we take him against his will, and then it gets ugly. The only question is, how ugly? I say we go in there and yank him off his stool and drag him out, four-seventeen anyone who makes a move."

"I don't like the idea of drawing guns unless we have to," I said. "But I think you may be right about the rest."

"Nobody expects him to hit a woman cop," Josie argued. "I say you guys stay back and let me bring him out."

I shrugged.

Floyd said, "Whatever, dudes. Let's just go, see what happens." He turned on his heel and started for the front of the bar, and Josie and I followed.

It was dark and cool and musky inside like the back of a high desert cave, a black hole in a mountain of red clay. We paused inside the doorway, allowing our eyes to adjust as the heavy wood door closed behind us, stealing the only shaft of sunlight. I liked the song on the jukebox, a Five Finger Death Punch remake of Bad Company's flagship song, *Bad Company*. Death Punch did it better. It was just beginning, and I wondered if it had been played with a purpose. It would go well with an old-fashioned barroom brawl, something that happens in places like this on a regular basis.

As my eyes adjusted, I could see that everyone was looking at us. The bartender, a small bald man, glared through the rising smoke of a cigarette dangling from his mouth. Smoking in restaurants and bars had been outlawed decades before. Maybe I'd mention it to him before we left. The tramp from the pickup was sidled up at the far end of the bar next to a skinny, long-haired man who wore a scraggly beard and reminded me of Willie Nelson. She was lighting a smoke of her own while Willie was stabbing one out in an overflowing ashtray, his beady eyes looking straight at us. An older, heavyset woman with an orange crush of hair sat a few stools from Willie and his tramp. She had glanced over but now seemed to have lost interest and was back to doing something on her phone. Hopefully not texting for reinforcements. Two typical bikers in jeans, heavy black boots, and black t-shirts with Harley emblems leaned on their pool cues on the far side of a table, balls scattered across the threadbare green felt. A bottle of beer and an ashtray sat on the far edge of the table, smoke rising from a disregarded cigarette, everyone in the joint oblivious to the smoking ban.

There was one man who hadn't watched us. His back was to us as he leaned over the jukebox that sat at the far end of the bar, not far from the pool table. Basically, beyond the gauntlet, down the walkway with the bar on one side and the pool table on the other. I knew instinctively this was our man, without even seeing his face. He was big and hairy—like a bear —and he had known who we were before we'd ever seen him. I knew this by how he didn't turn to see who came in, as everyone else had. He already knew, and now he was avoiding eye contact to confirm my suspicion. He not only knew we were the cops, but he knew we were there for him, and he was probably considering how far to take things so that he didn't blow his cover, but also so that he didn't end up with a cracked head or leaky chest cavity.

Floyd started across the floor, heading straight toward him. As usual, we were on the same page. Josie followed Floyd's lead and I brought up the rear. The tramp spun around on her barstool as Floyd passed by. She was looking at his ass when Josie grabbed her by the collar and pulled her off her seat. The tramp landed facedown on the sticky floor and was looking up with a scowl, saying, "What the—" when Josie stuck her gun in Willie's face and said, "Freeze, asshole," while placing her foot on the tramp's back to keep her from coming back up. So much for keeping it peaceful.

I veered off toward the pool table as the two bikers started to come around it with their pool cues at the ready, just as Floyd was reaching the jukebox. Following Josie's lead, I yanked my pistol too, and waved the muzzle from the nose of one nasty biker to the other. The song lyrics repeating, *bad, bad company, till the day I die...* I said, "This is none of your business, boys—back off or die ugly."

The big man at the jukebox turned and said something I couldn't hear over the music as Floyd threw a kick that landed on the biker cop's leg. It was a Muay Thai kick, one that I had both used and experienced myself while sparring with Floyd. When properly applied, the kicker's shin striking his opponent's outer thigh, the shock to his sciatic nerve would drop him to the ground. Bear dropped to his knees, and Floyd grabbed his hand, stepped past him, and in an instant stood behind him with the man's wrist twisted into some unnatural position that had the man stooped forward, grunting in pain. Floyd maintained his control of him with one hand while pointing his pistol toward the bartender, saying, "Let's see those hands, pops." The bartender removed his outstretched hands from beneath the bar and slowly raised them. I pictured a sawed-off boomer within his reach, and was glad Floyd had seen the subtle move while dealing with Hairball.

I quickly scanned the room for other threats. Everyone in the place was covered and controlled. I looked at Floyd and he met my gaze. I indicated the front door with a nod, and he gave a slight nod to affirm my plan. He said, "Get up, dickhead," and for an instant I was hurt that he used this term of endearment—normally reserved for me—on the big fat biker cop. I dismissed the thought; we had work to do. Floyd had started him toward the door, controlling him by applying pain to the contorted wrist.

As Death Punch reached its crescendo, the lead singer shouting, *bad, bad, company, 'til the day I die… until the day I die… eye for an eye, tooth for a tooth, blood for blood, we've all gotta die, we've all gotta die…* and I thought, *not today, motherfuckers. Not today.*

Backing toward the door myself, essentially covering Floyd's back while alternately pointing my Glock at the two assholes by the pool table and the bartender with the itchy trigger finger. I came alongside Josie who hovered over the tramp while still pointing her gun at Willie, and said, "Come on." She stabbed the barrel of her pistol at Willie and said, "Stay put, asshole," and then stepped on the tramp with all her weight before joining me hip to hip. The two of us backed out slowly while covering down range, having Floyd's back as he led Bear toward the door.

The front door flew open, but I knew we hadn't reached it yet. I heard, "Freeze, fucker" and "Ahhhh" and *pop-pop, pop-pop-pop*, and a wave of smoke rolled over me and the smell of burned cordite replaced the smell of sour beer and cigarette smoke. I spun to my left and found Floyd crouched over Bear, the big man sprawled on the floor, a pool of crimson spreading rapidly from beneath him. Floyd's gun was trained on a man who sat slumped against the wall adjacent to the front door, his legs splayed straight out in front of him. It was another biker, this one with two holes in his leather vest and an expression of surprise on his face. Nobody ever expected it would happen to them; that was both the cruelty and magnificence of unexpected death.

Two more gunshots rang out next to me and the music stopped. I turned again, quickly scanning the crowd as smoke trailed from the barrel of Josie's gun. The two at the table were upright, the bartender stood with his hands high in the air, his eyes wide. Willie still sat on his stool, his arms shielding his head as if something was about to fall on him. The tramp was still on the ground, though now she sat up, her arms braced against the floor. Nobody was dead, nobody was even bleeding. I looked at Josie and frowned. She indicated the jukebox. "I didn't want to yell over it." Then she raised her voice. "Everyone on the floor, face down. Now!"

Floyd said, "Dickie, I think we're going to have to call this one in."

38

When LAPD rolls to assist their cops or anyone else's, it is a beautiful sight to behold. Within minutes the parking lot was full of black and whites, doors left open as blue suiters charged in and took control of the scene. Everyone still alive became involuntary witnesses. They were separated into the backs of several LAPD units, where they waited while a sergeant and I discussed transportation. He insisted they go to Foothill station since it was an LAPD handle, the bar being located in their jurisdiction. I argued it was an LASD handle; it was our investigation, and of course we were involved in a shooting there. He keyed his mic and radioed for a watch commander. I shook my head and said, "Sarge, I appreciate the roll, and we are grateful for your help. But when it's all said and done, this is still the County of Los Angeles, and we don't relinquish our shootings to anyone."

Josie stood a few feet away, speaking into her phone, saying, "...and LAPD is trying to take the handle on it...uh-huh...okay, got it. I'll let him know. Thanks." She disconnected and moved closer to me and the sergeant, while still looking at the screen of her phone. She looked up. "All of Team Three are rolling, along with the captain, a commander, the shooting review team, Internal Affairs, and the DA's office."

"And the ATF, I'm sure," I said.

She nodded. "Also, they're sending units from La Crescenta and Altadena stations to assist." Josie looked at the sergeant. "Sergeant, my lieutenant wanted me to express his thanks for your assistance, and he asked if you could spare a couple of units to have them stand by until our patrol cars show up."

The sergeant furrowed his brows, obviously unhappy with the situation but likely realizing he would be fighting a losing battle. He said, "I can spare two cars," and turned on his heel.

As he walked away, I said, "They never do well with the fact that the bear goes everywhere," a reference to the grizzly on our badges.

Josie shook her head. "I don't know why anyone would volunteer to handle this clusterfuck. If I could leave right now, I sure would."

I watched as the LAPD sergeant went from one officer to another, apparently giving orders or direction. A couple times he and an officer he was speaking to would both look over. I nodded and smiled but got no responses. I said, "Yeah, you wish you could leave, but you're stuck here with Floyd. You're a shooter."

She rolled her eyes. "I shot the jukebox, for Christ's sake. It's hardly worth mentioning."

"Still—"

"And it's not like they're going to let you go anywhere."

Normally, she would have been right. All of us would be required to stay and give our statements to the investigators. Especially after a cluster like this, where an undercover was killed by one of his biker friends, who in turn did not survive Floyd's return fire and was not available to give his side of the story. I wondered what his story might be. He either just happened to come in gunning for Bear, or the redhead on her phone had sent a text to him. I would bet on the text, since he clearly came in ready for a fight. But why?

Josie was pecking away at her phone with both thumbs. I watched her until she finished and looked up, likely feeling my eyes on her. I said, "Why do you suppose that dude came in shooting?"

She shrugged while tucking her phone into a pocket. "Because he's an asshole?"

"Was."

"One thing about old Bear, he made a good shield," Floyd said, walking up behind us. "If nothing else."

Josie and I each made a quarter turn to face him. I said, "Do you think that dude was shooting at you?"

"Absolutely. How the hell do you think Bear ended up catching his bullets?"

I waited, still watching, until Floyd said, "Holy shit, you think Bear was the target."

Josie said, "Wow."

A moment ticked by while I sorted my thoughts. "I don't know, but it's something to consider. A better question is why would he come in gunning for the cops? Everyone there knew we were the cops before we stepped inside. Whoever sent that shooter a message—that reminds me, we need to see what's on Big Red's phone."

"The old broad?" Floyd asked.

I nodded. "She was texting as we walked in. We need to see if she's the one who alerted dipshit, and if so, find out exactly what she said to him."

"You don't want to wait for Team Three?" Josie asked. "I mean, they have the handle on this. I'm not sure how happy Hoss is going to be with us going through the evidence before they get here."

Hoss was a new lieutenant at the bureau, a bear of a man himself, but affable and easy to get along with as long as you were on the right side of him. He had worked Century when Floyd and I were still there, and I once saw him pick up a gangster and throw him over the hood of a car—and the gangster was a healthy young man, not a little pee-wee. Floyd, who had been partnered with the big man and considered him a good friend, had given him the moniker due to his similarities in size and demeanor to Hoss Cartwright from the old western television show, *Bonanza*.

Floyd said, "I'll deal with Hoss."

"Okay, good. Let's do it then."

The three of us marched over to the LAPD unit where the redhead sat handcuffed in the backseat, a scowl on her face, black streaks of mascara down both cheeks. Before opening the door, I said to the officer nearest the car, "Has she been searched?"

The officer was a young female who appeared to be new with her crisp uniform, a fresh-out-of-the-academy shine on her leather gear, and the blank stare of a youngster looking at a parent. She said, "I think so. Let me ask my training officer." The rookie started toward the bar, where I assumed her partner might be, but then stopped, unsure if she could abandon her post. She had obviously been told to stay at the car and keep an eye on the witness that sat in her back seat.

"That's okay," I said, "We'll just have a quick look."

The officer didn't respond. She probably felt a bit overwhelmed and certainly overpowered by the three of us. Floyd went to her and introduced himself. He was never shy about meeting attractive women, but this move had a tactical element to it and would serve a purpose that reached beyond Floyd's ego. While she was distracted by Floyd, Josie and I brought Red out of the car. Josie searched her as I asked a few direct questions. "Do you know that asshole that came into the bar shooting?" No response. "Did you text him and tell him to come to the bar?" She looked away. "Where's your phone?" No answer.

Josie said, "She's clean, no phone."

I grabbed her by the arm and squeezed. "If you texted that asshole and told him to come, you're going to face murder charges unless you start talking."

Red glared at me for a long moment, and then dropped her head. She wasn't going to say a single thing to us—maybe not to anyone. Looking across the lot toward the bar, I said, "Put her back."

Josie shoved Red back into the car while I looked at the front seat and on the dash to see if her property had been taken from her already. There was nothing there that appeared to be hers. Floyd was doing a great job of distracting the young officer, now telling her that yeah, he was one of the shooters, but it wasn't his first time and it wasn't a big deal. I worried we wouldn't be able to get him back now if we needed him.

Across the parking lot, the LAPD sergeant emerged from the bar. He looked in our direction and started toward us. I turned my head slightly and whispered to Josie, "Okay, your turn to run a diversion. I'll be back in a few."

I turned and started in the opposite direction, toward the side of the bar where our cars were parked. As I did, I looked back and, for the sergeant's benefit, said to Josie, "I'll check our car." It would be up to Josie to come up with the rest of that cover story should the sergeant inquire. I didn't look back as I heard her greet the sergeant and engage him in conversation.

When I rounded the corner, out of the view of all of those in front of the bar—my partners and the LAPD sergeant among them—I hastened my step as I passed Floyd's and Josie's cars, went around another corner and ducked into the back door of the bar. I knew there would be one, and as I had hoped, it was unlocked. Things were looking up.

An LAPD officer was posted just inside the front door, preserving the scene. He must have heard me come in, because he turned and called out, "Sir, you can't come—"

I flashed my badge. "Sheriff's Homicide, partner," I said authoritatively. My old friend Johnny Braxton used to say the sheriff's badge was a brass pass, something that could be used in any situation: speeding, no problem. *"It's okay, sheriff's department."* Drunk driving. *"Sorry, officer, but..."* and just flash the badge. He once opined that you could be caught with the mayor's daughter, and just whip out the brass pass. *"Sheriff's department, everything's okay here."* The LAPD officer lifted his chin and furrowed his brow, questioning... It dawned on me then that this was likely the training officer of the lady cop outside, and certainly no rookie who could be buffaloed or run over. I said, "Just have to check something really quick, sir." With Johnny's theory fresh on the mind, I added. "The sheriff himself asked me to confirm something for him." The LAPD officer nodded, satisfied with the excuse for a blatant breach in crime scene integrity.

It was the luck of the Irish, finally. I had struck gold, and the irony that it happened inside a bar didn't escape me. A cell phone was on the ground near where the redhead had sat and where she ended up prone on the floor after the shooting, having followed Josie's orders. I saw the officer had turned his back, so I grabbed it and headed out. "Thanks, officer," I called out over my shoulder while hurrying toward the back door.

The sergeant was gone. Floyd was still entertaining the young officer, taking this assignment more seriously than usual. Josie stood nearby. As I drew nearer, I said, "Get her out again."

Josie took Red out of the back seat and stood her up. I glanced around to make sure the sergeant wasn't watching, but I couldn't tell where he had gone. I pulled the phone out of my pocket and held it up for Red to see. At first she was puzzled as she stared at the screen, but then the phone unlocked, and she said, "You motherfucker."

I smiled at Red and said to Josie, "Put her back."

Josie shoved the woman into the black and white. Then she and I hunched over the phone and began looking through the text messages. The last one she had sent had been to someone stored in her contacts as "*La Jefa.*" The message was a direct one: *Those sheriffs are here.*

I took a picture of the message with my phone, then thumbed the Info icon to find out more about the contact. There was nothing other than a phone number, one with a Los Angeles area code. There were no other text messages of importance, so I clicked over to check her call log. I had no idea if any of the numbers there had any relevance, so I snapped a picture of that screen as well for future reference. I quickly thumbed around the home pages and looked for anything else of interest but found nothing that stood out. The text message was enough, and it confirmed what I believed, that Bear's killer had been summoned by the redhead. Now what I needed to know was if he had come to kill Bear, or if that was an accident. And who sent him. Who was this "*La Jefa,*" an obvious code name for a woman boss.

Josie waited with Floyd as I went through the back door again, gave the "Sheriff's Homicide" greeting and magic phrase to the LAPD officer at the front. After he turned his head, I returned the phone to its original location. "See ya, partner," I called out and started toward the back door. On my way out, I glanced at the jukebox and grinned at the thought of Josie blasting it to quiet the room. It sat silent now, darkened, dead as the two bikers up front, an innocent bystander and random victim of violence. But what about Bear, I wondered… innocent? Random? Or was it an assassination? And if so, why? I knew who would have the answers: *La Jefa.*

I hurried back to the parking lot and wrangled Floyd away from his new friend and signaled Josie that we needed to move away. We huddled near the car. "Okay, here's the deal." I looked at Floyd and said, "Josie shot the jukebox—"

"Last night," Floyd sang, finishing the line of a country western song about Bubba shooting a jukebox.

"—so she's not really a shooter, per se. She and I are going to split. Tell Hoss we had to handle an urgent matter, something related to our case. We'll be at the bureau later to give our statements."

Josie said, "He's not going to like that, and the captain will lose his shit."

Floyd shook his head. "Don't worry about Hoss, I'll handle him. Now your captain, that's another matter."

A moment of silence ensued, each of us considering the mess we were in. I indicated Floyd and said, "Are you okay, partner?"

He looked back at me through his shades. "Me? Well, yeah, Dickie, why wouldn't I be? Money for nothing and chicks for free."

"Well, you just killed a man..."

"I just killed a biker asshole. One mustn't mourn forever, Dickie. Now go on, you and Jukebox Bubba here go figure out why that asshole came a gunnin'."

I chuckled. Josie gave him a shove. Moments later we were burning rubber on Foothill Boulevard and not looking back at the disaster we were leaving behind us. I didn't want to think about that right now, since I knew that the day's events could spell the end of my career at Homicide.

3 9

"WHY ARE WE GOING BACK TO INDUSTRY?" JOSIE ASKED. SHE HAD HER left foot propped on her seat as she drove her hotrod Charger twenty-five over the speed limit but remained cool and in control, no big deal. We had just survived a potential barroom brawl and a shooting, and now we were sailing along knowing our jobs were in jeopardy as we left a chaotic scene against protocol.

"I want to take another swing at Tony. If that SOB wasn't so big, it'd be literal. I have a feeling he might know more than what he told us."

"Internal Criminals was with him when we left. You think they're going to be done?"

I thought about it for a moment. I didn't know, that was the answer. I didn't even know what they would do with him when they finished interviewing him. Would he be free to go? They didn't have a reason to arrest him—not yet. Would he be asked to wait at the station, left in the interview room for another round of interrogations? I was about to admit I didn't know, and that maybe I was swinging blindly because I was frustrated and didn't know what else to do, and then it hit me like a brick against my forehead. It might be a longshot, but... "I want to check the contacts in his phone for this *La Jefa*."

Josie glanced over at me but didn't respond.

I said, "Check it by name—*La Jefa*—and number by number. Ideally, that number's in his phone too, but under a different name. Like maybe 'Tammy Rae's Burner.'"

"Oh shit, do you think?"

"I don't know, but we'll find out. If that doesn't work, I'll get ahold of Ty and see if he can get us a subscriber. I guess I could get him working on it now anyway, in case we don't come up with anything. But I'd bet it's a burner, regardless of who it belongs to."

"Give him a call," Josie said, now checking her rearview mirror as she put a little more into the throttle.

By the time we reached Industry station, Tony was gone. He had left without restriction, so it was anyone's guess where he had gone. But the black El Camino would be easy enough to spot, and I had another idea.

The way I saw it, this was my last hoorah. There was almost no way my career would survive this because of all of the policies I had broken and the rogue ways I had pursued the Officer Gomez investigation. It seemed I was being self-destructive, and I silently questioned the reason for it. Perhaps I was burned out, done, but unwilling to admit it. You never knew when you would hit the wall, but almost all of us would. The burnout rate left most of the A-type hard-chargers limping off the field as if they had spent their entire lives in a vicious battle. Some of us had. Not necessarily in the physical sense, but it wasn't ever the physical ailments that steered you into the wall. It was the psychological toll of the job that did you in, that drove you to the brink of self-destruction, that caused many to crawl into their bottles and others to cram the barrels of their guns into their mouths. I had no suicidal intentions, yet here I was living as if my days were numbered, and unable to stop myself.

All of these thoughts rattled around in my head while I also began thinking of my future with Emily. Josie and I had come out of the station and sat at the picnic table outside, just as we had earlier today, though it seemed like a long time had passed, as we both had lost an entire night's sleep. I punched in the number to Personnel, and while I waited for the ringing phone at headquarters to be picked up, I stared at Josie and silently questioned why I hadn't yet told her everything.

The phone was answered, and I used the authoritative Dickie voice again: "Yessir, Captain Stover, Homicide, I need a home address for a deputy from Narco. It's an emergency."

I waited while the sergeant at Headquarters made some verifications, probably just checking the roster to see if there was a Captain Stover and where he was assigned. He came back and said, "Are you ready, sir?" I scribbled the address in my notebook, anxious to get off the phone before any questions were asked. When I disconnected, I closed my notebook and slapped it down on the table. Josie waited patiently, likely anticipating that I now planned a personal visit to Tony's house. Finally, she said, "Well?"

I said, "Emily's pregnant."

"Jesus, Richard, you tell me this now? With everything we've got going on? How long have you known?"

"A while."

"Well, congratulations, I guess. Are you guys okay with this?"

I nodded. "It took us a while but yeah, we're good. We're more than good. We're going to have a family." And suddenly it seemed crystal clear to me why I was throwing caution to the wind. I was done with it, all of it. I wanted to do something else now. I had stood over enough dead people to last me several lifetimes, yet I had only one to live. This was, in fact, my last hoorah. Maybe I knew subconsciously it would be easier if the choice to leave Homicide was made for me, and that was why I had handled this case with such reckless disregard for protocol, policy, and even the law.

Josie said, "You got the address?"

I shook my head. "He wouldn't give it to me."

She cocked her head. "Really?" she said, her tone indicating disbelief. "What did you write in your notebook?"

"He gave me a name and email address where I could send my request."

Josie reached for my notebook, but I snatched it away. "Why don't you head back to the office so you can give your statement, then go home and get some sleep. It's been a long day."

She stood up and stepped closer to me, looking down at me now with her hand held out. Through her clenched jaw, she said, "Give. Me. Your. Notebook."

"Why?"

"Because you're full of shit. You have Tony's address and you don't want me to go with you. And frankly, I'm offended, and I'm also pissed. Give me the fucking notebook."

"Josie—"

She reached for it and I pulled it away again. She climbed over me, trying to grab it, smothering me with her breasts. I started to think this was the most intimate moment we had shared until she slammed her knee into my ribcage. I dropped the notebook and grabbed my side while trying to catch my breath. Josie quickly moved a safe distance from me and flipped through the pages of notes. She tore a page out and tossed my notebook onto the table, then turned on her heel and started away.

I stood up, still holding my side. It felt like she broke a rib, or at least bruised one. "Josie, wait…"

She flipped me the bird and quickened her pace. I tagged along behind her but I was in pain, moving slowly. "Come on, partner… Josie… Hey, look, I was only trying to protect you—"

She stopped in her tracks and spun around, then came at me. I flinched like a battered woman on Saturday night after the Pabst had run out. But she didn't hit me again. She put her finger in my face and said, "Quit treating me like your girlfriend and pretend I'm Floyd. You wouldn't try to protect him by ditching him when there was work to do."

"It's not about that," I tried. "I'm convinced this is going to get me kicked out of the bureau or fired, depending on how ugly this gets from here. I'm only trying to protect you."

She took another step toward me and we stood nose to nose, inches apart, our gazes locked in a stare down. There was an intensity in her eyes I hadn't seen before, and I wasn't sure what she was going to do next. She had already thrown a knee into my rib cage, and I didn't doubt she would do it again. Only this time maybe she had in mind to punch me in the face or slap me across it. Knee me in the nuts. Break my nose with a headbutt. Anything was possible.

But she did none of those things. Instead, Josie grabbed the back of my neck and kissed me on the lips. Or had I imagined that in some twisted fantasy. No, it actually happened, I realized. And now she was looking me in the eyes again when she said, "Dickie, you drive me insane at times. I love you, I honestly do—but not like that. Not like Emily loves you. I don't know why I did that. But listen, you're the best partner I've ever had, so stop pissing me off. Don't pamper me, and let's go kick Big Tony's ass and find out what the real deal is. Got it?"

Josie turned and started for her car again. I stood still for a moment, shocked. And I realized Floyd had been right all along; they really were all crazy.

"HOLD ON."

Josie stopped the car just before pulling out of Industry station. I thumbed through my notes for Tony's cell phone number while she watched. She glanced in her rearview mirror, said, "Shit," and then pulled forward and to the side, clearing the path for a radio car that was coming out in a hurry.

I punched in the number and hit send. "I never knew Industry could be so busy."

"What are you doing?" she asked.

"Calling him. My bet is he didn't go home."

Josie started to say something, but I stopped her by raising my hand as Tony answered the phone. I asked how he was doing, and he said okay, considering. I told him our day had gotten really bad, and we needed to talk, now. He said, "I don't know, I'm—"

"We're at Industry. Pick a spot or we can come by your house."

He hesitated, so I upped the ante. "That might not be the best thing because part of the conversation we need to have might include Tammy Rae."

"Man, I told you guys everything—"

"Tony, stop being a pussy." Big guys always hated it when I said that

267

to them, but it hadn't failed me yet, nor had it cost me a beating so far. "Give us a place to meet you or I'm going to your house."

"Who's 'us'?"

"Just me and Josie."

He sighed, paused a beat, and said, "Okay, man, just meet me across the street from the station in the helipad parking lot. I'm about ten out."

I pointed across the street for Josie's benefit and said, "Helipad parking lot. Sounds good, Tony. Thanks."

Josie pulled across the street and started to pull into a spot. I said, "How 'bout over there, in the shade." She jerked the wheel and followed my request with a huff.

She backed us into a spot and left the car running. I said, "He's ten minutes out." Josie reached over and turned on the radio. Now there was tension between us. I wanted to say, Hey, you're the one who locked your soup coolers on me, lighten up. Then I considered joking with her that I was thinking about filing a sexual harassment complaint. Or maybe I'd ask for another kiss, since we'd now crossed that line. Instead, I said, "Hey partner, thanks for setting me straight back there."

She continued to stare through the windshield while apparently collecting her thoughts. After a long moment, she said, "If our careers survive this, I think we need to split up after the dust settles."

It was the last thing I expected her to say. Josie and I worked well together and I loved having her as my partner. I trusted her and knew I could count on her in any situation. She was a damn good cop, and the last thing I wanted to do was switch partners, if we survived this. But the truth of it was, we weren't likely to come out of this unscathed. Not me, anyway. I would insist on taking the brunt of any punishment, and the captain would be happy to oblige. So it was probably a moot point, but I had to say it anyway. "I don't want to split up, Josie. There's no one else I want to work with."

"You didn't want to work with me at first either."

"I didn't know you."

"Maybe you and Floyd could partner back up."

"The captain would never allow that to happen."

"Well, I don't know what to tell you. I think it would be best, since you're getting married."

I frowned. "Why? What's that got to do with anything? Look, I didn't mistake what happened back there for anything other than what it was. Okay?"

She nodded toward the driveway, and I turned to see the black El Camino turning into the lot. I looked back at her and said, "Seriously."

Josie turned the car off and we both popped our doors open. As I started to get out, Josie said, "But I'm not sure what it actually meant. That's the problem."

We looked at each other across the car's interior, each of us with one foot on the ground. But I didn't know what to say. The things that went through my mind were best left unsaid, especially since there *was* an Emily, and since she and I were about to tie the knot and start a family. So I said nothing until after we had both stepped out of the car, closed our doors, and started toward the front of the car where we would wait for Tony to join us. I smiled and said, "You don't have to worry about all that other stuff, partner; you're way out of my league when it comes to broads."

Josie smiled ever so slightly, then turned to Tony as he tromped up to us in his biker boots and jeans. She stepped in front of him and held out her hand. "Let's see your phone, big guy."

"HOW ARE WE GOING TO DO THIS?"

She had her foot propped on the seat again while sailing along the La Canada Freeway at about eighty-five, the Charger moving like a cat across the asphalt jungle that was the southland. It seemed we spent three-quarters of our careers looking through windshields, burning county gas and wearing out county cars. I said, "The same way we'd do it if she was a postal worker or a stripper or a welfare mom—we're going to walk up and spin her around and put her in cuffs. We can flip for who gets to hook her up."

Josie looked over and grinned. "Just like that, huh? Walk into the crime scene full of executives from our department and hers, and just throw the hooks on her like she was a crackhead and not a federal agent."

"Yep. She deserves no better."

"And just how exactly will that help our careers survive this?"

I was leaned back in my seat with one leg crossed and my arm stretched across the center of the car, my hand on her headrest. I had never been so at ease with anything in my life, even though I knew the outcome would be disastrous. I said, "It won't. Which actually settles the argument of who gets to hook her up. I'll do the honors. This whole thing needs to fall on me."

"No, we're partners. We stand together and fall together."

I had no intention of allowing that to happen, and she likely knew it. "Okay, Josie." I glanced at my watch. "I just pray she's there."

"She'll be there. Tony said she was on her way out there just before he met us. That's how he knew it was all coming apart. She had told him about Bear getting killed right before you called him."

Josie was right, just reiterating what I already knew. But I had no Plan B, so if she wasn't at the crime scene, I wouldn't know where to look for her or how to proceed from there. Not to mention, we were walking back into a lion's den. As soon as Stover spotted us back at the scene, he'd come steaming over yelling about what the hell we had been thinking, and it would be a huge mess. The one thing that would silence him would be us hooking up an ATF agent right in front of everybody. He'd be so stunned, he wouldn't know what to do or say while he tried to figure out if we had finally—actually—lost our minds, as he had always figured we would. Or at least that I would. Or had.

WHEN WE PULLED UP AT THE BAR IN SUNLAND THERE WERE FEWER LAPD cars, but the lot was now full of sheriff's radio cars and unmarked sedans, detectives and executives everywhere. There were uniforms and suits on both sides of the yellow tape that now encompassed half the parking lot and the entire front of the bar. Josie crossed the opposite lanes of traffic and pulled up at the curb to park facing the wrong way.

We both stared across the lot at a small gathering of suits that included Captain Stover, our lieutenant, and a couple of ATF agents, Tammy Rae among them. "There she is," Josie said.

I popped my door open and drew in a breath. "And here we go, partner."

We marched across the lot together and I imagined it might have looked to others like we were headed to a fight. Neither of us were taking in the sights; we were both laser-focused on our target, and it likely showed. The group seemed to stop whatever they were doing, and opened up, prepared for our arrival—knowing we were coming right at them with a purpose. It felt like an old-fashioned showdown, but I didn't expect there would be much of a confrontation. A dose of shock and awe, but no fight, no chase, no gunplay. Hopefully.

Tammy Rae watched our approach and glanced at her boss who stood just a few feet from her. It was Ms. Gray Suit from the meeting, the Assistant Special Agent in Charge, or ASAC Donner as she had been introduced. Tammy Rae's eyes flicked back to us, but her mouth remained uncharacteristically shut as we drew nearer, her expression a mask of apprehension. When we were within a few feet of the group, I said, "Hello, Tammy Rae Moore." She didn't return my greeting, just continued to stare. Josie walked right past her, bumping her with a shoulder as she did. I continued past her myself, diverting my eyes toward my captain for just an instant, and nodding as a way of greeting him too. Josie had stopped inches from the nose of Ms. Gray Suit, and I circled around behind her. Josie said, "You're under arrest for murder, *La Jefa*."

WHEN THE SMOKE SETTLED IN THE PARKING LOT OF THE SUNLAND biker bar, Ms. Gray Suit was wearing my handcuffs. Mr. Gray Suit, who had seemingly appeared from nowhere and had come to her defense, and who had mistakenly put his hands on me in the process, wore Josie's handcuffs and an impression of her ring on his left temple. Stover looked like he needed a drink, so I led him through the back door of the bar, bellied up to the far end of it, and poured him one while he watched, skeptically. I said, "You looked like you could use a snort," and then I poured one for myself. On the other side of the room, Forensic Identification Specialists worked around the two corpses near the front door, marking, photographing, and collecting evidence, while homicide investigators from Team Three documented the scene. Stover said, "This is very unusual."

I wasn't sure if he meant that the two of us sharing a drink in the early afternoon at a crime scene was unusual, or if he meant that my having arrested two high-ranking federal agents was unusual. Maybe he was referring to the fact that two dead bikers—one of whom was a federal agent himself—lay on the floor a few feet from where we drank. For all I knew, he was referring to the fact I put ice in his Jameson. I waited for more.

He said, "It's an awful thin case if all you have is the text from the woman in the bar to the ASAC's burner phone, alerting her that you guys had arrived. I hope you have more than that and Tony's statement."

"Her burner will show that after she got the text from Big Red, she sent a text to that dead biker over there on the floor, telling him to take care of it. Tony said she never trusted Bear and she panicked when she found out we were closing in on him. She ordered his murder, and we're going to be able to prove it."

Stover stared at his drink. "Ordered her own agent killed."

"Sounds insane, I know. But you have to remember, she 's in charge. She apparently oversaw everything that happened and figured if someone talked—someone like Bear—that she'd be on her way to prison."

Stover took a sip, his gaze set on the activity at the other end of the bar. "Well, I hope she is. I didn't like her from the minute we met." He looked at me again. "Just how confident are you in Tony's statement? How self-serving do you think it is?"

I held his gaze for a long moment as I considered the question. "Tony's not a dirty cop, he's a dumb one. Had he never gone to be with Skanky Rae, he'd still be putting good cases together the old-fashioned way, working informants and gathering solid evidence. I'm not saying he didn't fuck up, because clearly he did. I just don't think he needs to be prosecuted, and I'm pretty sure he'll testify against the others to keep from doing time. He knows he's finished as a cop."

Stover took another drink and seemed to be considering all of it. "And the Gomez case? Do you think they'll call it a homicide? That's still pretty weak, isn't it?"

I nodded, grabbed a dish towel and wiped around our drinks. "I'm not sure they'll ever call it a homicide, even with all of this new information. I mean, he died of a heart attack when he ran into that apartment searching for his kid. It's really that simple. If someone had been in there, and there had been some kind of altercation…"

"Which is what I tried telling you all along, and why I told you to put it down. I'm not always a prick just for fun."

"I hear ya, skipper. But on the other hand, if I hadn't pursued it, those ATF agents would still be committing crimes in the name of justice."

"Yeah, and the agent over there on the floor would still be alive."

I thought about it a moment. He was right, but was that on me? No, I didn't think it was. It was on two people, Donner the ASAC and the biker that Floyd had ventilated by the door. But there was no use arguing the point. He was right, Bear would be alive had I put the case down in the beginning. But that's not what bulldogs do.

I said, "We might also want to turn Tammy Rae. The only thing she's guilty of is breaking in to install a camera in the apartment, and being an idiot. And Tammy Rae is all about Tammy Rae, so she'll cut a deal and give us all the dirt on the rest of them."

Stover finished his drink and rattled the ice around in the tumbler. "I wish you didn't have to use her testimony against the others. She should go down with them."

I took another sip and pondered it briefly. "You know, some people just naturally avoid the karma they deserve, and she's one of those people. I'd like to think she'll have hers coming someday, in some way. The bottom line is, right now we need her, and we have to treat her with kid gloves. She puts it all together for us, all of it. So she gets a break, but she has hers coming. Someday."

He pushed his glass toward me, and I tipped the bottle over it again, and hit mine while I was at it. We drank in silence until Stover finished his drink and slid his glass toward the business side of the bar. He stood up from his stool and said, "The video of your partner spitting in the game warden's face doesn't exist."

"What!" I was stunned.

"Before Lopes ever had a chance to inquire about it, the bailiff made it disappear."

How would he know all of this, and did I want to know? It turned out I had to know. "How do you know this? I didn't even know that she did that."

"She didn't tell you?"

I shook my head.

"I don't blame her, with what that asshole put her through. The bailiff is my wife's nephew, and he called to tell me what he had done. He was afraid Lopes would figure it out, and he began regretting what he had done. The kid means well enough. I told him it never happened, and to take it to the grave or he'd go down for tampering with evidence."

I downed the rest of my drink and set my empty glass next to his. "Does she know?"

He shook his head. "There's no reason for her to know. The fewer who do, the better. Lopes doesn't know either. Just me and you and my dumb nephew."

"I can live with that. He didn't take the emergency exit because of anything she did or said. He knew what would happen to him in prison."

Stover nodded and started toward the back door, then stopped. "You know I'm going to have to hand down some discipline on this mess we have here. You were way out of line on this, disobeying orders, taking—"

"Yeah, I know, boss. No problem. I'll add some vacation days to the suspension and make it a honeymoon.

"You're getting married?"

I nodded. "Also having a baby."

"No shit, huh?"

"No shit."

We pushed through the back door and walked into the bright sunlight. I stopped and began fishing in my jacket for my sunglasses. Stover turned and faced me again while shielding his eyes from the sun. "Richard, while you're on that suspension—vacation, honeymoon, whatever you want to call it—I want you to think about taking a spot in Unsolveds. I don't think I'll be able to keep you on the floor after all of this, so it's that or Missing Persons and you're too good a detective to be stuck back there."

I didn't think it could have worked out any better, all things considered, so I just clapped him on the shoulder and said, "I get it, boss. I get it."

4 1

EMILY AND I WAITED BENEATH A FITTINGLY GRAY SKY AFTER THE SERVICES for Elizabeth "Lizzy" Marchesano concluded and mourners headed back to their cars, a hundred or more lining the narrow, winding roads of Forest Lawn in Glendale. Soon others from the bureau began joining us and before long there were twenty or more long-faced bulldogs gathered together in the shade of a giant eucalyptus. There were other clusters spread about and I assumed they were self-segregating by departments, units of assignments, and civilian friends and loved ones.

Rich Farris remained graveside along with Lizzy's husband, an LAPD Metro cop, and a few other family members. They became a topic among our gathering.

"He's really taking it hard," Floyd said.

Josie nodded, her eyes still glassy and red. "He loved her—as a partner." She glanced at me when she said it, and Emily gently squeezed my hand.

Mongo nodded and said, "Dude works Metro, badass."

I said, "I can't imagine losing your wife."

Davey Lopes said, "She was too goddamn young."

Joe Black, clutching a Bible, said, "She's in a better place now."

We remained, but the conversation had stopped. There were sounds of

267

car doors closing, engines starting, and muted voices all around. Life went on for the rest of us, though for how long, none of us knew. Lopes said he was going out for a drink. Floyd said, "I'm with you, Lopes." Several others joined in, and the conversation turned to where they should go, Chinatown or somewhere close, something here in Glendale or maybe Burbank. Lieutenant Black said he would see everyone Monday, and turned away with his head hung low.

I had continued watching Farris, but when his shoulders began shuddering, I could no longer watch. I announced that we were going to take off and head home. Nobody protested, not even Floyd, who would normally have insisted I have just one or two cocktails with my partners and friends. It was the beginning of a whole new me, and even he knew it. Emily and I turned and walked away, together, hand in hand. She was now my partner.

IT WAS COOLER WHEN I RETURNED TO WORK A MARRIED MAN AND expectant father. It had been nearly six weeks since the Sunland barroom shooting, and I used the time to think about the captain's ultimatum, Unsolveds or Missing Persons. I had also considered another job somewhere else in the department, maybe Arson/Explosives or even returning to Metro. But Emily and I had discussed it at length, and I had mulled it over even more, and Unsolveds would probably be the best fit for me. Monday through Friday, nine to five, still working murders but not being called out at night. It was just the job for a recovering homicide detective turned family man.

I made it across the squad room with few distractions, greeting some of my closer friends but keeping my eye on the ball, so to speak. I went straight to Stover and told him my decision.

"Good, Richard, I'm glad you're okay with it. I was right about you not being able to stay on the floor. You have no idea how many meetings I've attended because of that ATF cluster. The chief had the final word, and he agreed you could stay in the division and at the bureau but needed to come off the floor. At least until this blows over and everyone forgets about it."

The idea that someday I might be able to go back out on the floor and be assigned to a team hadn't even occurred to me. It was something I would think about over time, though not likely discuss with Emily anytime too soon. I said, "Thanks, skipper. I appreciate it."

He pointed in the direction of Unsolveds. "Better go claim a desk, that unit's just about filled up now."

I nodded, feigned a salute, and went straight to my new office. I could clean out my old desk and move in after I figured out where I was sitting and with whom I might be partnered. Lopes was on my mind. The detectives in Unsolveds didn't necessarily have assigned partners, but certain detectives would tend to partner up unofficially nonetheless. I couldn't imagine working with anyone better than Lopes back there, and it was what I planned to do.

I stepped into the Unsolved Homicides office and saw two empty desks, side by side, ready for two newly assigned investigators. One would be mine, and I wondered who would get the other. Then I realized one of the two had already been claimed. A name plate sat dead center atop the otherwise bare workspace. I turned the plate around to see who it belonged to. *Sergeant Josefina Sanchez.*

I tossed my hat on the desk next to hers and smiled. We were back.

Independent authors count on word-of-mouth and paid advertising to find new readers and sell more books. Reviews can help shoppers decide about taking a chance on authors who are new to them.

I would be grateful if you took a moment to write a review on Amazon.

Thank you!

Danny R. Smith

AFTERWORD

I love staying connected with my readers through social media and email. If you would like to connect, find me on BookBub, Amazon, Goodreads, Facebook, Instagram, and Twitter. You can also sign up for my newsletter and receive bonus material, such as the Dickie Floyd short story, Exhuming her Honor.

As a newsletter subscriber, you will receive special offers, updates, book releases, and blog posts. I promise to never sell or spam your email.

Danny R. Smith

Dickie Floyd Novels

THE DICKIE FLOYD SERIES

- A GOOD BUNCH OF MEN
- DOOR TO A DARK ROOM
- ECHO KILLERS
- THE COLOR DEAD
- DEATH AFTER DISHONOR
- UNWRITTEN RULES

SHORT STORIES

- In the City of Crosses - A Dickie Floyd Detective Short Story
- Exhuming Her Honor - A Dickie Floyd Detective Short Story
- Harder Times: A Cop Goes to Prison - Not a Dickie Floyd Story

AVAILABLE ON AUDIBLE

- A Good Bunch of Men
- Door to a Dark Room

ABOUT THE AUTHOR

Danny R. Smith spent 21 years with the Los Angeles County Sheriff's Department, the last seven as a homicide detective. He now lives in Idaho where he works as a private investigator and consultant. He is blessed with a beautiful wife and two wonderful daughters. He is passionate about his dogs and horses, whom he counts among his friends.

Danny is the author of the *Dickie Floyd Detective Novel* series, and he has written articles for various trade publications. He publishes a weekly blog called The Murder Memo, which can be found at dickiefloydnovels.com.

He is a member of the Idaho Writers Guild and the Public Safety Writers Association.

Made in the USA
Coppell, TX
11 November 2020

41165244R00157